I0783922

Shades of Darkness

Book Two

Trail of Lies

R.S. Raniere

Shades of Darkness - Book Two

Trail of Lies

Copyright © 2025 by R.S. Raniere

ISBN: 979-8-218-60802-6

Cover design by GetCovers.com

A special thank you to SM Davidson for her friendship, support, and invaluable assistance with the editing and formatting of this book.

DEDICATION

*To my remarkable Family for their unfailing love
and support.*

CHAPTER ONE

New York City

The Man in the Fedora

FEBRUARY 2020

The announcement of a flight delay to Dublin crackled over the PA system just as PJ closed her laptop, preparing to board. She groaned, unwillingly yielding to forces intent on making her life difficult. She had barely three weeks to submit the script for the debut airing of her national news program. She was beginning to feel the pressure. The thought of canceling the trip flashed through her mind, and was just as quickly dismissed. Although the timing was not optimal, becoming acquainted with what was left of her biological family was central to her recovery…so said her therapist. She opened her laptop and picked up where she'd left off.

"Damn!" the young woman sitting across from her grumbled, "I'll never make my connection." She looked up and her eyes landed on PJ. "Hey. Aren't you that news reporter on cable TV? Um, PT something? Haven't seen you in a while. Did you quit?"

Anxious to get back to her script, but not wanting to be rude, PJ offered a smile. "It's PJ. PJ Hollinger."

"Oh. Right."

PJ turned her attention back to the screen.

"That's too bad," the woman said, trying to talk over the squawking child on her lap.

"I really liked watching."

PJ sighed inwardly. "Thank you. I appreciate that," she said, hoping that would end the conversation.

The young woman, clearly worn out from the toddler squirming to get off her lap, unbridled the child. He plunked straightaway onto his bum emitting an ear-splitting scream that cast all eyes in the woman's direction. It took less than three seconds for PJ to secure her laptop and snatch the boy off the floor. "I think you could use a break," she said. "If you'd like, I'll keep junior occupied while you go and freshen up."

The woman did not blink. "OMG! Thank you," she trilled, scooting off without a second thought.

Having given up on accomplishing anything worthy, the babysitting stint cooled her frustration and became a welcome diversion.

Although PJ flew often, it was not one of her favorite things. For a moment, she thought about what it would be like raising a child, but the moment passed quickly. Not that she did not have small flashes of maternal instinct—this knee-jerk response, for one—but motherhood was conspicuously absent from her to-do list. Her life had not yet settled into a comfortable pattern of normalcy after having been abducted months earlier. The weekly therapy sessions helped, but she needed a break. And she'd put off this *family reunion* long enough. But was sojourning in Ireland with virtual strangers the break she needed? She had not entirely shaken off the traumatic events of the past months. The nettlesome feeling of walking through a minefield would not leave her.

Utterly engaged in the child's entertainment, PJ was unaware of the tall, burly gentleman leering at her from behind the Starbucks kiosk, a licentious curve to his lips. "Non Passerà molto tempo, mia dolce,"[1] he mumbled under his breath. Nattily dressed in a double-breasted, pinstripe suit, and wearing a gray Fedora drawn low over his face, he scanned the area.

Mama was taking her sweet time. *Who would leave their child with a stranger? What if she doesn't come back? Shit and double shit!* PJ breathed a sigh of relief when she spotted the short, stocky young woman scuttling toward her. By then, the boy had fallen asleep in PJ's arms.

An hour and twenty minutes later, passengers began queuing up for the boarding call. The man in the Fedora, still hidden by the kiosk, removed his hat revealing an *au courant* shaved head. Donning a pair of ultra-dark shades, he shrugged into his backpack and returned the hat to his shiny head. He made his way to the end of the line, all the while keeping his gaze on the stunning strawberry blonde now heading for the jetway.

Much mumbling and foot-shuffling erupted as the line was being held up by TSA officers randomly pulling aside male passengers and screening them with handheld wands. Seeing this, the man—known as Gino Carlotti—drew his hat lower and backed off the line.

---

[1] *It won't be long now, my sweet.*

CHAPTER TWO

Killarney, Ireland

The Cunninghams

That gut-wrenching quickening that streaks through the peripheral nervous system is a universal response at the point of realization—that moment of *knowing*. For Michael Cunningham, it came at the age of ten, in the last pew of St. Malachy's Catholic Church as he sat, mesmerized by the impassioned eloquence of a young visiting priest, an American. His name was Father Peter Francesco Romano, and it was in that moment that Michael knew in the deepest part of him, exactly what he wanted to do with his life.

Many years later, Father Cunningham steps up to the pulpit holding a bottle of Ballygowan sparkling water. He sets the bottle down, and in his customary irreverent style, greets his congregation. "Good morning, fellow reprobates. My name is Michael Cunningham, and I am a sinner!"

With a smile and a wink, the tall, carrot-haired priest begins. "Today I am going to talk about sex!"

A wet snowfall from the previous day, hardened by the frigid air, made the serpentine roads slick. Michael skidded several times on his way to the family farm after Mass. He felt somehow unsettled, and wondered whether it was the weather or this strange apprehension about meeting his recently-discovered niece from America. He knew little about PJ Hollinger other than the many fantasies fomented over back-fences and carried along on the breath of gossips: *she's a soul-less siren; she's sweet and shy; she's deceptive and will say anything for a story; she is brilliant and beautiful with a sterling reputation; she won the Pulitzer Prize*…and so it went.

Notwithstanding his vocation, or despite it, Father Cunningham was a bit of a skeptic. He believed none of it, preferring first-hand observation. This now-and-again emergent lack of trust engendered an ongoing battle with his faith.

"All right, where is she?" Michael bellowed with unusual verve, stomping the ice off his boots on the hall carpet. "And a good day to you, too, Father Cunningham," rejoined his mother, padding toward him for her weekly hug.

"She's not here yet, darlin.' Something about her luggage."

"Ach! Such a special visitor should have been provided for."

"To be sure, but I don't recall you volunteering."

"Surely you're not suggesting I abandon my flock?"

Fiona Cunningham scoffed. She took her son's coat, regaling him with the morning's events as they walked back toward the kitchen. "Mrs. Sullivan called a bit ago, complaining—as is her hobby—about the subject of your homily today. Sex, Michael? Truly? Sometimes you astound even me."

"Mmm. What smells so delightful?"

"Now, don't you go changing the subject."

To his relief, the front gate bells jingled, and the dogs began to yelp. Michael kissed his mam on the cheek. "I'll get it," and scurried to the door. He opened it wide, prepared to engage the beautiful young woman standing before him with his gifted oratory. Instead, he stood mute, his tongue as frozen as the icicles dangling from the eaves. After enough frosty seconds had passed, the woman spoke.

"Hello. I'm PJ. It's awfully cold out here."

Michael jumped as if someone had taken a match to his bottom. "Forgive me. I'm Michael. Please come in." Just as he moved to take her bag, Fiona stepped in. Pushing her son aside, she enclosed PJ in an ample embrace. After several long seconds, she stood back, holding PJ at arm's length.

"Jesus, Mary, and Joseph. Aren't you the spittin' image of my Mary," she blubbered, pulling PJ into the room. She hugged her again. Tears rimmed her eyes. "Oh, sweet Jesus," she sniffled, her speech thick with emotion.

PJ stood stock still, arms hanging listlessly at her sides, never expecting so effusive a greeting.

***

Kidnapped only months prior as a pawn in a game of revenge, orchestrated by the late Lucinda Russell, PJ's life would be forever changed. Following her return to New York after being rescued in Rome by her fiancè, she needed time to heal from the horrific events that spun her around like a game of Pin-the-Tail-on-the-Donkey, and thrust her blindly beyond the black stump. She was back to square one after thinking she had finally come to terms with who she was, and had successfully shooed away the ghosts of the past. After months of therapy and having dealt with her ancestry, and all the violence and death, somehow resolution and normalcy seemed out of reach. She had felt captive; frozen in a dream from which she could not wake herself. She needed to put it all behind her. But moving forward had become as torpid as wading through sludge.

The initial excitement of flying to Ireland to meet her *relatives* had waned. But it was more than simply elapsed time. For some unexplored reason, a growing sense of hesitation had crept in, a kind of foreboding. There was no denying its brewing presence. The percipient mind of a journalist was both a blessing and a curse. *Why was this push to meet her biological family suddenly surrounded by ambivalence,* she wondered? This was supposed to be the end of a quest, but felt like another divergence into a hornet's nest? It was far too late to change her mind. She shook off these dark thoughts and began to pack for her trip.

***

Fiona released PJ and dabbed at her eyes with the corner of her apron. "Forgive me. It's only that…"

"Please, don't apologize. It's an emotional time for both of us." PJ took in a breath. "To be completely honest, I'm not quite sure how to respond, or what I should call you." There was something about the woman's unabashed display that seemed inauthentic. PJ chided herself for being judgmental, but her instincts had always served her well. Anyway, it was much too soon to come to any conclusions about her *new family*. It wouldn't be fair…*should there be such a thing as fair.*

"Not to worry, darlin'" Fiona assured her sweetly. "You just need a bit of time to get used to us. And with this family being an itty-bitty daft, that may take some doing." PJ managed a smile.

"Call me Maw, or Fiona, if that's more comfortable for you. Maw," she explained, "is informal Irish for grandmother."

Usually not at a loss for the appropriate words, all PJ could think of to say was, "I see." An emoji of the Dopey Dwarf flashed across the screen in her brain. The lapse in conversation stretched a bit too long. PJ made no attempt to fill the vacant air. Perhaps it was jet lag, but the loss of motivation to engage was rare. It was Fiona who broke the silence. "You've already met

Michael," she said, scanning the room. "Although he seems to have vanished. Donnie, my older boy, and his wife Colleen will be here soon…with my precious little Sean."

PJ dug deep for something to say. "Sean would be your grandson?"

"And if he isn't ever the light of my life." Fiona made a quarter-turn. "Michael! Now where did that boy get to?" She sighed heavily. "Come, let me show you to your room."

Despite the warm greeting and homey aroma of home-cooking, PJ was not unaware of a certain tension that threaded the atmosphere. She could not put a finger on the basis for her discomfort, which she had to work at concealing. "Mmm. Something smells awfully good," she said, trying to sound cheery.

"That would be my lamb roast. Are you hungry?"

"Now I am."

Sadly, the Cunninghams had only recently been informed—rather perfunctorily—through American legal channels that their daughter, Mary, *missing* for nearly thirty years, was in fact deceased, and that she had given birth to a baby girl in 1993. When Fiona Cunningham opened the certified letter on that day, her hands were shaking. As she read, the specter of Father Peter Romano rose before her. Her body shook with sobbing, tears spilling down her cheeks until she could no longer see the words on a report that was brief and ambiguous. There were no supporting documents to be had. But Fiona Cunningham knew the story that documents could not tell. And her lips were sealed.

Michael had brought PJ's bags to the guest room then slipped away to his own room, kept for times he wearied of the church compound and its dim, claustrophobic surroundings. Kneeling at the foot of the bed, his mouth moved quietly in prayer. Through the closed door, he could hear the muffled strains of his mother's call. He continued to pray. "Forgive me, Father, as only you can. Please, lift this curse from me. In the name of Christ, I pray. Amen." He crossed himself, rose, and finger-combed the shaggy crop of red hair that defied controlling. He stood a moment before opening the door. "Coming, Mam. No need to get your apron in a twist."

Michael was what PJ would describe as *hot*. Ginger locks highlighted hazel eyes that gave the appearance of the sun rising behind his irises. Hypnotic. His slim, muscular frame seemed out of place for a priest. Once again, PJ scolded herself for her judgmental appraisal. Certainly, priests take care of their bodies as well as any man would. As he approached the women, he stretched out his hand toward PJ.

"I don't believe we've been properly introduced," he said, smiling. "I'm Michael." PJ took his hand, returning the smile while inwardly shaking her head at the idea that he was her uncle.

"Oh, for the sake of heaven, Michael. What sort of greeting is that? Give your niece a hug."

Michael's brief hesitation did not go unnoticed.

PJ took a step closer and put her arms around him in a gentle squeeze, then stepped back. "Lovely to meet you, Michael."

His eyes glued themselves to her face before he could speak the words gathering on his tongue. "I was only ten, but what I remember of my sister's face has been imprinted on yours," he said. "The resemblance is uncanny."

"Unfortunately, I did not know her—my mother— I was hoping I might be able to see some family pictures."

Fiona and Michael glanced at each other in a moment of awkward silence. "Of…of course," Fiona jumped in. "Perhaps after dinner."

PJ quickly replaced her questioning look with a smile. "That would be nice."

"Well, I hope my brother is on time. I'm starving."

PJ was not imagining the uneasiness in the room. She needed to breathe. "I would love to freshen up before dinner," she said. "If that's all right."

"Of course, darlin.' Let me show you to your room. It has a private bath."

Fiona passed Michael's room on her way back from settling PJ. The door was closed. She gave it a solid knock, then turned the knob. It was locked.

"Oh, for heaven's sake. Michael! Why are you hiding?"

"Taking a nap."

"Since when do you nap?"

"Mother!"

"Please open the door. I only want to chat for a bit."

"Can we do this later, Mam?"

She stomped off, humph-humphing her way back downstairs.

The remainder of the Cunningham family arrived shortly before dinner was to be served. Introductions were made. Colleen, a much-too-thin, but attractive blonde with sleepy blue eyes, took an immediate dislike to PJ, a nudge from the green-eyed monster for a life denied. She and Donnie were high school sweethearts. Colleen had a dream of living in America, a sought-after movie star . . . until she became pregnant. And that was that.

Donnie, a stocky fellow with a short beard he grew to hide his indelible freckles; he, too had a dream, and it was not sheep farming. But dreams get supplanted, and life becomes real.

"Wow!" was Donnie's spontaneous reaction on meeting PJ. "I would know you anywhere. You have my sister's face." He gave her a warm hug. There was no mistaking the angry look Colleen fired at her husband. It did not miss. He quickly backed off. *Unhappy wife, unhappy life.*

"What's a PJ?" little Sean chirped in, filling the awkwardness with bursts of laughter. PJ knelt and shook his tiny hand. "I'm PJ. Do you know what initials are?" "No."

"Well, an initial is the first letter of a name," PJ explained. "My name is Penelope Jane, but everyone calls me PJ for short. P is for Penelope, and J is for Jane." "Oh." Sean blinked. "Do I have a for-short name?"

"Well, let's see. What is the first letter of your name?

Sean took a moment to think about this. "S!" he exclaimed.

"Right. And what is your last name?"

"Cunningham."

"So, your 'for-short' name would be…"

"SC!" he shouted, pleased with himself.

"You are one smart young man, SC," PJ said, rumpling the boy's hair.

Sean hugged PJ's neck before his mother pulled him away. "That's enough Sean, go wash your hands before dinner."

"I learned my for-short name, mam!" he squealed as Colleen pushed him off to the washroom.

Liam Cunningham bore the formality of being introduced to PJ with stoic acceptance. A discomfort evidenced by barely looking at her. After shaking her hand, he dropped his eyes and turned away. Liam was not a hard man. He simply never overcame his grief. His daughter, Mary, regardless of her free-spirited nature, had been his angel. His look-alike granddaughter would not replace her. Rather than love, he felt resentment.

A hard-working, quiet man with sparse white hair and deep green, habitually narrowed eyes, Liam lived in his own private hell, never forgiving himself for a damnable agreement he had made so long ago. Handsome and gregarious in his youth, he now bears the dark, worn and weathered look of hardship and sadness, and too many hours in the fields under a blazing sun.

Liam Cunningham shut down when he lost his precious child, his engaging, outgoing nature, crushed by his daughter's *disappearance*—an event he refuses to talk about.

Fiona and Liam have been married for nearly fifty years. Other than farm-related issues, in which they are partners, they rarely say a word to each other. They have kept separate bedrooms since that life-shattering day when their daughter was taken from them.

Liam did little to contribute to the dinner table conversation, clearly uncomfortable in the presence of this stranger they say is his granddaughter. Colleen, as chatty as always, took charge, apparently determined to dig her claws into PJ. While Liam was relieved of having to engage in table-talk, he was not thrilled with his daughter-in-law and her unyielding tongue. Colleen seemed to take juicy pleasure in tearing into the innards of others, while her own were as rancid as week-old roadkill. She was not in the least reticent about her dislike of PJ Hollinger, her feelings poorly cloaked in innuendo and sarcasm.

"From the little I've read, Penelope," Colleen said, sipping her third glass of wine. "You don't mind me calling you Penelope, do you?"

PJ took a beat before answering. "PJ is fine."

"Well, in that case, Penelope, tell me how you managed to find us."

Liam squirmed in his seat. He cleared his throat. "Donnie, pass the biscuits," he said, giving Donnie a clear look of warning.

Colleen made a face, and reasserted her question. "Penelope?"

"If you're asking how I managed to find my grandparents, I can tell you that I was trained as an investigative reporter. And I am very good at my job."

"Oh, I am sure you are, having had to…pay your way up, as so many career women do to reach the top."

PJ gave herself a mental commendation for having restrained the expletives smoldering on her tongue from escaping her mouth. "I think you have a rather dated and uninformed view of successful women, Colleen," she said, calmly. "It's all about knowledge, experience, and hard work."

"So you say."

PJ just smiled and shook her head. Liam and Fiona exchanged a quick glance.

"How is your lamb, dear?" Fiona asked PJ.

"It's wonderful. I haven't tasted lamb this good since…since I lived at home." Colleen, the pout on her face obvious, poured herself another glass of wine. Michael asked PJ when her inaugural newscast would be airing.

"The actual taping is scheduled to begin in three weeks, but it will not air until the beginning of the following month."

"I hope we'll be able to watch it here," Michael said.

Colleen gave him an unapproving look. "Speak for yourself, Red."

"Unfortunately," PJ sighed, "NBC is not streamed outside the United States."

"Oh, what a shame!"

"Babe." Donnie looked weakly at his wife. "Go easy on the wine." PJ ignored Colleen's mocking tone.

"That's really disappointing," Michael said.

"You can get around that," Donnie offered, keeping one eye on his wife. "Just get a VPN service."

"When did you become so clever?" Colleen slurred. Donnie just stared at her. The room fell quiet.

"VPN stands for Virtual Private Network," PJ answered." It allows you to bypass the restriction."

"Well, there you are," Michael said, raising himself from the table. "Problem solved. Anyone for tea?"

Having fed her bibulous nature with far too many glasses of Merlot, Colleen would not let up. "Tell me, Penelope. A girlie pretty as you must have tons of fellas after her tail," she snarled. "Like mother like daughter?"

"Colleen!" Fiona shrieked.

Liam stood. "Donnie! Control your wife!" He tossed his napkin on the table and headed for the stairs.

"What? Was it something I said?" Colleen giggled. Donnie took the wine glass from her hand. "I think you've had enough." Colleen shrugged. "It was just a question."

PJ rose and pushed back her chair, glaring at Colleen, "I think I can use some fresh air. It's become rather noxious in here."

CHAPTER THREE

New York City

The Men in Her Life

Basil Romano, Sil to those he called friends, slouched in the corner of his favorite booth at McGarin's, tapping his fingers on the table as he waited patiently for his drinking buddy, a young man who persevered at being fashionably late. After fifteen minutes, his thirst got the better of him and he ordered a light beer. Another ten minutes had gone by when, draining the last drop of beer, he spotted Val Kendall over the top of his glass, walking toward him. Warned by the truculent look on Val's face as he slid into the booth, Romano shelved his intended reproach and ordered another beer. "What the hell happened? You look like you're about to commit murder."

"Ha! I might just do that," Val shot back.

"All right. Let's have it. What's gotten you so pissed."

Val removed a newspaper clipping from his breast pocket and tossed it across the table.

"Look who's having a grand time in Ireland," he said.

Romano put on his reading glasses, unfolded the clipping, and read the caption:

'American newscaster, PJ Hollinger, enjoying the local cuisine at Cassidy's in downtown Killarney.

Romano removed his glasses and looked up at Val. "Great picture of her. So, what's the problem?"

"What's the problem? Look at her, giving her coveted attention to some good-looking dude."

"Come on, Val. You know PJ better than that. You should be pleased. She hasn't looked so happy in some time."

"Exactly."

"The smoke coming out of your nose is not at all appealing." Romano said. "And how do you know he's good-looking? You can barely see the side of his face."

"I just know."

Romano refolded the paper and handed it back to Val. "I promise you; you're making a big deal over nothing. PJ is not like that."

"And how are you so sure? It took you nearly thirty years to find her. What makes you think you know her so well?"

"Believe me, Val, if PJ were going to cheat on you, she would tell you first."

"That's not very comforting, Grandpa," Val said, taking a long draught of Romano's beer.

Romano reclaimed his glass. "You cannot claim rights to call me that until you marry my granddaughter…and get your own beer."

"If I can only catch up to her long enough."

Romano sighed. "Give her some space. She's been through a lot." He was about to say something, but Val interrupted him.

"You need to understand, Sil. I love PJ more than my own life. And I will not lose her— not to her career, or her off shore family, and certainly not to another man."

"I do understand, son." He paused to look around. "What I'm about to tell you will change your focus."

"What are you talking about?

Romano ran his hand over his face. He leaned in and lowered his voice. "INTERPOL has lost eyes on Gino Carlotti."

"What!?" Val's face turned a cadaver's shade of gray.

"Hang on. She's covered. I get daily reports from Simmons. All is well."

Val took another swig of Romano's beer. "That's not going to cut it, Sil. You know how Gino operates," he said, slipping out of the booth.

"Where are you going, son? Come on, sit down. Let's work on a plan."

"I am working on a plan…and this is step one."

"Wait. Where are you going?"

Val did not look back as he strode toward the door. "Ireland."

Romano slammed his hand down hard on the table. "God dammit!"

"Something wrong, Mr. Romano?"

He looked up at the inquiring waiter. "Nothing a straight bourbon won't fix. Make that a double!"

Romano had ended his intimate relationship with hard liquor years before. By the time he arrived home, his eyes were watering and his head pounding. There was nothing more he wanted to do than stand in a hot shower and go to bed. Instead, he punched in Fred Simmons' number. Simmons, a former Secret Service Special Agent, now a private investigator and bodyguard, picked up on the third ring.

"Yes, boss."

"I assume you've heard that Gino Carlotti has gone underground."

"Just this morning."

"You know that you'll have to double surveillance." Romano reminded him.

"You know I know," he said. "I've got this."

Romano suddenly felt ill.

"There's something else," Simmons said.

"I'm afraid to ask."

"The number two person of interest has been released from prison."

"What!" Romano shouted. "Why?"

"Word is the Vatican chooses to stay in the background, what with Cardinal Montini's less than righteous activities. They've worked out a *mutual legal assistance* agreement with the Italian Government, who will now be handling the investigation and prosecution of the case. The good news is, Candace Baker has been warned to remain in the country until everything is cleared up."

Romano wiped the beads of sweat from his forehead with the heel of his hand. "What kind of bullshit is that? I don't understand."

"Apparently, Candace Baker is off the hook. They're focusing attention on their number one suspect, and they're not letting that cat out of the bag yet. That's all I've got, Sil."

"Jesus H. Christ." A surge of nausea overtook him. "Call me back in ten." Romano dropped the phone and made a bee-line for the bathroom, disgorging just short of the bowl.

While the nausea subsided, the gnawing in the pit of his stomach did not. Romano's thoughts circled his brain in disquieting waves. *Candace fucking Baker…or Russell…or whatever she's calling herself now. How could this have happened? And where is Gino? Most likely not far behind. But maybe that's a good thing. Maybe it will be easier tracking them together…maybe.*

After several tries, Simmons finally reached Romano. "Where'd you go, Sil. I was about to call in the FBI."

"Consequences, my friend. Consequences of one bourbon too many," he said. "But enough about me. I'm tired of dealing with this monkey on my back. We need to put these people down before I kick the bucket, or I will never rest in peace."

"Are you saying what I think you're saying?"

"No ambiguity here, Simmons. It's a matter of survival. They need to vanish from this ugly Tableau!

Silence.

"I don't know what to say, Sil. I know there's a lot hanging in the balance." Simmons said. "I think you need to sleep on it. It just doesn't sound like you."

"Trust me. It's me."

"Look. This is assassin territory. I know PJ's your granddaughter and all, but…"

"There are no buts. Don't you get it? It's kill or be killed. I have spent nearly half my life searching for her, and I will not lose her now!"

"I understand, Sil. But I'm only a bodyguard. And you know I will protect PJ with my life. That's what I do. But I am not an assassin."

"I'm not asking you to assassinate anyone, Fred. All I want is your expertise…and your arsenal."

"What arsenal?"

"Come off it, Simmons. It's common knowledge you have a collection of the latest and greatest fire power around."

"Listen, Sil. You've had too much to drink. Sleep on it and we'll talk tomorrow."

Romano was about to utter some uncensored words when he heard the muffled sound of sirens through the phone. "What's that?" No response.

"Simmons, what is that? Simmons!" The call disconnected. He threw the phone across the room, his heart thrumming in his ears. Not knowing what to do next, he picked up the phone and was about to call Val when it rang in his hand.

"Simmons. Thank God! What happened? Where are you? And where is PJ?"

"I'm at the farm, about 15 meters from the sheep stalls. There's a fire truck and a couple of local police cars near the main house."

"Simmons! Where is my granddaughter?"

"Been trailing PJ over hills and dales in this freaking cold. She apparently felt the need for a walk. She's safe. I'll check back with you when I find out what's going on."

"Tell her to call me for God's sake!" The line had already cut off before Romano's words could reach Simmons' ears.

CHAPTER FOUR

Killarney, Ireland

Inspector Doyle

Still seething from Colleen's caustic tongue, PJ had gotten more than half a mile from the farm proper when she heard the wail of sirens. She slowed her pace listening for where the sound might be coming from, but the shrilling stopped suddenly. Apparently, it was close by. She heard the crunch of boots behind her and spun around to find Michael bent over, gripping his knees, and panting for air. "My God, woman, you must have winged feet."

"Are you all right?"

"Just need a minute to catch my breath." He stood, inhaled deeply, and blew out a long stream of frosty air. "Guess it's time to join a gym."

"Seems so. Why the chase?"

"Something's happened. I wanted to make sure you were okay. Sorry about Colleen," he added, still breathless."

"Quite a character," she smirked. "What's happened? Does it have anything to do with the sirens?"

"Someone slashed the necks of two ewes. Nearly decapitated them, then set fire to the barn."

"Oh, my God, Michael! Was anyone hurt?"

"No. Thank God."

"And the other animals?"

"They were grazing. And the fire was put out pretty much before it got started. Mam insisted on a sprinkler system some years ago. A brilliant idea as it turns out."

"Who would do something like that?"

"Not a clue." He took her hand, as would a father guiding his child across the street. "I think we should go back now."

When they reached the farmhouse, the area was overrun with Gardaí.

"You may have to show them some identifying documents." No sooner had Michael said that, a Garda trotted toward them.

"Good day to you," he began benignly. "I am Inspector Doyle." He flashed his credentials. "Would you tell me who you are and what your business is here?"

Michael gave PJ a quick look and then addressed the inspector. "I'm Michael Cunningham. My parents own this farm. This is my niece," he said, nodding toward PJ. "We're here for Sunday dinner."

"Do you have some ID, sir?"

"Of course." Michael took out his wallet and gave him his identity card. And you, miss?

"It's in the house."

"Lead the way," Doyle moved aside, signaling them to go ahead. As they approached the front walk, another Garda ran up to Doyle and whispered something in his ear. Doyle nodded and turned to Michael. "Please go in. I'll be with you shortly."

Recently promoted to Inspector, Brian Doyle had been a member of the National Police Service of Ireland for eighteen years. He was a diminutive man in his late forties, perhaps a few inches thicker than he would have liked. His thinning chestnut hair was overcompensated for by a wildly thick stache that blanketed his upper lip and dipped around the corners of his mouth like a swath of rusty wool. Doyle was married with no children. It had been a condition of his marriage— to which his then fiancé agreed—to not bring children into this "blooming murderous world." He was a no-nonsense, but respectful officer with a reputation for solid police work.

Other than the local Gardaì, the only people ambling about in the cold were Liam, Donnie, and a few of the farmhands. Fiona and Colleen remained in the house.

After removing her boots and coat, PJ followed the drone of voices into the living room where Michael had already seated himself by the fire. The women were sipping tea, absorbed in quiet conversation that stopped abruptly when PJ entered the room. For an instant she sensed that something about Fiona had changed.

Fiona's smile was not convincing. "There you are!" she said. "You must be sprouting icicles. Would you like some tea?"

"Yes, that would be nice."

Colleen scowled at PJ, but said nothing. The front door slammed shut behind the two men as they scuttled into the house.

"In here," Michael called out. Liam headed upstairs without a word. Donnie joined the family, unzipped his Parka, and removed his wool cap. "They haven't found anything yet," he informed them. "No footprints, no weapon. Nothing."

"Do they know how the fire was started?" PJ asked.

"They suspect kerosene was used as an accelerant, but they can't say for certain until they run their tests."

"I don't get it," said Michael looking at Donnie. "I can't think of a single reason why someone would do this. Can you?"

It was a simple enough question, but apparently Donnie took exception to it. "How the feck would I know?"

"Donnie!" Fiona hollered."

"Sorry, Mam." He put on his cap and coat and went back outside.

"What's his problem?" Michael said, looking to Fiona. A loud knock on the door interrupted them before Fiona could offer an excuse for Donnie's outburst. "Probably the Inspector," Michael whispered. "I'll get it."

Donnie had given up smoking after Sean was born. He really wanted to be a good father, set the right example. After slamming the door behind him, he walked over to one of the officers. "You wouldn't happen to have a spare fag, now, would you?" The Garda accommodated with a nod, and lit it for Donnie.

"Thank you." Donnie slogged behind the house and sat on a cold rocker on the back porch, puffing away. He knew that what had happened today was a warning. And it had everything to do with the weird encounter he'd had several days earlier while making a repair to one of the perimeter fences.

"The north perimeter fence needs fixing," Liam had told his son in his customary irascible tone. "See to it before you head home today, Donnie."

Donnie was not happy about missing the football game, but he knew better than to make excuses. He loaded some tools into his rucksack, saddled the mare, and road out to the north end of the farm. He had to be quick about it as it would soon be dusk.

As he was about to tie off the last piece of wire, he felt a burning crack at the back of his head. He dropped to the ground, groaning in pain. Through his peripheral vision he could make out a short, slight figure standing over him dressed entirely in black, including a black ski mask.

"I have a job for you," said a gruffy, feminine voice.

A woman! It shouldn't be too hard to bring the bitch down, he thought, then he noticed the

Glock 19 she was holding uncomfortably close to his head. "Who are you?"

"Not important. I need your assist, sweetie."

"Find somebody else. I already have a job."

The woman kicked Donnie in the ribs. "You are not indispensable," she told him. "But I don't have time to shop around. Get up!"

Donnie staggered to his feet holding the back of his head, which was now bleeding down his neck. "What is it you want from me?"

"You have a visitor staying in the main house."

"A visitor?"

She jabbed the muzzle into the soft part of his gut. "Don't play games with me; I'm not in the mood. You know who I'm talking about."

"If you mean PJ, she's not a visitor. As mam would say—she's *family*."

"Yes. So I've heard." After giving Donnie explicit instructions, the woman in black tossed a mobile phone on the ground, about three feet behind him. "This is how we will communicate. It's untraceable. Now pick it up and get the fuck out of here."

"I have to finish this."

She jabbed Donnie again. "I said, get lost. Do what I told you to do, and quick. I'll be in touch."

Donnie heard his name being called through the haze of his recollection. He stomped out his cigarette and went back inside.

Doyle questioned each member of the family separately in another room. Fiona went to fetch Liam, who obliged reluctantly. Doyle spoke with Liam first, then Donnie, then Michael. He seemed satisfied with the responses of the first two. Michael's interview was several minutes longer than the others.

"I understand, Father, that you were all in the dining room when the incident occurred...all except the senior Mr. Cunningham. Is that correct?"

Michael hesitated. "Yes. That's correct. My father had gone upstairs." Doyle gave him a sidewise glance.

"Are you sure Mr. Cunningham was the only one absent, Father?"

Michael scratched his brow. "As far as I remember."

Doyle let the air hang for a few seconds, giving Michael opportunity to change his answer.

"Isn't it true, Father, that Miss . . . " he flipped over a page in his notepad. "Miss Hollinger was not in the room? In fact, she was not even in the house at the time of the incident?"

Michael was cornered. Long-practiced in caginess, however, he quickly recovered. "You know, Inspector Doyle, you are absolutely correct," he said, a boyish ring of innocence in his voice. "When Joe came running in about the stall being on fire, I realized PJ—Miss Hollinger— was not in the room, so I went to look for her."

"Mm Hmm." Doyle made some scratches in his notebook. "And who is Joe?"

"Oh, Joaquin. He's the farm manager."

"Right. I have already spoken to him."

Doyle next interviewed the women, whose responses were less than enlightening. Mrs. Cunningham, not particularly forthcoming, and the daughter-in-law, Colleen, rude, but more than willing to expound on the baser qualities of PJ Hollinger, which he found remarkable since they had just met. He saved PJ for last.

"Miss Hollinger. I understand you are an American newscaster."

"I am."

"And what brings you to Killarney?"

"Visiting family."

"What exactly is your relationship to this family?"

"Liam and Fiona Cunningham are my birth mother's parents—my grandparents."

Doyle's surprised look begged qualification.

"I was adopted, Inspector Doyle. I've only recently discovered that I had family here."

"Ah. I see." Doyle made a quick note. "Tell me, Miss Hollinger, where were you headed when you left the house?"

"For a walk. The air in the room had become quite...unbearable."

"Unbearable?"

"Unendurable, according to Merriam-Webster," she smiled.

"I know what unbearable means, Miss Hollinger." He gave her an admonishing frown, his thick brows coming together forming a single line above the bridge of his nose. He then reached into his pocket and pulled out a small plastic bag, removed an object dangling from a chain, and handed it to PJ. "Can you identify this, Miss Hollinger?"

She stared at the object for some time before answering. "It's...it's a Pectoral Cross." "Explain, please."

She swept her hair off her shoulders and looked up at the Inspector. "A Pectoral Cross is worn by certain Catholic clergy." "Certain clergy?"

"Only the pope, cardinals, and bishops are permitted to wear this cross...but you must know that, being Catholic."

"And how do you know I'm Catholic?"

PJ closed her eyes against the unnecessary and inane question. "You have the insignia of the Knights of Columbus engraved on your jacket collar."

Doyle, his cheeks turning a slight shade of pink, held his ground. "Please take a look at the other side of the cross and tell me what you see."

PJ did as he asked. The insignia consisted of three laser-engraved letters, R.A.M. The cross fell from her trembling hand. Doyle bent over and picked it up.

"I thought handling evidence without protective gloves is against protocol," she said, covering her uneasiness.

"You're diverting, Miss Hollinger," he said, slipping the cross back into the bag. "The *evidence* has already been dusted for fingerprints and swabbed for DNA. Now, my question. Can you identify the initials engraved on the cross?"

She looked away, then back at Doyle. "Yes."

He waited for the rest of her answer until his impatience spoke. "Would you care to elaborate, Miss Hollinger?"

She stared over Doyle's head through the window at the magnificent mountain range in the distance.

"Miss Hollinger?"

Roberto Alphonse Montini. The initials are those of the late Cardinal Roberto Alphonse Montini."

CHAPTER FIVE

An Unexpected Visitor

The flight from New York landed Val in Dublin at 5:55 p.m. He thought he would stretch his legs and kill his thirst with a beer before making the three-and-a-half-hour drive to the Killarney Park Hotel. He stopped at the first watering hole he could find, and took a seat at the bar. After being hit on by a male patron, he took a closer look around and thought it curious that the customers were men around his age or younger. Not a female in sight. When he realized his error in choosing this bar, he smiled sheepishly and shook his head. On the stool next to him, watching with amused interest, was a red-haired gentleman in a leather bomber jacket. He turned and spoke quietly into

Val's ear. "I believe you'd be more comfortable in a different type of establishment." Val looked at him, and they both laughed.

"Obviously, you are not from here."

"Obviously," he said. "Actually, I've just flown in from New York."

After a brief conversation, Val shook the red-head's hand. "Good meeting you," and left the bar, a bit embarrassed by his faux pas. He got into the rental and sat for a moment, still bemused by the incident. He laughed it off and started the engine, anxious to get to Killarney.

***

The morning sun with its warm blinding glow did little to meliorate the frigid air that bit at PJ's cheeks as she stood on the front porch wrapped in a furry afghan, taking in the majestic view of snow-capped mountains that transported her to a place of calming peace.

"Spectacular, isn't it?" Michael said, sidling up to her.

"Breathtaking."

"You see that peak in the middle?" He pointed. "It's called *Carrauntoohil*, the highest peak in Ireland, about 3,400 feet above sea level. There's an old myth that says it can be seen from every part of the country."

"Have you thought about climbing it?"

"Actually, I've tried a few times. Got a little further each time, but always turned back before I could complete it. It's a challenge."

The two remained silent for a while, taking in the magnificent vista.

She turned to Michael. "Maybe we should try it together sometime. Before I head back to the real world."

"Adventurous, are you?" Michael chuckled.

"Well, I've hiked Mt. Marcy in the Adirondacks once. Took me almost nine hours."

"Good God, PJ, you're as spirited as a wild Mustang. Easy girl, I'm a bit older than you."

Fortified by two strong cups of coffee, PJ coaxed herself to her room to work. While her contract specified one month's vacation, to be taken in two increments, she asked to have the entire month before beginning her anchor position, promising to do the research and reporting responsibilities remotely. She could hardly believe that two weeks had already gone by, and she was behind. The image of Roberto Montini filled her thoughts, hindering her efforts to accomplish any work. The pectoral cross could mean only one thing; someone was sending her a message. And the most likely candidates were Candice or Gino. But Candice was locked up in an Italian prison, and Gino was under heavy surveillance, hunted by any number of local and federal agencies, including Interpol and the FBI. Of greater concern were the veiled inferences Inspector Doyle seemed to make concerning her connection to Montini and ultimately…to his murder.

After an hour or so, she'd had enough of trying to work and accomplishing little. In frustration, she closed the laptop and buried her face in her hands. When done with her pity party, she showered, dressed, and scurried downstairs. She found Fiona in the kitchen preparing lunch for the farmhands.

"Good morning, Fiona"

Fiona swiped her hands down her apron and opened her arms for a hug. "Good morning my darlin.' Did you sleep well?"

"As well as I usually do."

Fiona frowned, but did not question. "Well, dearie, I must get this lunch done. Help yourself to anything you want. This is your home."

"Thank you," she half-smiled. "I'm good. I was thinking about going into town. Would you have the number for a taxi service?"

"Don't be silly. Take the pickup. Keys are on the hook by the door…and do be careful."

It was getting close to supper time. The skies were beginning to darken and PJ had not returned. Fiona tried her cell, but the call went straight to voicemail. She heard the gate bells clanking and breathed a sigh of relief. "Coming." She swung the door open expecting PJ. "I was beginning to . . . " Her smile melted as she stared into the face of a handsome young man in a very expensive cashmere coat.

"Hello," he smiled back. "I'm Val." He waited for the invitation to enter, but instead received a questioning look. Apparently, his assumption that PJ had told her family all about him was mistaken. He introduced himself. "I'm Val Kendall. PJ's fiancé."

Fiona raised an eyebrow. "Oh? She did not say."

Val, hiding his annoyance, dug his hands into his pockets. "Would you tell her I'm here, please."

"I'm sorry, but she's not home, young man."

Val winced inwardly at the word "home," but remained congenial. "Do you know when she's expected?"

"Soon, I hope."

Val shuffled his feet.

"My husband is out in the field, but I suppose you can come in and wait. It is a bit chilly outside."

"Thank you."

Fiona moved aside to let Val in.

"I promise, I'm not a serial killer. And frankly, I don't understand why PJ hadn't mentioned me." He followed Fiona into the living room.

"Well, it's been an exciting couple of weeks, and she's always so busy with her work, you know."

"Yes, I know."

Fiona's cell phone buzzed. "Maybe that's PJ. Oh, dear, where is that phone?" By the time she located it on the kitchen counter, the call had gone to voicemail. She rejoined Val in the living room. "PJ left a message. She's on her way back. Thank God!"

Liam had already entered through the rear of the house and gone upstairs to wash for supper. It was nearly dark.

"Supper is at seven," she announced. "I'm sure PJ would want you to stay."

Let's hope, he thought.

Fiona trudged upstairs and knocked on her husband's door. "We have a guest for supper."

"Then that makes five," he grumbled.

"Five?"

"Joaquin is staying for supper tonight. We have some business to discuss...and, of course, there's your granddaughter."

"Can you at least make an effort to be civil, if only occasionally?" she barked. "She's your granddaughter, too. And she is not a guest...she is family."

He looked at her incredulously. "Mark my words, this will not end well."

Fiona turned in a huff, then turned back. "And what business would you be discussing that would not include myself, dear husband."

Liam looked at her with irritation in his tired eyes. "Do I have to spell it out for you? You do the books. What is not clear…dear wife."

"You can just go to Hell!" she snarled, slamming the door behind her. Val and PJ were sitting on the sofa, holding hands when Fiona entered the room.

"Oh. I did not hear you come in. I'm so glad you're back, dear. I was beginning to worry."

PJ released Val's hands. "Fiona, this is Val Kendall. I think you've already met." She turned to Val. "This is Fiona Cunningham…my grandmother."

Val stood and extended his hand. "A pleasure to meet you—officially—Mrs. Cunningham."

"Oh, don't be so formal, you're practically family," and she wrapped him in one of her rib-cracking hugs.

During supper, Liam, occasionally engaged in conversation with his field manager, barely acknowledging the additional guest. His rudeness, as usual, went without comment from his wife. While PJ was learning to accept it as *his way*, it was irritating. She knew she should hold her tongue, but the little honey badger that occasionally takes up residence in her prefrontal cortex, began nudging.

"Liam," she said, staring directly at him. "I think I've been remiss in not properly introducing you to my fiancé. This is Val Kendall…in the event you would like to say hello."

He looked at her crossly. "Didn't know you had a fella." He said simply, and refocused his attention on his dinner.

With dinner concluded—and not a second too soon for Val—Fiona suggested that PJ and Val take tea in the sunroom while she cleared the table. "Well, that was awkward," Val remarked when they were alone.

"Fiona tries," PJ sighed. "So many years, but Liam still has not crossed the chasm that lies between his daughter's disappearance and the present. While everyone has pointed an accusatory finger at my father, I just know there is more to it."

"This is new. You've never before referred to Cardinal Romano as your father. Does this mean you've come to terms with all the history that's still a mystery?"

"Clever. You should try your hand at sonnets, darling."

"I love the way you so often avoid answering my questions with some diversionary response."

Too jittery to sit any longer, PJ got up and walked over to the window. "What's the point of denial…there's no doubt that Mary Cunningham and Cardinal Romano were my biological parents." She turned toward Val. "I've gotten so many different views of Mary Cunningham, it's hard to know what to believe about her."

Val got up. He took PJ into his arms and buried his face in her neck. He kissed her gently on the lips. "You can believe this: I love you. I've missed you so much."

"I've missed you, too, and I'm sorry for Liam's…unfriendliness."

"It's not just his discourtesy and the obvious disdain he has for his wife that troubles me," Val said. "The entire atmosphere seems awkward, strange even. Don't you feel it?"

"I'm still trying to get used to the fact that I have a family. Yes, I do feel…uncomfortable I guess would be the right word, but–"

"There is always that *but*."

After a moment of silence, PJ said. "The tea is getting cold."

The atmosphere, as well as the tea, had cooled down markedly, arousing Val's shrouded anger. "It certainly is."

PJ fixed the tea for Val and herself, ignoring the comment. They both sat down.

"PJ. We really need to talk."

"I know."

"Come back to the hotel with me. There's something about this place I don't like."

"Wouldn't that defeat the purpose of this trip, getting to know my family?"

"You cannot cover thirty years in one month," he said. "What do you say we build our own family?"

PJ did not miss the sarcasm in his tone. She knew he was upset. Throwing more wood on the fire would only spark the flame. "I need to be here," she said, without explanation. "But it would be nice to hide away with you for the weekend."

It felt good being with Val…too good. She had really missed his presence, his humor. And his body. They held hands the entire twenty-five-minute drive to the Killarney Park Hotel.

"Why didn't you tell the Cunninghams about me? And why aren't you wearing your engagement ring?" he blurted.

PJ took a minute. "Val, I know we have a lot to talk about, but can we please hold off on that. I'm really horny, and that's one fire I do not want to throw cold water on." She squeezed his hand. "We can talk all you want later…much later."

Val chuckled. "In that case, your wish is my command," he said, flooring the accelerator.

The hotel valet opened the car door for PJ. "Good evening, Miss."

"Good evening."

Val grabbed her overnight bag from the back seat and tossed the keys to the valet. As usual for a Friday night, the lobby was abuzz with arriving guests. He led PJ to the elevators, which seemed to take forever to get to the third floor, and even longer to find the room, insert the key card, and cross the threshold. Val dropped PJ's bag onto the floor just in time to catch her in his arms. Her lips were warm and sweet. He gently stroked her cheek and ran his fingers through her silky hair. He slid his hand down her back. "God, how I've missed the feel of you," he moaned into the crook of her neck. She pressed into him; he squeezed her bottom and lifted her off the floor as she wrapped her legs around him and began unbuttoning his shirt. He carried her to the bed and they undressed each other slowly—almost ritualistically—touching, caressing, exploring. His tongue nibbled and nuzzled and teased every part of her until she could barely breathe. When at last he entered her, he could feel the explosion. They made love throughout the night, and slept in until noon when awakened by PJ's mobile phone.

"Ugh," Val groaned. "Don't answer it."

PJ looked at the screen. "It's Fiona." She swiped the green icon. "Hello."

"PJ, dear. I am so sorry to bother you, but something has happened and . . . "

"What is it?"

"It's Sean," Fiona said, her voice cracking. "He's gone."

"What do you mean gone?"

"He wasn't in his bed last night when Donnie went in to check on him. Everyone is frantic. We're getting a search party together. Sean has taken such a liking to you, I thought maybe–"

"Of course. I'll leave now." She tossed the phone onto the nightstand and jumped out of bed.

"Wait. Talk to me. Where are you going?"

"Sean is missing. I have to go."

"Who is Sean?"

"Fiona's five-year-old grandson, my little cousin," she said, pulling on her clothes.

"Hold on, Ms. Horny. You're not going anywhere without me."

CHAPTER SIX

Candace

Donnie stood in the middle of the partially burned barn anxiously awaiting the call from the mysterious lady in black. He swiped the green icon on the first ring.

"Greetings," the woman said, cheerily."

His nostrils flared in rage. "You bitch! Taking my son was not part of the deal." The call disconnected.

"Hello? Hello! "SHITE! Shite, shite, shite!" Donnie paced, wiping the sweat from his face with his jacket sleeve. The phone rang again.

"I trust you've calmed down and are ready to talk."

"Where is my son?"

"Did you do what I asked?"

His heart beat to the rhythm of a pending cardiac arrest. "Please, just tell me where he is."

"I will ask you for the last time; did you take care of business?"

"No! Not yet. I haven't had the chance. She takes that fecking laptop with her wherever she goes."

"I will give you until Monday. And I am being generous." The call ended.

"Wait…my son! Fecking bitch!"

Donnie had no clue who this crazy woman was, but her manner of introduction left much to be desired. He had three fresh stitches at the base of his skull, and a missing child to prove it.

PJ could hear Colleen's hysterical screams from the walkway. No sooner had she stepped inside the house than Colleen sprang at her. "This is your fault, you bitch!"

Donnie and Fiona were quick to drag her away before she could do damage.

"Calm down, Babe."

"How dare you!" Fiona screamed. You apologize this minute!"

"Apologize? My God, you are all so blind. I knew from the first day that you were nuts to allow her to come here. Dead sheep, burning barns. And now my sweet little boy is gone. I tell you, she's a witch!"

Donnie sat Colleen down and tried soothing her with a back rub. While Fiona continued to hassle with her daughter-in-law, Val grabbed PJ's hand and pulled her out the door. They joined the crowd of volunteers that had begun to gather.

"Who was that?" Val asked.

"Meet Colleen, Donnie's wife." PJ pulled her collar up against the wind. "Donnie is the Cunningham's oldest son…my uncle." *This whole relationship stuff is bizarre.* She shook her head at the absurdity of it all.

"Poor guy. His wife is a nutcase."

"She's not entirely wrong."

"What are you saying?"

"I think we both know I'm being targeted, and I've put these people in danger."

Val put his arm around PJ's waist and drew her close. "Stop that. She's hysterical, and a bone fide nutcase." He swept a strand of hair off her face. "You know, we never did get around to talking."

PJ held back an irritable response. "Yes. I know. But now is not the time. If we don't find that child, I don't know what I'll do."

"We'll find him."

The craggy voice of a woman—apparently the organizer—barked instructions through a megaphone, dividing the volunteers into groups that would first cover the areas and stalls within the twenty-acre perimeter, then spread out through the fields and hills surrounding the Cunningham farm.

"This could take days," PJ said, staring into space.

"Uh, oh. I know that look. What are you thinking?"

She did an about-face. "Come this way."

Ignoring the frosty wind pinging their faces, they walked around to the rear of the farmhouse, past the greenhouse, the outer barn, and across a narrow, planked bridge that led onto a makeshift stone path. "There's a creek at the base of the path that takes you to what's known as *Devil's Ladder,*" she said. "It's one of the routes to a hiking trail up Carrauntoohil Peak."

"Wow! You've certainly been busy getting the lay of the land."

"Carrauntoohil is the highest mountain in Ireland," she said. "I've been toying with the idea of hiking it."

"Of course you have."

The wind picked up. Given the serried profusion of Hazel, Scots Pine, and Silver Birch trees, they were not making their best time. They called out the boy's name as they hiked.

"What happens when we get to the creek?"

"I haven't thought that far."

"Oh, good. Maybe we can sit down and talk."

"Val!" "Sorry."

The farther they walked, the less certain PJ became of finding Sean. She only hoped he was sheltered. Was it just wishful thinking that he would be there, playing with rocks; oblivious to what was happening around him? She refused to give space to the idea that someone had taken him. Finally, they reached the water's edge, straining their necks from right to left…but no Sean.

Val put his arm around her shoulder. "We will find him. You have the sharpest instincts of anyone I know."

"When things get personal, instincts fly out the window."

"Don't be so sure." He was not convincing. "What made you think he would be here?"

She took in a breath and let it out slowly in a misty cloud of cold air. "I was sitting on the porch, working on the script when Sean found me. He had 101 questions. When he couldn't think of another one, he asked if I'd play with him. Of course, how could I refuse such a charmer. He took my hand and led me here. We spent the better part of the afternoon building rock castles and…"

Val waited for her to finish the thought. "And?"

"And playing hide-and-seek…Oh, my God." PJ vaulted and began to run along the edge of the creek toward higher land that eons of wind and rain had carved into dozens of craggy shelters, some overhangs, others deeper caverns.

"PJ, wait!"

She pressed on, stumbling over loose stones and pebbles as she made her way up and down the hillside shouting the child's name, her heart hammering in her ears. "Sean! SC!" Val followed a couple of yards behind. Eventually, they separated, searching every nook and crevice they could find. Hours had passed. The sky was darkening making it difficult to see. Suddenly, Val's voice cracked the frigid air. She turned in its direction and scrambled down the hill to the edge of the creek. She could see him running toward her shouting out words she could not understand. He was carrying something.

CHAPTER SEVEN

Key West, Florida

A Killing

Gino Carlotti—aka Mr. G—while expelled from the family enterprise in Sicily for certain self-interest activities, maintained one or two *amici* he could depend on for favors, usually at a goodly price. Finding a safe-haven and arranging for the necessary *exit* papers had not been easy. Having Candace meet him in Key West, he realized too late, was a mistake. Since his financial stability depended on her now dead mother, Candace was no longer useful to him. She'd become a millstone around his neck. He had every intention of ditching her before reaching Cuba.

*****

Candace Baker, nee Russell. Witty, affable, endearing…and vicious. A bad apple fallen from a rotting tree. The pigeonhole of a room had been arranged through the cellmate with whom Candace had struck a deal while imprisoned in Rome. The space was in an Airbnb located at the end of a dirt road about three miles from the Key West marina. It was dank and musty and barely livable. But it would do nicely for her purpose. She arrived a day early just to stay ahead of the curve. The room, and her set up in Cuba were part of the deal—a deal that cost her the last of the ready cash she had socked away, with a promise to pay the balance out of the *proceeds* she intended to extricate from PJ's off-shore account.

Gino, she suspected, had lost interest in her. She no longer trusted him. They were, however, in the same boat…literally and figuratively. They both needed asylum in a non-extradition country. And so, they, too, had a deal. She would provide the means of transportation, and he, the passports and necessary government documents to get them to Cuba.

They were to meet at a small bar on a quiet side street not far from the Airbnb. She was intentionally early, and found a corner table at the far end of the room, her eyes fixed on the entrance. Her stomach lurched when Gino walked through the door. She took a long draught of the bourbon she'd ordered to calm her nerves, and gave him a phony smile as he sat down.

"*Ciao, Dolcezza*," he said, returning the smile in kind.

She leaned forward. "Come off it, Gino. You know enough English to sidestep that unctuous crap."

He chuckled, pulled her hand to his mouth, and kissed it. "Meese you too, *amore mio*."

"Yeah, right. Just give me my documents."

"*Que?*"

"You heard me…my passport, the papers."

He stopped smiling. "*Non adesso*."

"Then when?"

"*Dopo*."

"No. No dopo! Now!"

He slammed his hand on the table causing it to wobble. "*Dopo!*"

Fuming, she said, "I hear the bane of your existence is still alive. It seems PJ Hollinger slipped through your clumsy fingers…once again. Losing your touch, Mr. G?"

His face turned a shade of red that would make a boiled lobster seem undercooked. He grabbed her wrist and squeezed so hard she winced. She jerked it from his grip, ignoring the pain, and glared at him. "Let's order so we can get the fuck out of here."

The café, as it turned out, was an excellent choice. There were few other customers to contend with, and most of those were street derelicts who had begged just enough money for another drink. When the food arrived, the greasy smell of it brought bile to Candace's throat. She picked at her fries after drowning them in ketchup, and downed the last of her drink. "I have to pee," she announced, scuffing her chair back. Gino simply grunted, gnawing his cheeseburger,

The powder room was several seeds below the overall seediness of the bar. Candace locked the door behind her and took out a small zippered pouch from her purse. She extracted a syringe and loaded it with enough Ketamine to knock out a large boar, then carefully capped the needle and put it in the side pocket of her blazer. When she got back to the table, Gino was sitting back in his chair, apparently fully satisfied with his meal.

"It's getting late," Candace said. "We should go to the room and get things ready for tomorrow."

Gino gave her a nod of agreement and tossed two twenties on the table. "*Andiamo.*"

The drive to the Airbnb took less than seven minutes. He parked the rental car behind the house. He took their bags out of the trunk while Candace went ahead to unlock the side door that opened into the room. When he joined her, he threw her bag on the floor, and set his own on a small table in the corner.

"Now, may I have my papers?"

He grinned, pulled her roughly into his arms, and kissed her neck. "*Dobo*."

She pushed him away and moved back several steps. "No fucking until they're in my hand."

He gave her the bird, and went into the bathroom to shower.

As soon as she heard the water running, she opened his bag and began rifling through his belongings. There, in a side pocket, was a zippered leather pouch thick with cash and documents. She transferred the cash to her purse and flipped through each of the documents several times. Not one of them was in her name. Neither was there the passport he was supposed to have provided for her. "Son-of-a-bitch!"

When Gino came out of the bathroom, a towel wrapped around his waist, Candace was holding his passport in one hand, and her cigarette lighter in the other. He lunged for her just as she tossed it into the wastebasket, its pages ablaze. As he kneeled over the trash can desperately trying to smother the flames, she plunged the needle into his neck. He hit the floor with a ponderous thud.

"Sweet Dreams, you prick!"

There had been no margin for error. Living the good life in Cuba was now a faded dream. But she had been through worse—far worse—and survived. She ransacked the room, gathered all identifying documentation on Gino Carlotti and threw them into her carry-on. She also took his Glock 19. Before she left, she flipped open a seven-inch Zancudo knife she'd stolen from Sawyer, and unlovingly sliced Gino's throat from ear to ear.

CHAPTER EIGHT

Rebibbia, Italy

Women's Regional Prison of Rome

THREE MONTHS EARLIER

The registry listed the arrival of five new prisoners, one of which—already notorious among the inmates for allegedly murdering a high-ranking cardinal—was an American by the name of Candace Baker, a petite, dimpled, short-haired blonde who hardly looked the part of a cold-blooded killer. But, of course, looks can be deceiving. Following her intake, she was brought to the warden's office for the orientation spiel.

Grazia Rinaldi sat straight-backed in her Boss, top grain Italian leather chair, hands folded on the desk. Rinaldi, a seasoned veteran of the prison system, was a short, stout woman of 62 with clipped salt-and-pepper hair and wire-rimmed glasses that rested just below the bridge of her nose. While bearing the image of one's sweet, adoring grandmother, it would be a mistake to confuse Warden Rinaldi with the same.

"Welcome to Women's Regional, Signorina Baker," Rinaldi said in English with a discernable Italian accent. "You have created quite a stir here, having become something of a celebrity, in fact, even before your arrival."

"Is that so," was Candace's snarky response.

"That is so, Signorina Baker. We do not get many Americans visiting our establishment. And by-the-way, you will address me as Warden Rinaldi at all times."

Candace cracked the gum she was chewing and said nothing. The warden looked over at the guard standing behind Candace, who swiftly slammed the back of her head with his baton. Candace flinched, but steeled herself against the pain.

"It is quite simple. I say something, and you say yes, Warden Rinaldi, or no, Warden Rinaldi, and so on. Do we understand each other?"

"Whatever you say…Warden Rinaldi."

"I see we are going to have some fun with you," the warden smiled. "Officer Dale, please help Miss Baker dispose of her gum," she said in Italian.

The guard grabbed a chunk of Candace's hair and snapped her head back. She then squeezed her jaw open and caught the ejected gum in her hand.

"Now, do we understand each other, Signorina Baker?"

When Candace remained silent, the guard rapped her with the baton once again, this time on the side of her face.

"Fuck!" she cried out in pain.

"What was that, Signorina Baker? I did not hear you."

"Fuck you!"

"I see," Rinaldi said, standing. "It appears that you will have to be broken, like a wild mare." Rinaldi addressed the guard. "Put her in isolation until she learns to be more…agreeable."

"Yes, Warden Rinaldi."

"Ah, you see, Signorina Baker, that is a perfect example of respect." She pulled a tissue from the box on her desk and handed it to Candace. "I am so sorry we are off on a bad note. Your cheek is bleeding."

Isolation was a small, narrow room with four walls and a rectangular, shatterproof window carved into a steel door. The only amenities were a cot that could barely support a child, a toilet, and a sink. The prisoner was given only one meal a day consisting of a protein, a starch, and a vegetable. She was also provided a gallon jug of water to prevent dehydration. Often, inmates would not drink. After several days without water, they would dehydrate and be taken to the infirmary. Candace was above such games. She had her own well-set footprint, and would never resort to devices of the chickenhearted.

Candace shared a cell with an inmate known as *Sawyer*. A large woman with a dyed-blue buzz cut and deeply pocked face. The word was that she had murdered her husband with a chainsaw…hence the pseudonym. She had been given a relatively light sentence. Her attorney convinced a jury of mostly women that Sawyer had killed her abusive husband in self-defense. She had already served fifteen of her twenty-five-year sentence, and was due for a parole hearing.

During her time in prison, Sawyer had achieved a certain level of 'respect.' Her sphere of influence was extensive, and the word around the cell blocks reverberated clearly…*don't fuck with Sawyer!* As improbable as it would seem, she took a liking to Candace almost immediately, no doubt seeing something of herself in this newbie. Sawyer's on-going trust issues had been heightened to levels of paranoia that controlled her responses in some ungainly ways…like not thinking twice about jamming a shiv into someone's gut who had looked at her the wrong way. Credit some other-worldly twist of fate for the curious connection these two women developed. They shared an acerbic wit and snarky attitude that drew them together. And neither of them would think twice about taking a human life. It was an unusual occurrence, out-of-cell time, not to see one without the other.

Sawyer educated Candace on how things worked in prison; who to associate with, and who to keep away from, which guards were easily manipulated, and which she should avoid. Abuse was not rampant, but it was a part of this world, particularly from several of the male guards, although some of the female guards were no less likely to engage in such activity. "You need to have eyes all around you," Sawyer told her. "Especially back of your head. This is prison. There is no honor here, only one rule—survival. If someone comes for you, they will come from behind, surrounded by their *soldiers*."

Candace, having picked up some of Sawyer's felonious traits, lost whatever moral compass she may have had. As their relationship grew tighter, Candace opened up about her well-known news reporter half-sister in America, and her plan to extort two-million dollars left to Hollinger by their father. As she listened, Sawyer's eyes lit up, her brain tingling with thoughts of a promising future.

After suffering through nearly four months at Rebibbia, waiting for her trial, Candace was released when the Procuratore della Repubblica, unable to build a case, dropped all charges against her with the proviso that she not leave Italy until the investigation was concluded, as she remained a person of interest.

Visions of thousand-dollar bills danced in Sawyer's head. Candace Baker had become her *ticket to ride*. She told Candace that for a split, she would arrange an exit plan to Cuba for her friend…an offer Candace would have liked to refuse, but what choice did she have? There was no one she could go to, nowhere to live. She had just enough change for an espresso.

"How can you possibly do that?"

"Not your concern. Do we have a deal?"

Candace stood there, staring at her prison-mate until Sawyer shrugged and turned to go.

"Deal!"

CHAPTER NINE

Killarney, Ireland

The Confession?

The brash lighting in the hospital corridor gave PJ a headache. She grabbed Val's hand and dragged him to the end of the hall where the lights were dimmed, a penny foolish attempt at saving energy perhaps. Nonetheless, it relieved her tension a smidge.

"I can think of more appealing places to get me alone, babe," Val grinned, easing her into the corner.

"Stop that."

"No."

PJ gave him a slight push. "Inappropriate."

"I wish you would relax. The boy will be fine."

"Shit and double shit," she muttered, catching Colleen from the corner of her eye speed walking toward them. *This should be interesting.*

"How did you know exactly where my son was, you…you…"

Val stepped between them before PJ could use her balled fists on Colleen. "I found your son. And you're welcome."

Colleen's mouth dropped. But it did not still. "And who are you?" she asked, a bit less militant.

"I'm the fiancé."

"Oh," was her tenuous response. With that, she did an about face, and marched off.

"My hero," PJ chirped. "Saved from Satan's clutches."

"Yes. Remember that the next time you find me annoying."

"I'll try." *He should only know how much I love him.* "Let's see if there's any news," she said. *Before things get too schmaltzy.*

The resident physician was surrounded by the entire Cunningham clan with the exception of Donnie, whom PJ assumed was with his son. They clamored around him for a status report. It was clear that Sean was out of danger as they were all smiling. PJ caught the last of the doctor's assurance. "...keep him overnight, just to be safe."

PJ thought it best to make herself scarce. "Let's go back to the hotel," she said.

"Now you're talking."

"I need to stop by the house first to pick up my laptop."

"Of course you do."

She sniggered. "You only get one pass at being annoying."

Val followed her into the house and headed for the kitchen to get a drink. "Can I get you a bottle of water?"

PJ was about to accept the offer when she heard a thump from above. She took the stairs two at a time and turned the corner to her room. Her door was slightly ajar. She was certain she had closed it before she left. She pushed it all the way open and stood there, stunned.

"What are you doing in my room, Donnie?"

He swung around. "PJ. I…I thought you were at the hospital."

"Really. I thought the same about you. Seems one of us was wrong. What are you looking for?"

"Oh. I, um, I…nothing, really." He grasped for some excuse quickly. "Just, um, a toy Sean may have left here when he slept over last month." He side-swiped her as he flew out the door and down the stairs. She took a few steps forward and gave the room a 360 sweep. Nothing seemed out of place. *"Damn!"* She ran to the bed, lifted the mattress, and breathed a sigh of relief. Her laptop was exactly where she'd left it. She dropped the mattress in place and smoothed the coverlet as Val popped into the room.

"Here," he said, handing PJ a bottle of water. "You haven't had anything to drink in a while."

"Thanks."

"Was that Donnie tear-assing out of here?"

Mystified by what just happened, PJ looked at Val blankly. "Yes. That was Donnie," she said, more to herself than to Val.

He took a sip of water. "A man on a mission, apparently."

"Apparently." Just then, her cell phone pinged. She pulled it out of her coat pocket and checked the message. She closed the phone and slipped it back into her pocket.

"Who was that?"

She hesitated. "Work." She pulled off her wool hat and shook out her hair. She remained silent for a while. Staring ahead.

"Are you all right, PJ?" No response. "PJ?"

"Yes, I'm fine!" she said, not meaning for it to sound so harsh. "Sorry. A lot going on."

"You think?"

Managing a faint smile, she stood, stuffed the laptop in its case, and hung the strap over her shoulder. She placed a gentle hand on Val's chest. "Let's go."

They spent the rest of Saturday and part of Sunday in and around the hotel, checking out some of the finer points of the village. They stopped at *Lir Café*—which claimed to offer the finest coffee in Ireland—before heading back to the farm for Sunday dinner.

On the drive back, PJ was in an unusually quiet mood. Deep in thought about whether to tell Val of her findings at the Land Registry—which had opened another can of worms? But even she did not yet know what it all meant. She'd have to dig deeper, and some assistance would certainly help. Time was running out faster than she could catch up. As much as she did not want Val involved, the fact that he was also in the business of finding things out kept invading her thoughts. He, too, had a sixth sense, and was just as discerning as she. Perhaps more so, not being in the thick of the forest. And he does have certain connections she doesn't.

"Val?"

He gave her a side glance.

"I need to talk to you."

"Finally!"

"No," she tried to show him a smile. "It's not what you think."

Big sigh. "Oh."

"I spent the day in town Friday. At the Muckross House Research Library, and the land registry office. She paused to form her thoughts before she answered the question on Val's face. "I don't really know why I decided to go there. Journalist's instinct, I guess. But beyond that, I have this pesky nudging to know more about the Cunningham family, their history, and by association…my history."

"And did you find anything interesting?"

She took a deep breath and snuggled into her coat. "I'm not sure. But enough to have raised some questions. And that's what I want to talk to you about."

"Uh, oh. Sounds like another toe-dip in quicksand."

"Possibly more than a toe-dip."

"Dammit, PJ! Not again."

"I would like your help."

Val fell silent. After driving half-a-mile, he pulled into a small shopping area and parked.

"Okay. Tell me."

PJ relayed the details of her village excursion, and the history of the Cunningham property.

"What is now a sheep farm," she said, "was originally a two-thousand-acre land estate, handed down from generation to generation."

"That's a whole lot of grass."

"I traced it back to the mid-nineteenth Century," she continued, her voice dancing with excitement. "Over time, portions of the land had been parceled out. Divided among heirs, sold, or confiscated."

"You've certainly done your homework. Why was the land confiscated?"

"I hadn't gotten that far. I assume because of debt. All that's left is the twenty acres the Cunninghams have settled on."

"It all sounds reasonable," he shrugged. "Must be more to it than that, though. It's not like you to be so excited over a land grab."

"There's a lot more. And that is where I need your matchless skill."

"I love when you butter me up."

"I'm serious, Val."

He leaned over and gave her a peck on the cheek. "Do tell."

"The land is owned by a shell corporation. Now why, I thought, would Liam Cunningham, the heir of these twenty acres, have need of a shell corporation?"

"Hmm."

"Exactly. And get this," she turned to face Val, her eyes shooting emerald sparks. "The shell corporation is owned by another shell corporation!"

"Obviously, someone wants to remain meta-anonymous."

"Exactly."

"The million-dollar question is, who? And why the subterfuge?" Val had always been understanding about giving PJ the space she needed, albeit not always without qualm. But his bottled displeasure could not be dismissed.

PJ waited for Val's response, becoming a touch annoyed when he closed his eyes and leaned back against the headrest. When he finally did speak, she turned away, not at all pleased with what he had to say.

"Why, PJ? Why is this so important that you need to crack open another Pandora's box? I don't understand. Your career is about to explode, and here you are..."

"I guess that means you're not going to help."

Val groaned. "I didn't say that."

"Never mind."

"PJ."

"Let's save it for another time." She forced a smile. "I don't want your visit to end on a sour note." She decided then, she would not tell him about the text message she'd received from Candice Baker that morning.

They drove the rest of the way to the farm in silence. PJ was the first to spot the rotating beacons atop the police car as they approached the driveway. Every nerve in her body came to attention. *What now?* Before Val could bring the car to a full stop, she threw open the car door and jumped out, tires still crunching over the gravel. Nearly slipping on a patch of ice hiding in the shade of the portico, she grabbed onto the door handle to keep from falling. She stepped into the foyer and stood a moment before heading toward the muted voices coming from the sitting room.

"Ah, Miss Hollinger." Inspector Doyle stood, turning toward PJ as she entered the room. Another officer was standing off to the side of the fireplace. "Not a moment too soon."

PJ slipped out of her coat and threw it over the armchair. "What's going on? Where is Fiona…Mrs. Cunningham?"

Doyle stuffed his hands into his pockets. "It seems that several more lambs have been silenced." He wisely withheld a burgeoning smile and apologized for the pun. "Mrs. Cunningham is in the office with Mr. Cunningham, presumably addressing the impact of this latest incident."

PJ dropped onto the sofa. *Jesus!* "Do you have any idea who…"

"We are working on a few things." He took a seat opposite PJ. "You should also know that the room you are currently occupying here has been ransacked."

"What? But why?" *Donnie!*

"I was hoping you could tell me, Miss Hollinger."

She looked away for a moment, then directly into Doyle's eyes. "I am just as much in the dark as you are," she lied.

Doyle just looked at her. "The forensics team has completed their sweep of the room. I would like you to go through it yourself, very carefully, and tell me if anything has been taken."

"Right now?"

"Please. And when you're done, Miss Hollinger, I would like you to come with me to the Garda Station. There are a number of details that have recently come to my attention concerning your relationship with the late Cardinal Montini that I would like to discuss."

Her veins turned to ice. A barrage of troubling thoughts swept through her mind. *This cannot be happening.* She needed time to think. She rose slowly, fearful her legs would cave beneath her. "I am an American citizen," she reminded Doyle, drawing from her well of bravado. "Unless you are charging me with a crime, Inspector Doyle, I am not going anywhere with you."

Val stood in the wide arch of the threshold between the foyer and sitting room. Having overheard most of the conversation between PJ and Doyle, a deeply cut frown appeared on his usually unruffled face. He looked from Doyle to PJ. "What's going on here?"

The walls were closing in on all sides. PJ turned while she could still hold herself up, and rushed from the room.

"PJ?" Val stomped behind her, the blood rising to his cheeks. "Goddammit!"

Her room, as Doyle had indicated, was in shambles. She knew the reason the moment she saw the rumpled bedding and the mattress half off the bed. "My laptop! Where is my laptop?" Her hand flew up to her mouth covering a soft whimper. She crumbled to the floor. Val knelt beside her and put his arm around her. "PJ, calm down. Your things are in the car. You took your laptop with you. Remember.?"

She leaned against the dresser, facing Val. "You shouldn't have come."

Val clenched his teeth. "Now you're really pissing me off,"

"I don't want you getting involved in this mess, Val. You need to go home."

He got up and paced. "It's the Montini thing, isn't it?" She looked away.

"Listen. Whoever the guy downstairs is, he has no jurisdiction over you for something that happened months ago in another country. And now, because they let Candace Baker slip through their hands, they will try to look under every damned doormat for the key." The tension sucked all the air out of the room.

"I don't believe that Candace killed Roberto Montini," PJ said finally, weakly.

"And how do you know that?"

She moved away from the dresser and turned to look out the window.

"PJ?"

"I know because…because there is a strong possibility that I killed him."

Val swung her into his arms. "You did no such thing. It's simply not you. Besides," he looked into her tear-filled eyes, "You were traumatized. Not behaving rationally. Your memory is compromised."

Do I actually remember? She questioned herself. *Or am I reflecting my dreams?* "I remember only my father's brains splattering all over me," she said, her voice trembling. "Nothing before and nothing after, until I woke on the plane. The scene still gives me nightmares."

CHAPTER TEN

Could Things Get Any Worse?

PJ heard Michael calling from down the hall. She froze. He could not have heard her impromptu *confession*, could he? She and Val looked at each other. Before she could say a word to Val, Michael was standing in the doorway, his mouth hanging open. "PJ. What happened here? Are you all right?" "Yes. I'm fine."

He glanced around the room, his eyes finally falling on Val. He did a double-take.

"Michael, this is Val Kendall…my fiancé," she added, understanding with some annoyance that Val would be listening for those two little words. She looked at Val. "This is Michael Cunning…"

"Yes. we've already met," Val said, extending his hand, which Michael took with some reluctance.

"I'm sure you're mistaken."

"I don't think so. We met in Dublin, remember? You weren't wearing a collar though," he added with a slight chuckle. "But I'm sure…" Val stopped cold. "You're right. Forgive my mistake."

"Not at all. I'm often mistaken for someone else. It's the ginger top," he said, a bit too nervously. "Very common here."

Val scratched his head, while PJ looked from one man to the other, wondering what had just happened.

"What happened here, PJ?" Michael asked with a look of concern.

"We're trying to figure that out," she said quietly.

A stretch of uneasy silence filled the small room. It was Michael who finally spoke. "Inspector Doyle told me that another two ewes were killed," he said. "This is strange. People here just don't go around killing their neighbor's sheep. Sheep farmers support each other."

PJ made an instantaneous, but resolute decision. "I think it's best if I leave."

Val flung his hands up at the ceiling. "Thank God!"

"Why?" Michael took PJ's hands into his. "Why would you do that? This is not your fault. Besides, you are family."

"Maybe that would be wise, darlin," Fiona said, stopping just outside the room.

"Mam!" Michael gave his mother an incredulous look.

"It's for her own safety, Michael." She turned toward PJ. "You know that, dear, don't you? Inspector Doyle believes..."

"Inspector Doyle can go to the devil!" Michael spat.

"All right. Enough." PJ plunked her hands on top of her head. "You're giving me a headache. And I'll not be the cause of a family squabble."

Validating her decision to cut short her stay would be tricky, but she had to tell them something. She thought quickly. "Those in the public eye are sitting targets for criticism and judgment. There is a psycho fringe out there—although a small percentage—who will act on their perceived displeasure or disapproval of the target. It could be something I've said or written that ignited a reaction." Enough said. The atmosphere heaved with a shadowy thickness. No one spoke. She left it at that. Her need for clarity begged a word with Fiona before she left. But this was not the ideal moment. That discussion would have to wait.

***

Having taken over as CFO of *Kendall and Son* since his father's illness, Val could not absent himself from a critical board meeting scheduled for Tuesday morning. Assuming PJ would be returning to the States with him, he had arranged for their flights, which would land them in New York on Monday evening. PJ, though, had other plans.

"I can't, Val. I need a few days to sort out this shell corporation business."

"What! Why would you want to spend another day here? I thought you said..."

"I've taken a room at the hotel."

Val's anger rarely manifested by trashing things or punching walls. His usual response was to close his eyes and take a deep breath. He'd made a vow to himself that PJ, as infuriating as she could be at times, would never be a target for his anger.

"Please don't do that eye-closing thing you do when you're upset. I will fly back on Wednesday. I promise."

Val took a turn around the room. "Okay. What time shall I pick you up at the airport?"

PJ was not happy about the tension that had settled between them on the eve of Val's departure. She could have gone back to the hotel with him for the night. She could have eased his mind with a bit more graciousness…maybe a lot more graciousness. She was who she was. Once a thing locked onto her brain, she would not let it go until satisfied it had been effectively resolved. She will not be controlled. Not even by the man she loved, especially by the man she loved.

***

Penelope Jane Hollinger had been a dysfunctional five-year old when adopted by Karen and Brett Hollinger, a bundle of insecurities with a dark, if brief, history. It took years of love and attention, and ongoing counseling before she was able to shed her dark past and walk in the light. Once that happened, there was no stopping her. She excelled in everything she undertook, from sports to academics. She lived each day as though it were the last and met, then exceeded every challenge. She would not be vanquished. Not by childhood trauma, not by the murder of her adoptive parents, not even by attempts on her own life. She had become the quintessential overcomer. But always, there is a cost.

***

Initially, PJ ignored the text from Candace. But, of course, the need to know what this bitter little sociopath was up to overruled her good sense. She agreed to meet her at the edge of the creek on Monday at noon.

She pulled up to the farmhouse before the road turned onto the driveway, and walked around the side of the house to the back. She crossed the wooden bridge leading to the path that would take her to the creek, wondering all the while why she was doing this. The sun made an occasional appearance through a thick, cloud-laden sky, but the scent of snowfall was in the air. She turned at the sound of movement behind her. A startling blow to the head brought her to the ground. Before her brain could register what was happening, a heavy boot slammed into her ribs. She winced, swiped the boot away, and jumped to her feet. She leaned against a boulder to steady herself and cursed her unpreparedness. She should have known better. "What do you want, Candace?"

"Good to see you, too, Sis."

"How did you manage to get to Ireland?

"You're not the only one with friends in high places."

PJ clenched her teeth. "You didn't get me down here to renew acquaintances. What do you want?"

Candace slapped PJ hard across her face. "I've been wanting to do that since the day we met." But for the gun pointing at her head, PJ would have loved to deliver a push kick to the sternum that would put Candace out of commission for a good while. "Well, now that you've gotten it out of your system, why am I here?"

"Jesus, you've become so slow, PJ." She swung the pistol away from PJ's head and into her gut. "I want the bequest that is rightfully mine. I want to put *you* behind bars, I want to see you grovel. In short…I want to destroy you." Candace's anger grew incrementally stronger with each item in her litany of wants. She backed away several feet to calm herself, keeping her Glock trained on PJ. "Sorry, Sis," she chuckled. "I just become so excited at the thought of watching you burn." "I'm only your half-sister, thank goodness. You're as crazy as your mother."

Candace's face flamed. She slapped PJ again. Harder. Her lip began to bleed.

"So, you're the one creating havoc for the Cunninghams," she said, wiping the trickle of blood from her mouth. "I suspect Gino is up to his usual tricks."

"Ha! That fucker is dead!"

Surprised at the news, PJ remained stoic. "So sorry for your loss." "Shut up, bitch!"

"Explain what you mean by *bequest*," she asked, honestly not knowing what Candace was talking about.

"Don't play dumb with me. Peter Romano…His Excellency…was my father, too. But only you got his two million. I deserve at least half. But now I want the whole thing, just to make up for the time I spent in prison. Time *you* should have served."

Inflamed to the point of distraction, PJ lurched at Candace, and ducked to the side as Candace fired off a shot that whizzed by her ear.

"Careful now. The next one won't miss."

"You won't shoot me," PJ said. "If you kill me, your dreams of the good life on my two million dollars will go poof!"

Candace brought her face inches from PJ's "Don't be so sure," she said, jabbing the gun into PJ's side. "The satisfaction of killing you may be worth the price."

PJ pushed her away. "How did you find out about the money?"

"Never mind that. I also want your laptop. That will give me complete control. That, and the photo I have of you shooting Montini between the eyes should seal the deal."

PJ flinched. "You're bluffing!"

"I knew that would get your attention." Candace cackled. "When I got back to the house in Frascati, I was looking for Gino. I heard a commotion and when I got to the landing, I saw Lucy, my mother…remember Lucinda Russell, PJ? I saw her impaled on a long, thick slice of glass. And there you were, standing in front of the reverent Cardinal Montini, gun in hand. The next thing I knew, Bang! Right between the eyes. Then another, Bang! Through his black heart. Nice work."

PJ narrowed her eyes and waited for the chance to drop Candace to her knees. "You must think I'm an idiot. The whole soap opera was broadcast around the globe, and plastered on every front page…with all the bloody details."

"Whatever." Candace waved her gun. "Move."

"Where are we going?"

"We're going to find your laptop."

Propelled by a surge of adrenalin, PJ made a quarter turn and thrust a lead kick to Candace's torso, knocking the breath out of her. Candace fell to her knees, moaning in pain as the gun flipped onto the rocks and over the side of the railing.

One of the first and most consequential rules of journalism inculcated in PJ's mind during her years at Stanford, was *Document everything,* with a capital E. She raced back to the farmhouse for her car, her feet seeming inches off the ground. She needed to get back to the hotel where she could think, sift through everything that had happened from the moment she stepped foot on the Cunningham farm until today, and get it all on record. That was the only thought keeping her mind off the stomach-churning feeling that her life had been taken over by some evil, shape-shifting entity. She turned the key in the ignition, floored the gas pedal, and skidded away from the farm like a rabbit being chased by a hound.

***

On Tuesday morning, PJ received an encrypted email from Val containing the answers she was looking for. Having put Candace out of her thoughts for the moment, she drove out to the farm to confront Fiona Cunningham. She'd promised Val she would be in New York late Wednesday. And barring some unforeseen catastrophe, she would keep that promise using most of Tuesday and part of Wednesday to polish off a draft she'd been working on—an opening show script she was proposing for the *Breaking News* segment. Bringing certain truths to light about a nearly 30-year-old mystery would bring uncontestable closure. And undoubtedly secure a huge segment of audience. This was her hope. Of course, the vagaries of life do not always cooperate with hopeful intentions.

She found Fiona in her home office at the back of the farmhouse, leaning over a ledger. The door was ajar. PJ knocked and walked into the small, dimly lit room, cluttered with file cabinets and various size tables—two round and three rectangular—each one covered with file folders and small stacks of papers. "Not now," Fiona grumbled without looking up.

"Sorry to bother you, Fiona. We need to talk."

Fiona quickly closed the ledger, lifted her head, and adjusted her demeanor. "PJ," she said, forcing a smile that never reached her eyes. "I wasn't expecting you, dear." She looked tired, worn. Her salt and pepper hair, always neatly in place, was uncombed. An unruly gathering of short, springy tendrils framed her face. "Is something wrong?"

PJ's attention was drawn to the wide bay window overlooking the east end of the back porch. Outside a gust of wind speared through the Scots pines that ringed the backyard, juddering the window glass. A light snow began to fall. She turned to Fiona.

"I'm sure you've guessed, or heard, that I'll be leaving tomorrow."

"I…Michael told me. It's probably for the best."

PJ had the urge to shout accusations but held her anger in check. Whatever secrets the woman was holding, or lies she'd fabricated, her life had not been a joy ride. She deserved a hearing. "I need to ask you a question. And I'd like you to be truthful."

Fiona looked as if she were about to protest, but held her tongue. "All right. What is it?"

"Do you know who my father was?"

"Why are you asking me this?"

"Do you?"

Fiona looked away. "The Pope for a Day." she said, her voice dripping ice.

"Correct. Cardinal Peter Romano. And it was three days. Three days in which he managed to do some good, before resigning."

Fiona spun around, flushed. "Why are you defending him? You know who he was, what he did." Her eyes filled. "He ruined my daughter!"

"And you and your husband were culpable parties!" PJ knew as soon as the words flew out of her mouth that she crossed a line that could not be moved.

Fiona blanched. "How dare you!"

PJ sat on the only other chair in the room, a cushioned antique wooden rocking chair.

"Cardinal Romano," she sighed, "was certainly not on the short list for canonization…or the long list. But, like everyone else, he deserves a defense." The wind kicked up again, whirring through the branches creating a tightening of already strung-out nerves. "He may have been the worst sinner of the age, but whatever evils he committed, in the end, he made every effort to redeem himself."

"What he did was criminal," Fiona persisted.

PJ leaned in, their faces inches apart. "You and I both know that he did not kidnap Mary. Or lure her away to a secret harem of underage girls...as some have accused him of."

Fiona dropped her face in her hands. She said nothing for several beats, then, with renewed self-possession, she sat erect and looked directly at PJ. She raised her eyebrows and steeled her face. "I have no idea what you are talking about, PJ. I think it's good that you are leaving. Get on with your privileged life."

PJ could not hold back the burning anger. "I'm talking about how the Cunningham's were nearly bankrupt in 1991 and about to lose this farm. I'm talking about how you begged then *Father* Romano for help. I'm talking about selling your own child!"

"Stop it! Just stop it!" Fiona stood, wringing her hands as she paced the room. "She was better off. I saw how he looked at her. There were rumors about him. He would have taken her. I know he would have."

"No, Fiona You didn't know that, and I'm betting that when Liam made the offer, Peter refused."

"But not for long," Fiona shot back. "He couldn't forestall his urges for long."

Neither said a word. Fiona slumped in her chair. "She would not have survived living in destitution," she said. "She was made for so much more than that. We were giving her freedom from a mediocre life on a failing sheep farm. He promised to take care of her."

"And how did that work out?"

Fiona stared at PJ. Her eyes fired with anger. PJ had the uneasy feeling that Fiona was about to strike her. She sprang from her chair and stepped back. "My intention is not to exhume long-buried events," she said, calmly. "There is no fruitful end in trying to right the many wrongdoings of a so-called *holy institution.* I simply want to set the record straight."

"And turn against your own family."

"Biology does not make a family."

Fiona turned her head and swiveled her chair back around to the desk. "I think you should leave now…and never come back."

The words stung. But they would not deter her mission. The snow was coming down heavily. The walkway was slick. Gingerly, PJ made her way to the rental car. She was about to open the car door and get in when a man's voice summoned her.

"Miss Hollinger." Inspector Doyle jogged toward her, breathing heavily as he caught up to her.

"Inspector?"

"I need you to come with me, Miss Hollinger. To answer some questions and perhaps clarify some new information we have just received."

She immediately stiffened. "I beg your pardon. What new information?"

"I'd prefer to discuss that with you at the station."

Her breath hitched. Her insides clenched as though compressed in a vise. The blood rushed to her head with such force, she had to brace herself against the car, bringing her hand to her head.

"Are you quite all right, Miss Hollinger?"

She berated herself for showing weakness, but rebounded quickly. "I told you once before Inspector Doyle, unless you're charging me with a crime, you have no right…"

"Please, Miss Hollinger. Let's not make this more difficult than need be."

"Are you arresting me, Inspector?"

Doyle shuffled his feet. "Not just yet." He tightened the scarf around his neck against the wind. "You are, however, a person of interest."

"For what crime?" she asked, scrambling for composure.

The inspector did not hesitate. "The murder of Cardinal Roberto Alphonse Montini."

CHAPTER ELEVEN

New York City

The Getaway

Val arrived at the terminal on Wednesday evening at eight p.m. He had not heard from PJ since Tuesday morning when she promised to be on the Delta flight scheduled to land at LaGuardia at 8:55 p.m. He texted her earlier in the day to confirm. She did not respond. He felt uneasy. PJ always kept her promises, he reminded himself. He checked the flight board. It was scheduled to arrive on time. At 8:35, he checked the board again. No change. He bought a coffee and found an empty seat, took out his phone and scrolled his emails. He replied to only one, nervously tapping his feet. He couldn't concentrate. He then checked his text messages for the umpteenth time, and put his mobile phone away. He got up and paced, nervously jangling the keys in his pocket. At 8:50, he looked at the flight board again. *Landed.* He raked his fingers through his hair and breathed a sigh of relief.

The passengers began pouring out, slowly, at first, then in clumps. His eyes were glued to the exit ramp, waiting to rest upon that gorgeous face. When all passengers had deplaned, Val's heart sank. He rushed over to the flight desk.

"Would you check the passenger list for me, please. I was expecting my fiancé to be on this flight, but…"

"Name?" The desk attendant asked, blandly.

"Hollinger, PJ."

"Spell that for me, please."

Val did so. The attendant took an interminably long time. "I'm sorry, there was no one on this flight by that name."

Val began rolling his fingers on the counter, trying to order his thoughts. "What about the next flight?"

"The next flight from Dublin does not arrive until tomorrow, same time. And we do not have a passenger list yet."

Val stood there, immobilized. After several seconds, the attendant had to ask him to move on.

"Sir, I need to help the next person." He made no effort to move. "Sir, please step aside."

His ears finally picked up the more insistent tone. He walked off, steamed, and wended his way toward the exit. He sat in his car, resting his pounding head on the steering wheel. When his pulse returned to normal, he took out his phone and dialed PJ's number. It rang and rang and kept ringing until he finally hung up. "Fuck!" It took a few seconds for him to realize that the call never went to voicemail.

The next call he made was to Sil Romano.

"Slow down, son, I can't understand your blathering."

Val took a long breath and began again. "PJ's not answering her phone. And I'm unable to leave a message because apparently, her voicemail has been turned off."

"So what's the urgency? You know she does screwy things when she needs *alone time, a*s she calls it."

"Here's the urgency, Sil," he said angrily. "She was not on the flight she was supposed to be on, and I haven't heard a word from her in 36 hours!"

"Okay, okay. Let me get in touch with Simmon's and get back to you."

KILLARNEY, IRELAND

Doyle had no choice but to let PJ leave…with the promise that the next time they met, he would have an arrest warrant. He warned her not to leave the country.

PJ figured it would take Doyle at least a day to scurry up a warrant. After her confrontation with the inspector, she raced back to the hotel, packed, and gave the bellhop a hundred-dollar bill to return the rental car for her. She called a taxi and had it pick her up at the delivery exit in the event Doyle was having her followed.

She knew she should call Val, but she had neither the time nor the strength to deal with all the questions he'd have. She was adamant about not having him involved in this hot mess any more than he already was. She would call him once she was safely out of the country. She'd deal with his inevitable anger then.

The cab ride seemed interminable. Her hands clenched around the handle of the carry-on. She could barely string two plausible thoughts together. Her body felt the weight of a 200-pound anvil pressing down on her. She closed her eyes and took deep breaths, refocusing her mind to the tune of calm.

The taxi dropped her off at St. Malachy's Catholic Church. She needed to ask Michael for a favor. A big favor.

Knowing that Doyle would probably have Gardai at the airport, as she paced the rather confining rectory waiting for someone to locate Michael, PJ developed a plan that would get her to the UK where she'd get on a flight from Liverpool to Los Angeles. She had turned her phone off, and purchased a phone card using cash, trusting that would keep Doyle out of her hair, and give her the time she needed to drive to Dublin and take the ferry to Liverpool. She was in the middle of hatching her plan when Michael burst into the room.

"PJ! Is everything all right?" He gave her a warm embrace. "This is quite a surprise—A pleasant surprise to be sure, but…"

"Michael, I need to borrow your car," she said. "Please don't ask questions. I know we haven't had enough time to get to know each other well, but I believe I can trust you, and I'm in a bit of a mess."

Michael looked at her for a long minute. "Quid pro quo?"

"What?"

"You keep my secret and I'll keep yours," he said with a wink.

"I don't understand."

"Didn't your fiancé tell you about our…encounter?"

"What encounter?" They looked at each other in mutual confusion. "Never mind, then," he said. "Whatever you need."

She hugged his neck. "Thank you. I'll explain another time."

"I will look forward to that."

Michael gave PJ the keys to his Toyota. She told him he would find it at the Dublin ferry crossing, apologized for the inconvenience, and cautioned him not to tell anyone.

"My lips are sealed."

She kissed him on the cheek and left, a strong pang of fear and a cloud of uncertainty hovering over her like a thought bubble in a comic strip. Except, there was nothing at all funny at the recent series of events…or what providence yet had in store for her.

Ten hours later, PJ disembarked in Liverpool and grabbed a cab to the airport. So far, her plan was working.

***

Doyle did not actually have enough evidence to hold PJ. For the most part he was bluffing. All he had was a phone message they were unable to trace that claimed PJ Hollinger murdered Cardinal Roberto Montini at his residence in Frascati, Italy. Anyone could have made that call. There could be dozens of people with grievances against PJ Hollinger for exposing their respective foibles. Although he had the ability to interview her as a possible suspect, given her American citizenship, he did not want to overstep any bounds unless absolutely necessary. He did, however, alert the Kerry and Dublin airports to detain the potential suspect should she attempt to leave the country. On Friday, he decided to pay Miss Hollinger another visit and headed out to the Cunningham farm.

Liam answered the door. "Fiona is at market," he said, thinking Doyle was there to see his wife.

"As it happens, Mr. Cunningham, I am looking for Miss Hollinger." "Not here," he said, curtly.

"Do you know when she will be?"

"Fiona said she's staying at a hotel…The Killarney, I think."

"Oh?"

"Yeah. Seems the ladies had a tiff."

Doyle did not know what to make of that. He gave Liam his card. "Please ask her to call me if she should return."

Doyle sped straightaway to the Killarney hotel, where he was told Ms. Hollinger had checked out two days prior. "Fecking eejit!" he said out loud, smacking himself on the head.

Done with berating himself for his indecisiveness, Doyle issued a Blue Notice request through INTERPOL.

***

Candace was running out of money. If she didn't get her hands on some cash soon, her plan would fold like the first little piggy's house of straw. PJ had already slipped away…*bitch!* The car Candace had *borrowed* ran out of gas on the M8 to Dublin. She used every curse word she could think of as she thumbed her way along the highway. After an endless stream of vehicles whizzed past, an eighteen-wheeler slowed, brakes squealing as it pulled to a stop onto the right shoulder.

"I need to get to Dublin," she shouted up at the open window over the din of the highway. The driver, a scruffy looking dude she estimated to be in his mid-forties, looked like he hadn't showered in a month of Sundays. He motioned her to climb in, his eyes scanning her from head to toe not bothering to conceal his voracious intent.

"Thanks."

"No problem, sweetie."

She'd hoped she would have been picked up by someone with a car she could jack. But this was how things seemed to be going. She needed cash, and this guy was it. The creep asked her name. She sighed, then swallowed the churlish retort that was eager to spring off the tip of her tongue. She needed to play the game until she got to Dublin, or within walking distance.

"PJ," she told him, not knowing exactly why. It just popped into her head and out of her mouth. "What's yours?"

"Brian." Pause. "What's the PJ stand for?"

She blew out a sigh. "Just PJ."

"Whatever. What's a cute little thing like yourself doin' out here all alone?"

Candace was beginning to feel nauseous. The smell of him was getting to her. It was at least another two hours or so to Dublin. "You ask a lot of questions, Brian."

He gave her a lecherous side glance. "The better to know you, my dear," he said, then chuckled at his own wit.

Candace rolled her eyes. Adjusted her backpack.

"Why don't you lose that thing? Make yourself more comfortable. We got a-ways to go."

"I'm fine."

"Yes, you are, girl."

Oh, my God, she thought. *I don't know how long I can do this.*

They drove awhile in silence before Brian again spoke. "Not very friendly, are you?"

She looked out her window. "Depends on how you define *friendly.*"

Brian changed the theme. "How about if I make you dinner. My place is just outside of Dublin by three miles. And I've been told I'm a pretty good cook…among other talents." He had a foghorn laugh that made her want to gut him right there. But she held on. Just a few more miles.

Without a word, he pulled into a truck stop. A short strip of about fifty yards that included a slop house of a diner and a row of shanty-like cabins with *motel sex* written all over them.

"Changed my mind, sweetie. Time for dinner…and dessert." Again, that laugh.

Fuck! Candace was not prepared to make her move yet. She would have to play along until she could get her bearings.

The creep jumped down off the step and walked around the front of the truck. He opened the door for Candace. "Here we go." He grabbed the side handle, hoisted himself up, gripped her around the waist, and pulled her down with him. He was a big man. "Jesus, you're so light, like you're empty inside." Once her feet touched the ground, she jerked away. He pushed her ahead. "Come on now. You must be hungry." Brian guided her with his hand, fingers splayed across her back. He attempted to pull off her backpack. She elbowed him in the gut, which didn't even elicit a wince. She spun around to confront him. "Fuck off!!"

He put up his hands. "Easy, little lady. Just tryin' to make you more comfortable." They took a booth and slid in...Well, Candace slid; Brian had to wriggle himself into it. He ordered two steak dinners that came with mashed potatoes and green beans. Candace had two beers, but did not touch her food. He scoffed his down, then ate Candace's.

"Not hungry?"

She gave him a snotty look. "I need to get to Dublin before the second coming."

About thirty seconds had elapsed before Brian burst into raucous laughter. "I get it now. Funny. That's really funny." His laughter ended abruptly. "Enough chatter," he said, digging into his jacket pocket and pulling out a wad of euros that made Candace's eyes light up. He tossed a couple on the table and shimmied himself out of the booth. "Let's go."

The next morning, the motel manager discovered Brian's very dead body after he had failed to settle his bill. His throat had a four-inch gash in the well of his neck, just below the laryngeal prominence of the thyroid cartilage. Candace was gone...and about 600 Euros richer.

CHAPTER TWELVE

Los Angeles, California

The Sisterhood

Somewhere, about thirty-thousand feet over the Atlantic, PJ awoke with a start, trembling from icy beads of sweat that covered most of her body. She asked her seat neighbor if he would be good enough to lower the A/C blowing cold air directly on her. He obliged, but not without a grumpy comment.

She had been dreaming, again. Reliving for the thousandth time, a murder scene as it had been replayed under hypnosis. She had no conscious memory of holding a gun aimed at the head of Cardinal Roberto Montini. Immobilized as he was, tied to a chair, his life about to be snuffed out, Montini made the mistake of admitting to having PJ's adoptive parents killed, along with a series of other maleficent deeds. He recited these horrific acts as dryly as running down items on a grocery list. Somehow, PJ had left her body for the millisecond it took her brain to relay the message to her trigger finger. The bullet tunneled into Montini's head, leaving an ugly, bloody hole between his eyes before he could complete his litany of crimes. A second bullet…through the heart…followed.

The battle to unravel the mystery of her life still raged. If she could only shed her past like a Cobra sheds its skin, maybe she would find some peace. She had come so close. Now the dreams were back. And if that were not enough, she was probably being sought internationally for questioning involving a murder she had no conscious knowledge of.

She drew the blanket around herself and checked her watch. They should be landing at LAX in about an hour-thirty. She took out her laptop to check her emails. Finally, a reply from Reynolds' office.

Ms. Hollinger: Mr. Reynolds will see you at 11:00 a.m., Tuesday.

Short and sweet. Good enough. She closed the laptop. The elderly gentleman beside her...A/C man...was glaring at her, apparently his irritation still simmering. She was about to respond indelicately when she realized she'd been drumming her fingernails on the laptop. She returned the old man's glare. "It helps me think."

He pursed his lips and turned away.

She thought about Val. *He must be livid.* She sent him a brief email: *I will be out of reach for a few days,* she wrote. *I will explain everything.* She added an emoji heart and punched the send button. It would not go over well, she knew. But what could she do? She was, literally on the run, one impulse-reaction after another. Until she could cut back, slow her mind, and develop a viable plan, Val had to wait. Her first step was to see Jefferson Reynolds, the Hollinger's legal counsel and executor, the man controlling her financial position...and possibly her fate.

PJ had no idea what might be awaiting her at LAX. She stayed back until all passengers had deplaned, piled her hair into a men's felt Trilby hat she'd purchased in Liverpool, and put on a pair of oversized sunglasses. She grabbed her carryon from the baggage compartment and made her way through the jetway into the terminal without incident. *Thank God,* she whispered under her breath. She had turned down celebrity status travel arrangements offered by the network. They did not ask any questions when she'd advised them of her arrival date. They had, however, set her up for her stay in LA. *"Anything to get you back here next week, Ms. Hollinger."* And therein lay the rub…next week might not arrive if she did not gather up and dispose of all the debris she had accumulated…and quickly. Right now, she needed to get discreetly to the hotel and set her mind to the meeting with Reynolds.

The one checked bag containing a hard-sided gun box was waiting for her in her room at the Ritz Carlton…not a hostelry known for its anonymity, but if this is where the network people put her, she was not about to argue. How could she refuse such luxurious splendor? After settling in, she showered, ordered room service, and made due with a tank top and gym shorts to sleep in. She sat on the bed, propped against the headboard with multiple pillows in a sort of Lotus position, and opened her laptop. She reconsidered contacting Val with an explanation, if only to assure him that she was okay. *Liar! I am light years from okay.* She had installed TOR software, so felt fairly secure her emails could not be traced.

"Sorry," she wrote, then deleted and started again. "Please forgive me for being incommunicado. I'm in a bit of a difficult situation which should be cleared up after Tuesday. Will explain everything in detail when I see you." She read it over and added, "I love you." Then backspaced and deleted the I, not entirely sure why. In any event, this should satisfy him enough so he would not be chasing around the globe after her.

She jotted down some script notes, answered a few questions from NBC's legal department regarding her contract, and decided to call it a night. She left most of her dinner, but she needed sleep more than food. Before turning out the light, she took the revolver out of the gun box and placed it under the pillow beside her.

In her dream, the same dream she'd been having almost nightly for the past few months, she is being pursued by a hulk of a man in a red cap brandishing a knife. The blood dripping from the knife is a deep crimson, almost black. Suddenly, the face of a laughing Roberto Montini inserts itself. There is a gaping hole in the center of his forehead. As the hole widens and deepens, PJ begins to see an image of her own head floating in some kind of viscous fluid inside the hole. She's crying out in search of her body so that she can put the two parts of herself together when the hole slowly closes, swallowing her up. This is the point at which she usually wakes and jolts upright dripping with sweat. But this time there is a distant voice calling her name. She feels a strong pain in the muscles of her arms as the voice gets closer and louder.

"Ms. Hollinger. Wake up." The hotel manager on call is gripping her by the arms and shaking her. "Ms. Hollinger. There you are. Are you all right?"

"What? Let go of me. You're hurting me."

"I am so sorry." He released her and guided her toward the settee. "Here. Why don't you sit down." He poured her some tea.

She sat as directed, massaging her sore arms. "What happened?"

"You apparently had some sort of…episode. A nightmare?" He paused. "Oh, my name is Carl. I am one of the night managers. A guest in the next room complained about a banging noise coming from your room," he explained. "In your sleep-walk, you were pounding on the door, rather loudly I should say, in an apparent attempt to get out." He looked at her sheepishly. "Sorry if I bruised you. You are very strong."

"That's all right." She held her head in her hands. *Good God. It's happening again.*

"Is there anything I can get you, Ms. Hollinger? Do you require medical attention? I have to ask"

"No. No, I'm fine. Just an unusually realistic dream." She looked away. "I'll be fine. Thank you. Sorry to have caused a ruckus."

"No apology necessary. If you need anything more..."

"I'm fine now. Thank you."

Carl left and PJ got up, opened the mini-fridge, and found what she was looking for. She unscrewed the cap and downed half of the shot-size bottle of bourbon in one swallow. She poured the rest of it into her tea. *There, that's better.* It was now three a.m. She got back into bed, but sleep eluded her. She sat up, fluffed the pillows, and opened her laptop. A new email. It was not from Val. She had not received any response thus far from Val. He must be truly pissed at her. The email was from Charlie. She brightened up.

Girlfriend. Where R U? Y R U not returning my calls/texts? Did you lose your phone again???

Call, text, or write...or I'm coming after you!!!

PJ heard herself chuckle as tears welled. *Oh, Charlie, if I ever needed you, it's now.* She texted back:

Didn't know you were in town. I'm in LA. Need to see you! Don't have much time. I can drive up to Brentwood later today. Please be home! ☹

Given the hour, she did not expect a reply until morning. But Charlie—the night owl that she was—got right back to her.

OMG! Of course I'll be home! But Wally is in one of his restructuring modes...experimenting on a new architectural design. I need a map to find my way in and out of the polyethylene labyrinth that is now my home. Sounds like a drinking lunch is in order. Meet me at Sur Le Ver @ one. Can't wait to see you!!

Charlotte Fredericks Thurgood and Penelope Jane Hollinger had been inseparable since grade school. Wherever PJ was, Charlotte—shortened to Charlie at PJ's insistence—was never far behind, or ahead. Outwardly, they are worlds apart, but otherwise, two sides of the same coin. Charlie, gregarious, flippant, often indelicate, contrasts starkly with PJ's cultivated, intellectual, serious nature. Ever ferociously protective of each other, despite their differences, their sisterhood of two remained inviolable.

Parting after high school graduation had been traumatic. PJ went on to Stanford situated in the heart of *Silicon Valley*, and Charlie, an intensely beautiful, light-skinned Black woman, went on to become a popular, well-paid fashion model. She met Walden Thurgood, III while doing a modeling gig at the New York Auto Show. They married a year later, and bought a home in London in the Knightsbridge section, commuting back-and-forth to and from LA until the house in Brentwood was completed. Now London is more-or-less their summer residence.

Charlie married well. She and Walden, however, remained childless—by choice—as far as public knowledge is concerned. But PJ knows that Charlie is unable to have children. A condition she will only discuss with PJ, if rarely. Walden Thurgood fully supported remaining childless.

"Children bring untenable worries. And you, my darling, are quite enough for me to worry about," was Thurgood's response to this news.

Charlie gave up her modeling career soon after marriage, filling her time entertaining and managing The Thurgood Foundation, a philanthropical organization begun by Walden's grandfather.

Both stunningly beautiful women, their relationship hinged on a deep, time-honored love and genuine respect for each other. Charlie's arresting stature, exotic, deep chocolate eyes, and flawless, light caramel skin, and PJ's impeccably fair skin, perfect facial structure, and hypnotic emerald green eyes provide nonpareil eye candy; heads literally turn wherever they go. But beauty is a double-edged sword, at once a blessing and a curse drawing both admiration and envy.

Sur Le Ver is bouncing with the usual lunch crowd. Vibrating with angst, PJ is uncommonly short with the waitstaff.

"My, my, a tad cranky today, are we?" Charlie turns to the waiter. "Don't mind my friend,

Gregory. She gets a bit out of sorts when she hasn't been laid for a while." Gregory offers the obligatory smile. "The usual, Mrs. Thurgood?

"Yes, and my friend here will have the same…and lots of it." "I can speak for myself, thank you. And thanks for embarrassing me. Not funny." Nonetheless, they wrap arms around each other in a long-held embrace.

"That's enough, PJ, you're deflating my implants."

They had barely settled into their seats when the interrogation began.

"So how is your hunka-hunka love?"

"Val's fine."

"That's it? Val's fine?"

"Yes. That's it. He's fine. Can we move on?"

"Oooh, you *are* touchy today. Why don't you just marry the guy so you can avoid these long stretches of sexual fasting."

"Stop it, Charlie. Actually, he came to Ireland for a weekend."

"All the more reason to tie the proverbial knot. You know neither of you can stand being away from each other."

"Something's happened, Charlie."

Charlie leaned forward and put both hands over PJ's. "Something is always happening, my sista from a different mista. Just tell me that *you're* okay."

PJ gave her a wan smile. "I'm not sure. The dreams are back, Candace Baker is out of prison, and," she lowered her voice to a whisper. "And I think I may have put two bullets into

Roberto Montini…although I have no memory of it."

"And why wouldn't you have murdered that douchebag?"

"I'm serious."

"So am I."

"Can you stop being flippant, for once. I can go to prison for life…Or worse!"

Charlie squeezed PJ's hands. "You know how I get when I'm nervous. I didn't sleep a wink after your text. And you are not going to jail. That is ludicrous. Walden's lawyer will take care of everything."

"I have an attorney. The Hollinger's long-time counselor. I'm seeing him tomorrow morning."

"Good. But you always need an ace in the hole, and Walden's gal is tops."

"Thank you. We'll see how it goes tomorrow."

"I'll come with you."

"No!"

"Okay, okay. Just a thought. Wait! Did you say Candace Baker is out?"

"Yes. And with visions of my body in a casket."

"Shit!"

"And double shit."

Gregory brought their drinks and a light lunch plate. "Will there be anything else, Mrs. Thurgood?" Charlie put her elbow on the table and hooded her eyes, paying no attention to Gregory.

"Mrs. Thurgood is deep in thought, Gregory," PJ spoke up. "But I think that will be all for now, thank you."

"Very well, Miss."

Charlie sat erect. "What is she up to? Where is she?"

"She was in Ireland. Stupidly, I agreed to meet with her to *talk*."

"She followed you to Ireland? That's crazy. Did you report her stalking to the police?"

"Given the circumstances, Charlie, I really don't want to have anything to do with the police."

"But what will you do? The woman is a psycho."

"That may be a moot point," PJ said, taking a sip of her drink. "If I go to prison, I will kill myself before she has the pleasure."

CHAPTER THIRTEEN

The Lawyer

The law offices of Reynolds and Reynolds occupy the entire 18th floor of a 32-story high-rise on Wilshire Blvd. Just one of several imposing skyscrapers along the *Miracle Mile*. PJ could not remember the last time she'd been in LA, but it had been quite a while. Of course, some things never change. The morning smog, the bumper-to-bumper river of vehicles streaming their way along the freeway to some translunary destination. Nothing new here. She pulled into the underground parking garage, surprised to find an actual living person rather than a machine that spit out tickets before a slow rising guardrail.

"Good morning. May I have your name and a form of identification, please."

PJ complied and handed him her press pass. He checked it against his iPad. "Please take a left at the end of the ramp and park in the V.I.P. section," he said, handing back her card. "The elevator will take you to the 18th floor. Have a nice day." She thanked him and followed his instructions.

The tortoise-like movement of the elevator doors only added to PJ's apprehension as they inched open on the 18th floor, like a ponderous curtain on a Broadway stage between acts. They finally opened, onto a minimalist vastness in the center of which stood a blindingly shiny ebony circular desk with gold-plated edging. Suspended overhead on thick gold chains, like the sword of Damocles, hung an enormous matching ebony plaque with ***REYNOLDS and REYNOLDS*** etched in gold lettering, leaving no questions as to who occupied the premises.

The room was comprised of several ultra-modern seating arrangements overlooking an incredible view of the city through floor-to-ceiling, laminated glass panels. PJ stepped up to the desk and asked for Jefferson Reynolds. The young woman behind the desk took a moment to survey PJ before she spoke.

"Mr. Reynolds is expecting you." She swiveled out of her chair. "This way, please."

PJ walked around the desk and fell into step with the receptionist. "May I offer you something to drink, Ms. Hollinger?"

PJ declined.

Reynolds' corner office was at the end of a walkway, the length of which was extravagantly accoutered with handmade marble inlay flooring. A collection of original paintings obtained from various auctions and galleries around the globe rendered the walls on which they hung, arguably one of the most well-decorated…and costly…in the country, perhaps the world. The receptionist knocked on the hand-carved, rosewood door and waved PJ inside. With a broad, ultra-white smile and outstretched hand, Jefferson Reynolds walked toward PJ. "Wow! Penelope Jane Hollinger. And I thought all those pictures of you were photo-shopped."

PJ took his hand, despite her confusion. "I have an appointment with Jefferson Reynolds."

He gave her a questioning half-smile. "Well, here I am…in the flesh." He cocked his head. "Ah, you mean my father. He's cruising somewhere on the Mediterranean as we speak. Your appointment is with me."

"But..."

"Come. Sit. We'll talk. How about a drink? Bourbon? Scotch?"

She gave him a sidewise look. "It's a bit early."

"Well, then. Coffee, tea, or water?"

"Nothing. I'm fine, really. I don't mean to be rude, but I need to see your father. He's familiar with..."

"You're absolutely gorgeous. Did you know your right eyebrow goes up when you're tense?"

PJ turned to leave. "Apparently, this was a mistake."

"I don't think so." Reynolds immediately changed his tone. "But leaving would be. Please, sit down, Ms. Hollinger." He took a breath. Offered a smile. "My father is an estate lawyer. He would not be able to handle your case. I, on the other hand, am a criminal defense attorney."

"But, how did you..."

"I never see anyone before learning everything I can about a potential case," he said. "For example, were you aware that you're being sought for questioning by INTERPOL?"

"What! No! How..."

"Not to worry, my dear," he said with a sly curl of his lips. "I've already made a formal request to have the Blue Notice rescinded. Not a problem."

"How is that possible?"

"Anything is possible. If you have the balls to make it so."

PJ was not impressed by Reynolds. A crass, pompous ass who looked more like a surfer type than an attorney, although he was not hard to look at with his curly blonde hair and piercing blue eyes, which he used to every advantage. She turned away, needing to think about this. If she needed anything at this moment, she needed a savvy attorney.

He apparently picked up on her disapproving look. "I beg your pardon." He brought his hand to his heart. "I can see I have offended. It is just my way. You'll get used to it," he winked.

"I very much doubt that, Mr. Reynolds." Nonetheless, she took a seat on the teal blue Tetea-Tete. "I am in a bind at the moment, as you apparently know. I need to be back in New York by Sunday, and I do not want to be greeted outside my apartment by a swat team."

Reynold's chuckled. "Jeff," he corrected her. "Please, call me Jeff." He sat next to her and placed his hand lightly on her knee. "Let me assure you, PJ…may I call you PJ?" He did not wait for an answer. "Let me assure you that I have yet to lose a case. In fact, my colleagues on the other side have often accused me of sorcery." He waited for a response. An appreciation, perhaps, of his wit. When none came, he patted her knee, got up, and sat behind his desk.

"I'm going to be recording this." He pressed a button on his iPhone and laid it flat on the edge of his desk with the microphone facing PJ. "Confidential interview with Penelope Jane— PJ—Hollinger, fifth of May, 2020." He loosened his tie and sat back in his indigo aniline leather chair. "Tell me everything. And I mean everything. Start wherever…go back and forth if need be, but leave nothing out.”

After nearly ninety minutes of listening to PJ’s narrative, occasionally interrupting to ask a question, Reynolds turned off the recorder. “So, bottom line is…” He stood and walked slowly around the spacious, hexagonal room as he spoke. “Candace Baker, your half-sister—both of you having been sired by the late Cardinal Peter Romano—Candace is threatening to expose you as the murderer of Roberto Montini. Correct?”

“In a nutshell, yes. Unless I give her full access to the money being held in an off-shore account Peter had set up for me before he was killed.”

“Mmm…I can see perfectly well why he would favor you,” he smiled at her. “The question remains however, why wouldn’t the Cardinal—your father—be equally generous to his other daughter?”

PJ thought about this. Who could really understand the motives and actions of Peter Romano. He was, if not something of a mystic, certainly mysterious. “I don’t think he knew he had another daughter.”

“Explain.”

“Peter Romano had raped Lucinda Russell when they were both teenagers,” she said. “Candace was the result of that rape.”

Reynolds, though listening intently, showed no emotion. PJ continued.

“I don’t believe Lucinda Russell told him. She was obsessed with destroying Peter Romano, and I became a pawn in her game of revenge…and now they are both dead." The weighty silence that filled the room made PJ physically uncomfortable.

Reynolds sat down and finally spoke. "I should have recorded that. I might have you repeat that story at some point." He tapped the *record* icon. "Tell me more about your nascent relationship with the Cardinal, and what happened in Rome."

By the time PJ covered everything she could think of, it was approaching two p.m. Reynolds' face had the look of a man who had just been told the planet was about to implode. He leaned forward, elbows resting on the desk, hands clasped. "So, tell me if I have this right," he said. "Montini had your birth mother killed minutes after you were born, shipped you off to a convent, and some years later, the Hollingers adopted you, and you lived happily ever after…until that fateful meeting with Lucinda Russell, who was out for revenge against the erstwhile pope, Peter Romano." He took a long breath. "Then there was your abduction to Montini's secret hideaway in Frascati where Lucinda Russell attempted to use you to lure Peter Romano for her long-awaited revenge trip. Is my understanding correct?"

"For the most part, yes."

"What am I missing?"

"I have no memory of most of what went down in Frascati."

"I see. What do you remember?"

"I remember being brought down from the attic I was being held in to a lower level of the house by Candace…at gunpoint. And I remember feeling shocked at seeing Lucinda Russell there. Nothing after that."

"My God, PJ. This sounds like a Shakespearian tragedy played out in a soap opera. I would be laughed out of court if I told that story."

PJ's face turned white. "You're not thinking this will go to court?"

"Let's hope not. Truly, I cannot imagine myself explaining this scenario to twelve assumedly rational jurors."

"But it's all true!"

"Not to worry. It may take some doing, but I have ways of turning the surreal into the believable." Reynolds checked his watch. "There's lots to be done, PJ. But right now, I'm starving." He ordered lunch, along with a bottle of Catena Zapata Malbec.

PJ did not protest, her mind leaping from one foreboding thought to the next. When all was said and done, according to the wall clock, it was approaching four p.m. She sprang from her seat. "I've completely lost track of the time. I've got to go."

He walked her to the door, took her hand and kissed it. "Parting is such sweet sorrow."

Oh, my God!

He gave her a cheesy smile. "If you have questions, call or text me…night or day."

"I do have one question."

"And what would that be?"

"You haven't said whether you think I did, in fact, murder Roberto Montini. Why?"

"What I think is not important." To the incredulous look on PJ's face, Reynolds simply said, "My job is to defend you. Period."

She could not escape fast enough, or identify the mix of emotions coursing through her psyche. Discomfort? Confusion? What to make of Jefferson Reynolds? His demeanor could be off-putting. Yet, she could not deny a certain attraction. And clearly, he knew the ins-and-outs of criminal law.

When she got back to the hotel, she plopped on the bed, completely wasted from the intense meeting…and the wine. Val popped into her head. She had not heard back from him. She grabbed the burner and punched in his number. He picked up before the second ring. "Nice of you to call."

His irritation was expected, but she was not in the mood. "You never acknowledged my email."

"Where the hell are you, PJ?" His voice was angry and loud. "What's going on with you exactly?"

"If you continue to shout at me, I will hang up."

"I'm not shouting," he shouted. "I just cannot believe you've shut me out like this. You must know how upset I've been, and half out of my mind with worry, he bellowed again, "beginning with being stood up at the airport!"

"Did it ever occur to you that maybe I had no control over that?"

"Just tell me when you're coming home."

She took a deep breath and released it in a slow sigh. "Sunday."

"Good. I'll pick you up. And this time, please be there."

"The studio is sending a car. I have a meeting with the producer." She could almost hear the grinding of his teeth through the phone. "I'm sorry, Val. It can't be avoided. Things are not going well."

"You think? Are you still in Ireland?"

"I'm in LA"

"LA! Why are you in LA?"

"I had to see my dad's attorney."

He took a calming breath and lowered his voice. "PJ, please, tell me what's going on. Are you alright?"

She took a moment to think about that. "I don't know." Nothing felt alright. Telling Val would not change how she felt, and she didn't have time to survey the car wreck that had become her life. Each new day added another clunker to the pile-up. She had been working on a shoestring having promised a measure of productivity that was becoming almost impossible to fulfill. While the studio had been gracious enough to give her additional time to get through her personal commitments, the producers were quite clear as to their expectations. Their generous four-million-dollar contract...not to mention the thousands already spent on her welcoming campaign introducing PJ Hollinger as their new prime time *Night Watch* anchor...was a lot to live up to. And she was feeling the heaviness of the pressure. The good news, based on the pre-airing surveys, was that ratings would undoubtedly go through the roof...at least initially. Still, she had to produce. At this point, feeling the push to constantly look over her shoulder was not reinforcing her self-assurance.

And having to assuage Val's sudden insecurity was becoming a thorn in her side.

Trying to convince herself that her only priority was making it through the first week, was butting up against the overwhelming sense that her life was about to fall apart, and she had absolutely no plan. The image of sitting in a prison cell floated tauntingly in the back of her mind, keeping her stomach in taut knots. Reynolds had better come through!

After ending her conversation with Val, the long held-back tears began as she lay listlessly on her bed. She thought she would never stop crying. If she didn't pull herself together, and soon, she would never be able to pull herself up from this quicksand. She put Val out of her mind. Best to deal with him in person. She got up to take a soothing shower and stopped cold at the loud knock on her door. She tiptoed slowly to the door and looked through the peephole. There was no one there. She opened the door to snatch a peek up and down the hall. A sudden flash of light swirled around her before everything went dark.

It was the last thing she remembered when she woke the following morning lying on the cold marble floor, her head hammering. She heard a muffled groan. When she realized that it was coming from her own throat, she coaxed herself up from the floor and slogged to the bed holding her head with both hands. It took the better part of an hour, after four aspirin and a hot shower, before she was able to reason. She wanted to keep this as quiet as possible, but knew the police would be called.

Wholly overtaken by rising anger, PJ picked up a carved table lamp and threw it full-strength into the corner fireplace, then arm-swept a cut-glass vase off the coffee table, shattering it into delicate slivers splayed across the marble floor in translucent crystals. Calmer now, she went in search of her laptop. It was not on the bed, the first place she looked. She scoured the rooms. The laptop was not to be found. After twenty minutes of exhaustive search, she succumbed to the last straw and pulled the TV from the wall and threw it headlong at the window. "Fuck!" She found her phone and surfed for Charlie's number in her contacts. Charlie picked up before the second ring.

"I know that voice. What's wrong?"

"I've just lost my fucking mind."

CHAPTER FOURTEEN

Good News and Not-So-Good-News

"Your hands are shaking."

Charlie gave PJ a scornful look as she pressed an ice pack against the emerging purple lump on her forehead. "Of course they are. You scared the shit out of me, girlfriend. And I don't think you've told me everything. So spill!"

"Look at the shape of this room!" PJ shot back. "What more is there to say?" She pushed Charlie's hand away. "I'm losing it, Charlie. On my worst day, I'd brush things off and take the next step. Now, I can't even see what's in front of me. I'm swimming against the tide and my arms are getting tired," she said, in tears. "I have moments when I simply want to stop and surrender myself to the currents…moments like right now."

Charlie grabbed her by the shoulders and shook her. "Stop that!" she hollered. "This is not my PJ speaking. My PJ would not give in to a cabal of crazed lunatics trying to trample her."

"So tell me, what would *your* PJ do?"

Charlie did not hesitate an instant. "She'd put on her boxing gloves and utterly destroy her opponents." She drew PJ close and wrapped her in her arms. "We'll figure this out together."

They sat side-by-side on the bed as Clive Smythe, representing the hotel management, and officer Gary Jacobs, representing the LA police, asked their questions. All was amicable. The assumption was that the condition of the room was the work of a large, strong male. PJ and Charlie looked at each other. Charlie's eyes told PJ very clearly to keep her mouth shut. And PJ, her head still floating somewhere above her, did not correct that assumption. The officer was a bit taken up by the two women, despite his experience with celebrity types. His behavior was reserved and respectful, even timid.

"The motive for the break-in appears to be theft," he said. "A laptop containing confidential and valuable information. Would you say that's correct, Ms. Hollinger?"

Ms. Hollinger seemed to have lost her voice.

"Yes. That is correct, officer," Charlie answered.

"Ms. Hollinger," he said, subtly. "This does not feel like a random burglary. Do you have any idea who might want your laptop, and why?" PJ looked up at Jacobs, but did not answer his question. Charlie leaned into PJ. "PJ?"

"I…I do not."

After several long seconds of awkward stillness, Jacobs asked PJ the nature of its contents.

It was Charlie, reverting to a long-ago nervous habit of chipping off her nail polish, who answered. "Why is that important?"

The officer showed no emotion. "Knowing specifically what the computer contained may give us a better picture of the perpetrator…what he might have been after."

"Why are you dismissing the idea that it might have been a female?" PJ shook off her wooziness and took the reins.

"Oh, I'm not. Not at all. But statistically, most break-ins are perpetrated by men."

PJ left it at that and answered his question. "The laptop contained my notes and all my work, including confidential material. Material that has not yet been vetted. And personal financial information."

"Not to worry, Ms. Hollinger," Jacobs assured her, pencil-scratching across his notepad. "We have tracking software. We'll get your laptop back for you in no time."

"I'm not worried about that." PJ wished they would leave. She needed to get this over with. "I have a backup and recovery service. And the laptop is triple encrypted, so it's virtually impossible for anyone but myself to get in. It's about the inconvenience. There are deadlines I must meet, and it will take days to recover everything…maybe weeks." At that, she stood and walked to the window, tears welling. Charlie, too, was done. "I think Ms. Hollinger needs to rest now…if that's all."

Smythe, who seemed to be more concerned about a lawsuit for the lapse in security, offered PJ the penthouse suite. Without missing a beat, Charlie accepted for her friend. "That is very gracious of you, Mr. Smythe," Charlie said, walking the men to the door. "When will it be available?"

After they had left, Charlie sat on the bed. "Come. Sit." She patted the space next to her. "Tell me the latest cause of such grief."

"It isn't just one thing," PJ said, gazing out the window. "It's a heap. And I am overwhelmed.

"Well, you could have fooled me."

PJ chuckled softly. "That's what I love about you, Charlie, you could bring a smile to the lips of a corpse." She sat next to Charlie as invited, and *spilled*. "I'm being hounded by the Irish police, threatened by my half-sister, totally unprepared for my *Night Watch* gig, and to add seasoning to the mix," she turned her face, swiping away a tear. "My relationship with Val has hit a pothole."

"Oh, Posh. I wouldn't worry a notch about Val. The man worships the red carpet you walk on. Slip him off your worry beads."

"It's not him I'm worried about."

"I see. Having a cooling down moment, are we?"

PJ considered this. "N…no. Not exactly. I just haven't been able to put much of myself into our relationship. It feels like…more responsibility than I can take on right now."

"Geez! You need to give yourself a break. Let Val carry the load. He'd love that. He's a guy, and guys think it's their job to protect their women. He needs to be your hero. Let him have that pleasure."

PJ rolled her eyes. "Let's put Val aside for now. I really need to get myself together…and fast."

Over the next two hours, they moved PJ into the Penthouse, hashed out a rough plan, and prioritized PJ's next moves. Charlie was not particularly happy with PJ's decision concerning Candace, but it seemed to be the only way to satisfy the *evil twin,* and put an end to her threats. PJ would give her half of the bequest willingly. It seemed fair. After all, she was Peter Romano's daughter, too.

The next item on PJ's list was to contact the backup service and get to all her files. Then do some hard research and writing. She had to be prepared for her meeting with the executive producer on Sunday. As far as Inspector Doyle was concerned, well, that would have to be left in Reynolds' hands.

"By the way," Charlie said after hugging PJ and heading for the door, "I did some checking up on Reynolds. He does have quite an impressive success record. But his reputation as something of a Lothario precedes him." She walked back and kissed PJ on her bruised forehead. "And you are in a weakened condition. Be careful, my sista."

By the next day, miraculously, PJ had retrieved about half of her files from the backup and recovery service. Bolstered by a new surge of enthusiasm, she was making headway in her preparations for the first taping. She was feeling optimistic that things would come together when her phone pinged. It was a text from Jefferson Reynolds.

My driver will pick you up at eight. I'm taking you to dinner. You will need *sustenance. Have good news and not so good news. Wear something dazzling!*

Her first reaction was, *how impertinent*, upgraded to *shit!* Then finalized with *double shit!* So much for positive thinking. She'd promised Val they would speak that evening. Now she had to dash those hopes.

PJ purposely dressed down in a belted, black, Versace jumpsuit. Well-fitted, but nothing she would call *dazzling.* The driver knocked on her door at eight p.m. sharp, and escorted her to the limo. They reached Mastro's Ocean Club in less than ten minutes. Reynolds walked to the curb and took PJ's hand as she stepped out of the car.

"Dazzling, as usual, despite hiding those gorgeous legs."

Ugh!!

He gave her a peck on the cheek. "You will need a good steak dinner for this, and Mastro's has the best."

"My God, Jefferson, can you be any more disheartening?"

"Please, call me Jeff. And I'm not being disheartening, just realistic."

"What's the difference?"

"Exactly. But let's not sink into the abyss of legalities. I've brought you here to lighten up, enjoy excellent food and drink…and just be."

"I'm more than willing to relax, but you must know that I'm on the edge of my seat about the not-so-good-news."

"Enjoy the ambience," he said. "It can wait."

Dinner was a relatively short affair during which PJ buried her frustration with Reynolds' cavalier attitude, with several martinis. She hardly ate. Reynolds paid the bill and suggested they go back to his home office so "I can avail myself of your file while we talk business."

Having consumed, by all accounts, a liquid dinner, and not having eaten all day, PJ was quite buzzed when Reynolds wrapped his arm around her waist and walked her out the door. Whether or not she heard his suggestion was immaterial. She seemed to have misplaced her will, and moved along listlessly. When they were seated in the limo, she laid her head back and closed her eyes. *Oh, God,* she thought. *I must call Val.*

In addition to his beach home in Malibu, Reynolds kept a small apartment several blocks from his office. By the time they reached the 15th floor, and were cozily ensconced on the loveseat, PJ had gained a smidge of clarity. She slid over a bit to make some space between them. "Jeff," she said, her voice still woozy, "I need you to tell me what's happening." She tucked her hair behind an ear. "But first I need a strong cup of coffee."

"Sorry, dear. I only have wine and scotch."

"Oh, no. If I swallow any more alcohol, I won't be able to stand."

Reynolds smiled hopefully, and offered water.

"That'll work."

He got up and found a bottle of water in the fridge, unscrewed the cap, and handed it to her.

"Thank you." She took a long swallow. "Please, tell me what my fate looks like."

He groaned. "Work, work, work. You need to lighten up and relax, darlin'."

Still not in complete control of her mental acuity, her impatience took over. "Why are you stalling?"

"Okay. Have it your way," he grumbled. "I spoke to Inspector Doyle. The good news is, they will not be pursuing charges at this time. Apparently, they do not have a viable case against you."

She released her breath." That *is* good news. But what does *at this time* imply?"

"It means what it says; it's an ongoing investigation."

"That certainly puts a crimp in the good news. I can only imagine what the not-so-good news is."

Reynolds stood and dug his hands into his pockets. He cleared his throat. "The Vatican, under a provision of the Lateran Treaty, has requested that the Italian government handle the investigation and prosecution for this case so they will remain out of the limelight, given the numerous incidents of malfeasance and sexual misconduct within their domain. "

"I see." She swallowed hard. "So where does that leave me?"

"There's more."

The agitation broiling in her stomach reached its limit. "I need to use your bathroom."

Jeff jumped to the call and escorted her down the small foyer to the bathroom. "Are you alright?" She did not answer. Quickly, she closed the door behind her, held her hair back, and vomited into the sink. After about ten minutes, Jeff knocked on the door.

"PJ? Are you okay?"

She was sitting on the rim of an antique copper, claw-footed slipper tub, trying to get it together. "Give me a second, Jeff. Please." After throwing cold water on her face, and rinsing with a mouthful of Scope sitting conveniently on the counter, she was ready to hear the rest. She walked unsteadily back into the room and leaned against the wet bar.

"Why don't we continue this another time? Let's just relax for a while."

"No. I'm okay. Just tell me."

"Look. This is not the end of the world. There is still much recourse."

"Tell me!" She had not intended to sound so harsh, but she was long-past pleasantries. She moved hesitantly, and coaxed herself into a side chair, still a bit giddy.

He sat across from her and bent forward, resting his elbows on his knees. "While the Holy See will not technically be involved with the case, they are exerting their influence and have requested the Promoter of Justice, what we call the Chief Prosecutor, move forward with the extradition papers, given your person of interest status." He waited a few moments for PJ to digest what he'd said. She turned her head and looked out over the balcony, dazed.

CHAPTER FIFTEEN

Rebibbia, Italy

Sawyer

Having served more than half of her twenty-five-year sentence, Concetta Barone, aka *Sawyer*, was granted a conditional release from Women's Regional Prison of Rome exactly one week after having arranged Candace's *travel plans*. There remained in place, however, a proscription from the Surveillance Court—under whose watchful eye she was yet a prisoner—against traveling outside the city. Under her release plan, she moved into a furnished, two-room apartment in Rebibbia along the southeast edge of the town, within five miles of the prison.

Nearly everything had been put in place by way of Sawyer's select, if unsavory *connections*. All she needed was the means. And that, of course, was in the hands of Candace Baker, who apparently had chosen to remain incommunicado.

The murderous look on Sawyer's face when Candace could not be reached on the third try in as many days would stop a hungry black bear in its tracks. She hurled the phone to the floor, and pounced on it several times with the heel of her boot. "This is what I'm gonna do to your face when I find you, bitch!"

It had been agreed that Candace would contact Sawyer when she got to Key West, and again when she had safely arrived in Cuba. That never happened. Sawyer's cut for her troubles was one-million dollars...half of the Hollinger booty. Now, since Candace had not stuck to the plan, she would require the entire two-million. Sawyer was about to take matters into her own ponderous hands.

Done stomping around her lowly digs, Sawyer decided she could use a drink. She also needed to buy a prepaid SIM card. She snatched her keys from the wall-hook and left, slamming the door with a final burst of choler.

"She's in Dublin," mumbled a voice on the other end of the phone. "Trying to dig up enough scratch to get back to the states. What do you want me to do?"

"Nothing for now. I'll take care of this one. Dublin, heh?" she echoed under her breath.

"Send me the address."

"Sawyer?"

"Yeah?"

"I…um…I need to get paid. I'm sitting on my last coin."

"Be thankful, you lump of shit," she growled, "that you still have an arse to sit on."

DUBLIN, IRELAND

The chilly, grey morning was far from welcoming to the heavy-set, pocked-face woman in an ill-fitting business suit as she made her way down the Air Lingus gangway in Dublin. She stopped before exiting the terminal to adjust her mid-length black wig and got into a taxi that took her to the address she'd been given, drops of fury still trickling through her veins.

The apartment building in Blanchardstown was, at best, falling apart. She avoided the lift and walked the four flights to number 4H, knocked on the door and placed her thumb over the peephole. She waited. Nothing. Inside, all was quiet. She knocked again. She looked up and down the hall, took two paper clips from her pocket, and picked the lock. It was a shithole if there ever was one. A one-room studio with half a refrigerator and makeshift cook stove. The only furniture was a ratty, pea green sofa that apparently doubled as a bed, a coffee table strewn with newspapers and used Styrofoam cups, and a side chair and small dresser. *Jesus!* She was beginning to feel sorry for Candace. But then she remembered; the bitch was trying to screw her. She sat in the armchair, pulled off her wig, and massaged her itchy scalp.

Sawyer waited in the darkened room for two hours before she heard the key in the lock. Kicking the door shut behind her, Candace flicked on the light and went limp, dropping her grocery bag to the floor. She feigned a smile. "Sawyer! When did you get out?"

"Cut the shit, bitch. Where the fuck have you been? We had a deal. And you know what happens to assholes who break deals." She pulled out a 9mm Luger pistol and proceeded to attach the silencer.

Candace snorted. "Come on, Sawyer. You know me, if I were able to contact you, I would have. Look around you. I'm trying to get my shit together after Gino screwed me. I had no way to get to Cuba. I had to drop out of sight…and sound."

"My deal was with you, not Gino—and where is that douchebag?" Sawyer seemed to soften a little after hearing about Candace's misadventures in Key West and Killarney. But she was still simmering inside. "I want that money…and the ante has been upped to two million…my having to come after you like this."

"And what am I supposed to live on?"

"Who said you're going to live?" she sneered, brandishing the gun.

Candace did not tell Sawyer that she had put an end to Gino.

Based on Candace's description of Gino Carlotti, Sawyer understood him to be a member of an old-school Mafia gang, someone to be avoided. And Candace was not above using Gino—even dead—as her knight in this murderous chess game.

"So where's the laptop you were supposed to snaffle?"

Candace sat on the sofa, about three feet across from Sawyer, and swiped the perspiration from her face. She took a deep breath and explained how she found someone who, for enough money, would snatch the computer and ship it to her. Unfortunately, the encryption hacker she had hired to upload PJ's financial records failed to get through the second encryption level.

"He's the best there is," she said, "and he couldn't do it." Candace paused to check Sawyer's reaction. Her eyes were closed, but there was no missing the clenched jaw.

"Then he picked up a tracking alert," she said. "It was a lost cause at that point. There was nothing he could do except destroy the laptop."

Sawyer lost it. She flew up from the chair and back-handed Candace across her face with the pistol. "You screwup! You have a week…and that's me being generous. If I don't get that dough by then, you're a dead bitch walking!"

CHAPTER SIXTEEN

Los Angeles California

The Breakup

Still a bit light-headed, PJ stood and ambled to the glass doors that led out to a small balcony. She stared thoughtfully over the city. Reynolds went to her and put his arm around her shoulder. "It's not so much bad news, Darlin.' It's just not-so-good-news." He turned her to him. We'll deal with it."

A lonely teardrop trickled down her cheek. He gently brushed it away, his eyes locked onto hers. "I can barely breathe when I'm in the same room with you," he said, then kissed her softly on the lips. She did not return the kiss, but neither did she pull away. He kissed her again, deeply. This time, she accepted his kiss and pressed into his hardness. He began undressing her, exploring her mouth with his tongue. He had the top of her jumpsuit unzipped and slid her bra strap down her shoulder. He squeezed her breast. She drew back.

"No," she said hoarsely. "I can't do this." She tried to push away, but he had her locked in his arms. She pushed harder. "I said, No!" But he would not release her.

"I can't do this, Jeff…I'm with someone else."

"How unfortunate."

"Let me go. I'm not myself at the moment." She managed to muster some fortitude. "And fuck you for taking advantage! If you don't let me go, I will kick your ass to the next building." She gave him a forceful shove, and he relented, with a chuckle.

"And I bet you could. I've heard about your kickboxing skills."

It made her chillingly uncomfortable that he knew so much about her. "Maybe it would be best if I found another attorney," she said, adjusting her clothing. "One with far more propriety."

"I think you're smarter than that, PJ. Anyway, it's not my fault you're so damn irresistible."

"How smarmy." She sat, and buried her face in her hands. He sat next to her, wisely leaving some room between them. "I can't believe this is all happening. I don't even know who I am anymore. I feel as though my life is over just when it was beginning." She looked at him. "I cannot go to Italy, Jeff."

"Listen, PJ. I don't want you worrying about this. They've got nothing but hearsay, the word of an anonymous caller that you were at Montini's residence in Rome. That won't hold water. Even if they somehow can place you there, you'd been taken against your will and locked up in the attic. You have a solid defense. Besides, the US does not easily agree to extraditing American citizens."

This did not make her feel any better. She finished the last sip of water and leaned her head back.

"I think they're bluffing, " he said to ease her mind. "I promise, I will take care of it."

Emotionally exhausted, PJ had not the strength to say a word.

"There is one thing you should be aware of."

She closed her eyes, as if to ward off whatever might be coming. "Please, if it's not going to untie the knot in my stomach, don't tell me."

"I'm sorry, dearest. It has to be addressed." He softened his voice. "It's about the gun they found in the Cardinal's car. Is it possible your fingerprints could have been on that gun?"

"What? Why are you asking me this?"

"Because I have to."

She stood and paced anxiously, trying to corral her thoughts.

"PJ?"

"I don't know! I don't even remember there being a gun." They were both quiet for some time before PJ spoke again. "Please, be honest with me, Jeff. What am I up against here?"

He went to the mini-bar and poured himself a drink. "They found a partial latent print on the trigger."

"Oh, God." She tried swallowing, but her throat closed. "What does that mean?"

"Well, it depends, of course, on whose fingerprint it is, and if they can obtain a match."

"Can they match a partial print?"

"Mmm, yes and no. Matching fingerprints can be a tricky procedure. It's based on a point system. The print must come up to a certain level to be considered as viable evidence. And that depends on the qualifications and expertise of the forensic scientist."

As though she had not heard a word he'd said, she walked slowly toward the door. "I'm leaving for New York Sunday. I can't think of anything else until I've settled things with the studio." She turned to face him to find he was right behind her. She started, gave him a slight push. "About tonight," she said. "It's best we both forget it ever happened."

"You can forget all you want, darlin' but I'm not giving up."

Dear Jesus! Do I need this right now? It was pointless to go down that road. She groaned and left.

Reynolds followed her down to the street and helped her into a cab, but not before giving her a peck on the cheek. "I'll be in touch."

***

It was nearing midnight when she asked the driver to let her out several blocks from the hotel. She needed to clear her head, but all she could think about was her slip-sliding into perdition. What was happening to her? Had her relationship with Val reached an impasse? Even so, she could never betray him…*but she almost had.*

No doubt Jefferson Reynolds was a lecher. What was she to do? He'd already burrowed himself into her life. She had no choice but to stick with him…while keeping a safe distance.

When she was done mentally flogging herself, she turned down a side-street to shorten the distance to the hotel. The night air was thick with little light from a cloud-covered moon. The streets were empty. She thought she heard a snap behind her. A foot stepping on a twig. She turned. No one. She stepped off the curb to cross onto the main street, and was certain this time she heard footsteps. She did not look back. She picked up her pace. This was not the first time she sensed that she was being followed. She turned into the alley toward the side entrance of the hotel marked *Employees Only*. She pressed herself against the opposing wall, and waited. She had not imagined the footsteps. They quickened, then stopped abruptly just before the turn into the alley. After several seconds of this standoff, she took a deep breath and in a strong, controlled voice said, "Why are you following me? Show yourself!"

Familiar with her background, including, her expert kickboxing ability, he cleared his throat. "I mean you no harm." He advanced several feet and turned toward the alley with his hands in the air. "I am unarmed."

PJ took a few steps back into the light of the streetlamp. "Who are you and why are you following me?"

"Believe me, I am a friend, Ms. Hollinger, and my job is to keep you safe."

"It doesn't appear as though you're very good at your job seeing as it's so easy to pick up your tail."

The man smiled. "A bit of jetlag. You are one difficult person to keep up with. And I must admit, I did lose you for a while…which made my employer very unhappy."

A light began to dawn. "Did Val hire you to check on me?"

He took off his cap and brushed back his thick, black hair. "No, Miss Hollinger. My name is Fred Simmons, and I am doing this as a favor for your grandfather, who seems really worried about you. And for good reason, I might add."

She took a breath and held back her rage at this innocent guy just trying to do his job. "You tell my grandfather," she barked between grit teeth, "that if he doesn't take you off my trail, he has seen the last of me!" She strode out of the alley, pushing Simmons aside as she made her way to the front entrance.

The very minute she got to her room, she locked and chained the door. She picked up her phone to chew out Romano herself, when it vibrated in her hand. She hesitated, then swiped the green icon without looking at the screen. "Hello." Her voice carried the remnant of her anger.

"I thought that hearing your voice would make me feel better. And it does, I suppose. At least I now know you're alive."

"Val. I..."

"Please, don't say anything. You've put me through hell and back. You promised to call me at six, your time. It is now three-twenty a.m. New York time. I don't know when I last slept through the night. You don't talk to me anymore. I know nothing about what's going on with you. It's killing me to think," he said, his voice cracking, "that you would do this to me."

Something erupted inside. She tried with whatever remaining strength she had to control her anger. But it would not be shackled. All of the suppressed fear, worry and tension, just exploded out of her mouth. "You narcissist!" she screamed. "Not once during your poor-me monologue did you care enough to consider what *I've* been going through." In a fit of temper, she ended the call.

CHAPTER SEVENTEEN

Worse Things

Sunday was bounding forward faster than a racehorse out of the gate. PJ had barely three days to get her act together, finalize her script, and formalize her proposal for next month's programming while struggling to remain focused and calm. She could not shed the feeling that she was losing this battle. She sequestered herself in her hotel room and worked through the night. When she could no longer keep her eyes open, she lay on the bed, fully clothed, and slept for a few hours. Fortified by several cups of coffee, she went back to work, but before resuming, she checked her phone messages. Roy Warren, the executive producer had left a text: *Send what you have, ASAP. I want to take a look at it before you arrive.*

She frowned at the rather curt tone of the message. A noticeably different hue than the last time they had spoken, the note in his voice then having been a touch more exuberant. She shrugged it off as nervous paranoia, but she could not deny the sinking feeling that another battle loomed. When she thought she'd proofed and polished everything as best she could, she hit the send key, and hoped for the best. She spent the rest of the day organizing notes for her presentation and returning emails. At around one, she went down to the residents' gym, after which she showered, dressed, and decided to do some shopping to get her mind off the four walls that were closing in on her. She strolled along West Olympic Blvd. then grabbed a cab to

Raquel Allegra on West Third, a recommendation from Charlie: "You'll love it. Their clothing is stylish yet not too flashy. Just as you like. " The thought brought a rare smile to her lips.

After her shopping spree, she picked up some Thai food before heading back to the hotel. As she approached her room, she noticed something on the floor in front of her door. A closer look revealed a huge vase filled with red, white, and yellow roses. Before opening the door, she pulled the card perched on top of the flowers and read it:

Forgive me. I behaved like a Neanderthal. I was so worried about you, and yes, angry. I love you. I miss you beyond words. Come home to me.

She hadn't realized she'd been crying until she tasted the salty tears on her lips. She unlocked the door, brought her packages inside, including the roses, and slid to the floor, sobbing uncontrollably. Her life—and her dreams—were spiraling down a tube slide at full throttle.

As she packed for her trip to New York, her phone chimed indicating a text. It was Reynolds. She stiffened, then calmed herself before opening the text. It was short and not necessarily encouraging.

Taking the Red Eye to Rome. Will hopefully convince DiFaccio (representing the Holy See) to rescind extradition request. They must have sufficient evidence in order to proceed, which I don't believe they have.

P.S. I don't usually fly overseas for clients. I'm doing this for you, Babe. Will keep you posted. Jeff.

Why, she wondered, skeptical of his motives, would he do such an inconvenient, selfless act? Maybe she had him all wrong. She again read the text, more carefully this time, and closed her eyes tightly against the implication of *Babe*. She told herself she should look for another lawyer. But where would she find an ace defense attorney willing to cross an ocean for a client? She could not spend another second on this. For now, she would have to leave it in his hands and get back to focusing on her career, which was looking less and less optimistic. She shooed the negative thoughts aside and finished packing.

Jefferson Reynolds' reputation as a criminal defense attorney was renowned…as was his ruthlessness. His moral code of ethics was also well-known. He had no qualms about obtaining his objective—regardless of how unscrupulous it was.

Reynold's had no intention of wasting time and money on a trip to Italy. He instead had an equally disreputable *buddy* in the Justice Department gather all the information he needed had he made the trip—and lied about the rest. He spent the next week on the beach in Malibu.

DUBLIN, IRELAND

Using her well-honed theatrical skills, Candace talked Sawyer into supplying a phony passport. "You know a week is impossible. It'll take me that long to get to PJ. I can't do anything from here. Hollinger has to be in New York for her debut newscast. I need you to help me get to New York."

Sawyer roared with laughter, wiping imaginary tears from her eyes. But it wasn't funny. She glared at Candace. "You gotta be joking. Do you really think I would set you up again so you can disappear. You're a scream."

Fully aware of Sawyer's travel restrictions and the need to get back to Rebibbia in time to check in with her parole officer, Candace played the only card she had left. "Then come with me," she blurted.

"What kind of a moron are you? I'm already on the border of violating probation. Leaving the country to chase after you! It'd put me on every fucking wanted list in the world!"

"How would they know you left the country?"

Sawyer grabbed Candace by the throat. "They will when your body turns up dead with my knife in your gut."

"And there goes your million," Candace choked.

Sawyer released her with a forceful shove. "I want that money, Candace. I need that money."

"And so do I. You know as well as I do that we need each other. We can go our separate ways after, but I need your help to get it done."

Sawyer flopped onto the side chair. "I gotta think on it."

NEW YORK CITY

The studio limo picked PJ up at the Arrivals terminal. Her flight was twenty-minutes late, so of course, she would not be on time for the meeting with her producers. She whined inwardly. *Would anything ever again go right for me?* A question, she thought, best left unanswered.

The reception she received at the studio was not exactly overwhelming. Something felt decidedly off as evidenced by the Gordian Knot tightening in her stomach.

"Follow me, Ms. Hollinger," instructed the rather dour-looking seat warmer at the reception desk. "They've been waiting for you."

Yep. To paraphrase Shakespeare, something is decidedly rotten in Studio 4.

Miss Sourpuss led PJ through a set of enormous glass doors into a capacious conference room almost entirely taken up by an overly large oval table of highly polished teakwood. To her unhappy surprise, in addition to the producer, associate producer, and program director, the general manager sat at the head of the table. This was unexpected. She was under the impression that at the conclusion of the contract-signing, there would be no further interaction with the GM. She felt every organ in her body drop. The expression on the GM's face could only be described as…steely. Only Roy Warren stood and shook her hand. "Good to see you, PJ. Have a seat."

She did not feel at all welcomed, but forced a smile. "My apologies. The flight was delayed."

"Yes," offered the associate producer, "We'd been informed." The tension in the room was palpable. The silence lasted a bit too long. PJ took a deep breath and spoke up. "I assume you've received my proposed program outline and script."

"Um. Yes." Warren looked around at the others, then at PJ. "We've all read it. Great, absolutely wonderful," he said. After another stretch of silence, the program director, Melanie Young, spoke. "We loved it. Imaginative, intriguing, and forward thinking. Just great."

"Thank you, Melanie."

"Let's cut to the chase," the GM groused. "Roy, kindly explain to Ms. Hollinger our decision."

Warren cleared his throat. "As you know, PJ, your contract contains a morality clause that interdicts any…"

"I've read the contract, Roy. What is it you're getting at?" PJ gripped the arms of her chair as her apprehension was about to be realized. "My morals are above reproach," she nearly shouted, struggling to cover the tremor in her voice.

"Look, PJ..."

"Enough!" The GM pushed back his chair as though about to rise, but remained seated. "There's been some scuttlebutt that you are about to be arrested for some unthinkable crime, and we simply cannot have an association with..."

"With all due respect," it was PJ who stood, her rising anger poorly controlled. "That is utter nonsense. I don't know where you've gotten such information, but..."

"PJ," Warren interrupted. "Please sit down. We can work this out."

The GM finally stood. "I'm afraid I have another appointment and must go, but I will leave you in Roy's hands, Ms. Hollinger." He looked directly at Warren. "He will conclude this meeting as expected." With that, he left the room without a glance back.

With sudden and unexpected calm, PJ leaned back and sighed. "Just tell me about this *decision*, please."

"Can I get you a drink?"

"Water would be nice."

Warren stood, walked over to the server, and with his back to PJ said, "Bob has demanded we cancel your contract." He turned, water in hand, and placed it before PJ. "I am so sorry. We tried to talk him out of it until we were purple, but he is adamant."

"You cannot be serious, Roy. You can't simply cancel my contract. I will sue!"

"Be realistic, PJ. That won't benefit either of us. We have an option we want to discuss with you."

"I can only imagine," she said, sickened.

"Just hear us out."

"The only viable option is to fulfill my contract," she insisted.

"PJ." Melanie broke in. "That is not going to happen. Bob Starky will not change his mind." She stood and took the chair next to PJ and covered her hand with her own. "I can't tell you how sorry I am about all of this. We're trying to be fair and avoid any long-term repercussions."

"Fair? There is not a dust particle of fairness in this room. I *will* sue!"

"Please, PJ." Melanie removed her hand and sat back. "No one wants to create a media circus. Just listen, digest it, and then decide."

PJ took a long draught of water. "I'm listening."

"Well, okay." Warren chirped, a bit too cheerfully. "Firstly, we have been authorized to present you with a generous separation package which includes..."

"If it's not four-million dollars as per my contract, it will not be generous enough."

"We're already over budget on pre-airing costs, but you will be given a lump sum of 500,000 dollars, plus a benefits package for up to one year, allowing sufficient time to secure another position."

PJ swallowed the bile churning up to her throat. "I can't believe you are doing all this based on rumors. Surely there is something else going on here."

Warren cleared his throat. "They are more than rumors, PJ," he said. "It would be judicious on your part to accept this offer. That's all I will say."

She jumped out of her chair and headed for the door. "Excuse me."

She found the rest room and locked herself in one of the closets. Her breath was coming in shallow snatches. She could hear the escalating drumbeat of her heart. This was not a convenient time for a panic attack. The room was starting to dim. She put down the toilet cover and sat, dropping her head low until the moment passed. She sat up and leaned against the back wall, struggling to control her labored breathing…in two three four…hold two three four…out two three four. She did five sets until her heartbeat returned to its normal rhythm and she could breathe comfortably. *Fuck them!* She would not be tossed to the curb like litter. She kicked the door open, busting the lock. *Shit and double shit!* She went to the sink and threw some cold water on her face, patted it dry, and took several deep breaths until the color returned to her cheeks.

"Are you all right?" Melanie asked when PJ reentered the room.

"Just fine."

Warren looked at her sheepishly, then looked down at the papers laid out on the table.

"Shall I continue?"

PJ had never been one to accept her fate without a fight, but for the moment, the fight had been siphoned out of her. "Yes. Please."

"Firstly, will you agree to accept the benefits package as stated?"

"I will have to consult with my attorney."

Warren sighed and sat down. "I should tell you that the offer expires in ten days. There's really not much time."

Melanie stood. "Roy, can I speak to you privately for a moment?" He gave her a questioning look.

"Please."

Reluctantly, he marched to the door and held it open for her. When they were out of earshot, she glared at him. "When are you going to tell her, Roy?"

"Jesus." He looked away for a split second, tightened his jaw, and faced her. "She must accept the terms first. If I tell her now, it may blow the whole deal."

"If you don't tell her, I will."

"You're out of line here, Mel."

She turned and headed back to the conference room. "Whatever."

CHAPTER EIGHTEEN

Headlines

From his vantage point outside the building, Doug, the doorman, spotted PJ getting out of a cab a few yards down the street. The absence of her usual sprightly step—and the fact that she was wearing shades when the sun had already gone down—raised a red flag. Something was wrong.

"Evenin' Ms. PJ. Welcome back."

A listless, "Hello, Doug," was all she could handle. Not even the usual *thank you* as he held the door open for her.

"Everything all right, Ms. PJ?"

She continued to the elevator banks without a word.

Uh oh, he thought. *A bad day. A very bad day.*

She unlocked the door to her apartment and closed it behind her. She leaned against it, sobbing. *I need to call Charlie,* was her first inclination when she was finally able to calm her emotions. She reconsidered. She'd been leaning too much on Charlie's shoulder lately, and chastised herself for making her problems Charlie's. Instead, she placed a call to Jeff Reynolds. It went directly to his voicemail. She steadied herself, controlling the shakiness in her voice before leaving a message.

"Please call me. It's important." She checked her messages. There were two messages from Charlie, a message from Sil, and one from Val. Other than her attorney, she was in no shape to talk to anyone right now.

The stuffiness of the room took her to the one large window. She pushed aside the curtains and opened the side-panels as far as they would go, letting in the cool air. She was about to undress and get into the shower when there was a knock on the door. She jumped, as did every nerve in her body, and went quietly to the door. She peeped through the eyehole. It was Doug. She breathed a sigh of relief, and standing at a distance, opened the door.

"Um, the cabby brought in your luggage."

She took a minute for her brain to receive the message. "Oh, my God, I'd forgotten all about it."

Doug wheeled in the suitcase and placed the duffle bag on the floor just inside the door. He remained for a moment, hands clasped behind his back. "Is, um, everything all right Miss PJ?"

Her eyes red and swollen from crying, she avoided looking directly at him. "Yes, Doug. Just fine. Thank you for bringing my things up. Have a good night."

On occasion, PJ would invite Doug up for tea or coffee on his break, especially after she'd traveled. They'd developed an easy friendship. Tonight, though, Doug knew he should take his leave. "Good night, Ms. PJ. Call if you need anything."

After a hot shower and a warm brandy, PJ fell into an all too infrequent deep sleep…until the incessant chiming of her mobile phone woke her with a start. She swiped the green icon.

"Hello?"

"Sorry for the hour. I could never get these time differences straight. You sound groggy."

"I was asleep."

"I got your message, but unfortunately, don't have much to report…yet"

"That doesn't sound very encouraging, Jeff."

"I still have one more ace to play. Hopefully, I will have some good news for you tomorrow. Hang tight. Gotta run. Go back to sleep."

Fat chance.

Her first call the following morning was to Charlie after all.

"Finally! Where have you been?"

PJ couldn't dredge up the right words.

"PJ? You there?"

"Yes. I'm here."

"What is it, sweetie? Sounds like things are not going so well in New York."

She broke down, unable to hold back the tears. "They've canceled my contract."

"WHAT! For God's sake, why?"

"Apparently, I'm bad publicity."

"Those Bastards! What do you mean *bad publicity*? You're the best thing that's happened to that money pit of a time slot."

"I guess they've changed their minds about that. Something is going on beyond my ken regarding the Vatican affair. They seem to know something I don't. Charlie, I'm at the end of my rope."

"Stop that! I coming to New York."

"Don't you dare! I will not disrupt your life. If I can't cry on your shoulder, who then, can I turn to when I need to vent? You will just have to put up with me long-distance."

Charlie mumbled something under her breath. "What does Reynolds think?"

"He's in Rome as we speak, trying to negotiate with the Vatican to withdraw their extradition request."

"Well, he must be back, I saw him outside of Mastro's two nights ago."

"That's impossible, he called me from Rome last night."

Charlie took a minute. "I could be mistaken. It was from a distance…and it was dark."

"I'm devastated, Charlie. I expected some sort of admonishment for all the time I've been taking, but firing me? I just can't take another fiasco in my life."

"It's not a fiasco. You can sue them. I'm here for you, my sista. You know that."

"I do. And I'm sorry to keep dumping my problems on you."

"Well, isn't that just too selfish of you!"

"Selfish?"

"If that's what you believe, then you're saying that I can't dump my shit on you...which, by the way, I've done for half my life!"

"That's not what I'm saying, and you know it. And I didn't use the word *shit!*" There was a long silence before they both burst out laughing.

"Come home, PJ. Back to California, preferably Southern California"

"New York is my home now."

"If the shit–sorry–if the shit hits the fan, New York will toss you to the fishes. Canceling your contract is just one example."

"I'm settled here."

"So what will you do?"

PJ drew a long breath. "I don't know yet. I've contacted a contracts attorney."

"Oh, for heaven's sake. Your days are overrun with a parade of attorneys."

"What else can I do?"

Charlie moaned. "Negotiate."

"There is no room for negotiation!"

"Ok, keep your panties on. I'm just asking."

"They offered me 500k, a year of benefits, and a good reference to get out of their hair."

"Those miserly sons-of-bitches!"

"Oh, but there's a condition." Her voice cracked.

"They want the copyright to my program ideas and scripts."

"Swine! I hope you didn't accept."

"Of course not. If I'm going to be screwed, I want to enjoy it." Neither spoke for several long seconds.

"Come back," Charlie croaked. "Whatever you think you can do in New York can be done in California. Besides, I miss you. Please Think about it."

"I miss you too. You can't imagine. But I can't think about anything until all this legal muddle is cleared up, and I get my life back."

For two days, PJ lived on yogurt, coffee, and Ativan, waiting for some word from Jeff Reynolds. On the morning of the third day, her phone pinged a text message.

Will be arriving LaGuardia tonight. We'll talk then. Good and not-so-good news. Jeff.

This was not the word she was hoping for. A vise gripped her stomach. She returned the yogurt to the fridge and put a slice of bread into the toaster, just to have something to absorb the Ativan. She made herself some tea and picked up her mobile phone. She had to make the call. She could no longer put it off. She took a sip of tea and tapped the screen. The call was picked up on the first ring. "Val?"

"PJ!"

"It's good to hear your live voice," she said, meaning it.

"I miss you so much, and I am so sorry. I can't imagine what this news is doing to you.

"How did you find out? Did Charlie call you?"

"It headlined this morning's Post. And Newsday, and the Daily News!"

"Oh, God. It's not enough that those snakes fired me; must they throw salt on the wound by publicizing it? You would think there are more important events in the public interest."

"Wait. What are you talking about?"

"Those parasites cancelled my contract! What are you talking about?"

"Jesus. I am so sorry." He took a breath. "PJ, this has nothing to do with your contract."

"I don't understand."

"Have you read the paper this morning?"

"No. I've had other things on my mind."

"Where are you?"

"My apartment, but..."

"I'll be right there."

Val hung up before PJ could protest. *"Damn!"* She rang downstairs. "Doug, do you have this morning's Post?" No response.

"Doug?"

"I, er, yeah. Yes."

"I'd like to borrow it."

"Um..."

"I'll be right down."

"I'll be right down."

CHAPTER NINETEEN

The Reunion

Whatever had come between them dissolved the millisecond they lunged into each other's arms.

"My God, I've missed you," Val said, stepping back to look at her. "You still take my breath away…as if that will ever change." She took his hand and tugged him into the room, turned and kissed him deeply on the mouth. "I've missed you, too."

"We'll get through this together," he whispered in her ear. "Did you see the Post?"

"You mean the headline that says, '*Well-regarded news anchor, PJ Hollinger, a person of interest in the murder of Cardinal Roberto Montini*'? Yes, I saw it. But I don't want to talk about anything connected to this imbroglio. Just be with me."

He drew her closer. "I'll always be with you."

That was the last they saw of daylight. With lights off and curtains drawn, they spent the rest of the day in bed.

As the purple shadows of dusk appeared on the horizon, they realized how hungry they were. PJ sent out for dinner from the local Thai restaurant. Whatever was hovering over her, she refused to acknowledge it, safe at the moment in Val's loving arms, absorbing herself in the rapture of her lover's touch.

"I feel reborn," Val said, putting down his chopsticks and gazing into her glistening emerald eyes. He placed his hand on hers. "Marry me. Now. Tonight."

She chuckled. "So impetuous."

"Impetuous? I've been wanting to marry you from the day we met."

"Liar."

"Well, pretty close to the day we met."

"Sorry, the license bureau is closed."

"Not in Las Vegas."

She could not think of anything else to say. She slipped another shrimp into her mouth and ignored the comment.

"I'm not joking, PJ. After everything that's happened, I will not let you slip away."

"I'm not going to slip away, but I don't want you involved. I mean it. I've been trying to get that through your thick head. I am not good for anything until all this is behind me."

"You're good for me. And I'm already involved. Furthermore, when it comes to thick heads, yours takes the prize."

"One of the things we have in common, then. But we weren't going to talk about this, remember?"

He pushed his plate away. "Yes. I remember."

"Don't go sulky on me now and ruin my euphoria."

He got up, hoisted her out of her chair and carried her to the bed. "Wouldn't think of it."

Her phone chimed at 8:30 p.m. Jeff's number came up on the screen. She grabbed it from the nightstand. "Hello."

"Did I get you at a bad time? Your sexy voice is huskier than usual."

"Where are you, Jeff?"

"My plane just landed. I should be at your place in about an hour or so."

"My place?"

"PJ." He said gruffly. "I do not have a New York office. But don't worry, Sweetie, I will be staying at the Hilton. See you in a bit."

She nudged Val. "Val, it's getting late."

"What?"

"It's getting late."

He sat up. "Are you dismissing me?"

Too sated to be annoyed, she gave him a peck on the lips and headed for the shower.

"For now," she said over her shoulder. "My attorney is meeting me here in about an hour."

"Great! I'd love to meet the guy." She stopped mid-step, her hand on the door knob, and let out an unmistakable groan. She counted to ten. "Only if you leave immediately after. Don't make this more difficult for me than it is. There'll be another time, I'm sure."

"Dammit!" He got up and threw the pillow against the headboard.

"I'll leave," he hissed, "but I'm agreeing under protest."

"Duly noted."

Reynolds arrived at 9:40 with a resounding knock on the door. Much to his surprise, it was Val who opened the door, beating PJ by two paces. Val extended his hand. "Val Kendall." After a noticeable hesitation, Jeff shook it. "Jeff Reynolds."

Val stepped aside for PJ. "Hello, Jeff. Come on in."

"Good to see you, PJ. You look absolutely radiant."

Val winced inwardly as Jeff took a seat on the sofa. He opened his briefcase and spread a sheaf of papers on the coffee table. "What we will be discussing," he said, not looking up, "is highly confidential."

"Oh, don't worry about me…Jeff," Val said. "I've already been clued in." With that, Val put his arm around PJ, his hand firmly on her bottom. She pulled away discretely and gave him a look that said, *Seriously?*

"See you later, baby," he winked, and gave her a lingering kiss before leaving. PJ closed the door behind him.

"Can I get you a drink, Jeff?"

"Scotch and soda. No ice." PJ mixed him the drink, and poured herself a bourbon on ice.

"Your boyfriend is quite good-looking," he said. "You make the perfect Hollywood pair. The 21st Century Ken and Barbie."

PJ ignored the comment and sat next to Jeff glancing at the papers while leaving sufficient space between them.

Jeff would not let it go. "The jealous, possessive type, I see. Not very becoming."

"We're not here to discuss Val," she said, her last nerve pulsing. "What is all this, and what happened in Rome?"

Reynolds sat back, gathering his thoughts. "I met with both the Promoter of Justice for the Vatican, and the Public Prosecutor for the Italian Government," he said, not looking directly at PJ. "It took several tries, but the good news is you will not be extradited to Rome."

She put her face in her hands. "Thank God!" After a few moments of digesting the good news. She looked up, her eyes rimmed with tears. "And the not-so-good-news?"

He took a long swallow of his drink. "There is a condition."

Her throat, as if of its own volition, gave out a mournful groan. "Tell me."

"The Holy See, through the Italian Government, 'requests the immediate detention and prosecution of PJ Hollinger by the United States in full cooperation with the Vatican Legal Counsel, and the Italian Government.' Quote-unquote, or no deal."

PJ leapt from her seat like a skipjack. "How can they demand such a thing? With what evidence?"

"Please. Sit. You must remain calm and collected from this point on. No outbursts, especially in the courtroom. Leave the histrionics to me."

"Court? Detention? Prosecution? What does it all mean?

"PJ! Calm down. Please, let me finish." She sat and emptied her glass in one gulp. "I'm calm. I just don't understand how they can do this without cause."

Reynolds took a second. "They, the Italian Justice Department, claim to have an eyewitness."

"How is that possible after all this time?"

"Possible or not, that's what they claim." He sat back and locked his hands behind his head. "I believe, in their zeal to have this resolved, and perhaps some assurance that there will be a trial, they've leaked it to the Press, albeit prematurely."

"So that's where it came from."

"You've seen the papers."

"I have. My God! How will I ever be able to walk down the street without accusatory stares and snide remarks?"

It was Reynolds' turn to stand. He paced most of the square footage of the small studio apartment in silence, appearing concerned.

"What are you thinking?"

He turned to face her. "I'm thinking, one; how impossible can it be if you claim to have no memory of the event; and two..."

"Claim? You do think I killed him!"

"It doesn't matter what I think, PJ. My job is to get you out of this, with as little damage going forward as possible."

"Well, that's just great, Jeff. You could have told me this from the get go."

"Forget it. It's not important. What is important, though, is two; finding out who and where that witness is. I'm leaning toward the hope he or she is not a credible witness. So let's find out before we come to any unfounded conclusions."

"Don't the Italian police know who it is?"

"So far, he…or she…has remained anonymous." He sat close to her on the sofa and took her hand. "You must do everything possible to remember everything that transpired in that house in Frascati. Write it down. Every minute detail." He paused and squeezed her hand. "I would also like you to see Dr. Stoller again. Maybe under hypnosis…"

"How do you know about Dr. Stoller?" She slid her hand out of his. "That's supposed to be confidential."

"I assure you, PJ, Stoller did in no way break doctor-patient privilege. I happen to have an excellent PI who works with me. Let's leave it at that."

"Maybe for you it's easy to leave it at that, but it's my career, my reputation. And my life that are on the line."

"No need to panic just yet."

"Just yet? Well, that's very encouraging. I presume you will tell me when I should panic."

"Look, this may all be resolved tomorrow when I meet with the Attorney General." He put his arm around her and drew her close. "Let's drink to a positive outcome."

She pushed away, got up, and went to the door. "It's late, Jeff," she said as she opened the door. "I have a busy day tomorrow. I'd rather you go." She could almost hear his teeth clenching. He was not pleased. The way he glared at her sent a sudden chill up and down her spine.

"I had expected you would be more…appreciative of my inordinate efforts on your behalf." He collected his papers and walked out, leaving her with some sobering words. "It's in your best interests to stay on the good side of me, my sweet."

CHAPTER TWENTY

The Snitch

Candace, having died her hair black and chopped it into a boyish cut, left Dublin with a new identity and 300 Euros. But before leaving she sent off an anonymous letter to the *Rebibbia Prison, Women's Section, to the attention of Grazia Rinaldi, Warden*. Notwithstanding Sawyer's warning: "Screw me, girlfriend, and I will saw you into little pieces and watch you slowly die in agony," the letter briefly described how one of their parolees who went by the name of Sawyer, left the country to settle affairs with an ex-boyfriend, and his body could be found in an Airbnb near the Key West marina. *That should take care of Sawyer.* Candace smiled at her own cleverness.

Her next missive was addressed to Cardinal Vittorio Mangano, head Canon Lawyer on the Vatican Legal Council, a ploy that would nail PJ to the wall while covering her own ass. She sent this one via DHL Air to have it arrive in one day. *Amazing,* she thought, *the information one can extract from Google.* The wheels were in motion.

Meticulously planning her moves, Candace decided it best to fly into Newark rather than directly to New York. Two days after leaving Dublin, she landed at Newark Liberty International and took the Northeast Corridor line towards New York Penn Station. From there she grabbed a cab and was in Little Italy ten minutes later. A friend of a friend hooked her up with a cousin who could rent her a room above a pizzeria for seventy-five a week. Figuring she would need only two or three weeks, it fit into her budget...snugly. She took the room and waited for something to break.

For the first couple of days, she found the smells wafting up from the restaurant enticing. By the third day, she was literally sick of them. She went out early to grab some fresh air and an espresso. As she passed a newsstand, her eyes caught the huge banner headlining the New York Post. *Bingo!*

PJ's address was not hard to find. It would take her about half-an-hour to walk the nearly two miles from Little Italy to Battery Park City. She needed to be careful with her limited cash, but walking such a distance was not her thing. She took the 120 Bus line, which cost only two dollars, and was there in ten minutes.

She strolled for a bit along the Esplanade, delighting in being back in New York, even smiling at passersby. She had not realized until that moment how much she'd missed the city. When she'd had enough of waxing sentimental, she circled the area around PJ's apartment building, observing the doorman as he greeted those people he knew, and seemed to question those who apparently were unfamiliar. This may not be as easy as she'd anticipated, but she would give it her best shot. She took a deep breath, waited for the light to change, and crossed the street when the white hand permitted. Assuming the posture of a resident, Candace strode quickly past the doorman with a bright "Good afternoon," hoping she could slip by him. She got as far as the brass door handle.

"Er, excuse me, Ma'am," Doug called after her. She pretended not to hear, and went through the door. Doug followed her into the entranceway. "Excuse me," he called out again, louder. "Ma'am, I need to know your business here."

There was not much else she could do, but turn and acknowledge him. "I beg your pardon?"

"I don't believe you're a resident. I need to know your business here."

"Oh, of course. I'm visiting a friend."

"You'll have to come over to the desk and sign in."

He walked her to the desk and handed her the clipboard. "Who is it you're visiting? I will have to advise them."

"Oh, that won't be necessary," she said, thinking on her feet. "It's a surprise. Haven't seen her in some time, and I'm in town for only a short time."

"Yes, Ma'am. You will have to fill out the name of the resident you're visiting." He leaned over and pointed to the line where she was to do so. "Right there."

She had no choice at this point. She scribbled PJ Hollinger on the line, hoping that would satisfy him.

He took a quick look at the name. "Miss Hollinger is not in."

"Oh, dear. I was certain she'd be home." She put her hand on his arm, and turned on the charm. "I don't suppose you could let me in…that would be a really great surprise."

"Sorry, Ma'am. I can't do that."

In a last-ditch effort, she pulled out her purse and proffered a twenty-dollar bill.

"Please don't ruin my surprise," she pouted.

"Come back after five or six. Miss PJ should be back then."

She took out another twenty she could dearly afford. "I can't come back. I told you, darling, I'm only here for the day."

Doug took off his hat and rubbed his hand through his thinning hair. He put his hat back on. "There's no amount of money you can shove at me that'll get you into Miss PJ's apartment. I think you'd best leave now."

Candace so wanted to put a bullet between his eyes. Instead, she smiled sweetly, tossed the clipboard across the desk, and left.

Fuck this. She used most of the forty dollars on a cab back to Little Italy, and treated herself to a cannoli at Ferrara's. She walked the three blocks back to her room where she would hatch Plan B.

***

Doug's schedule did not always coincide with PJ's comings and goings, but he had a special attachment to her, in a sort of fatherly way, and made it something of a priority to look out for her. It pretty much fit nicely into his shift: eight hours on, eight hours off, with double pay on weekends. Today, Doug's shift ended at 5 p.m. Anxious to talk to PJ about the strange encounter he had with her *friend,* he hung around. PJ walked in at 5:40 p.m. Doug rushed up to her just as she stepped into the building's entrance, nearly crashing into her.

"Miss PJ."

In reaction, she stepped to the side. "Hi, Doug. Didn't expect you'd still be here. Don't you leave at five today?"

"Uh, yeah. I mean, yes, but…"

She put her hand gently on his arm. "Are you all right? You seem flustered."

"Oh. I'm fine, but I wanted to talk to you about your friend."

"My friend?" PJ began walking slowly toward the elevators with Doug in step.

"This woman. I'm not really sure she's a friend, but she said she was and that she was here to see you. Said she didn't see you for a long time, and wanted to surprise you."

PJ was about to press the up button, but let her hand drop. "Who was this *friend*, Doug?"

"Um, she didn't say her name." He rubbed his chin. "Oh. She did sign the log." He hurried toward the desk. PJ followed him. He took it off the hook and ran his finger up several lines to where she had signed. "Fiddlesticks! She wrote your name, but didn't write down hers."

PJ's brows furrowed as she scanned the log. "What did this woman look like?"

Doug took a minute. "Uh, she was not very tall. And she had dark hair, black maybe…cut short, like a guy's."

"Hmm. I can't say that I recall having any female friends with very short, black hair. Then again, I meet so many people in my profession, I couldn't say for sure, but I'm certain she is not a close friend."

"What do you think she wanted?"

"Nothing good."

"Maybe you should hire a bodyguard…I mean what with all that's happened."

She gave Doug a tight hug. "You're my bodyguard. Now go home and get some rest. You're dismissed for the night."

Doug chuckled, but he could not let go of the bad feeling he had.

Day two, and PJ had not heard anything from Jeff Reynolds. She was tempted to call his office, but wouldn't give him the satisfaction. She'd give it another day or so.

The four walls were closing in on her. She had to get out of the apartment. She tied her hair back with a scrunchie and donned a pair of shades and a Yankee baseball cap, pulling the ponytail through the opening. She left the building and jogged the nearly three miles to the gym. She slowed to a trot for the last couple of blocks. She breathed more easily knowing that other than a sidelong glance or two, no one seemed to recognize her.

Scarborough Kickboxing was a private establishment owned and operated by Jeremy Scarborough, graduate of Columbia University with a master's in business administration, and two-time kickboxing world champion. Scarborough specialized in American and Muay Thai training. While kickboxing does not have a specific ranking system, Scarborough had his own ideas about developing champions. He did not stray much from the required moves for Muay Thai, but he incorporated certain boxing techniques, and used the belt ranking system, from white for beginners, to black for those fully trained with perfect technical scores. He believed strongly that the belt rewards were highly motivational.

The gym was one enormous room, sectioned off into three large square training areas separated by immovable roped stanchions. Two of the three areas contained a punching bag and a banana heavy bag suspended from the ceiling. Scarborough employed two junior trainers, and therefore never had more than three trainees at one time, by appointment only. The changing room and office were in the northeast corner of the gym next to the rear exit.

PJ scanned the room. There were only two courts being used. She spotted Scarborough in one of them, working with a woman. She was practicing kicks. He looked up when the cow bells jangled as the door opened and closed. When he saw it was PJ, he excused himself and walked over. "Wherever have you been? Not turning to flab I see, despite your protracted absence." They hugged. "You've lost some weight. Not good."

"I'm fine. Ready to get back in the saddle."

"Wonderful! I have fifteen more minutes with this lady." He lowered his voice to a whisper. "Not a good candidate. Has no agility, and legs are a bit short. I'll have to work on a special program for her."

"I hope you didn't tell her that," she whispered back.

"Have you forgotten how charming I can be?" he winked. "I'll be back in a flash. Practice on the bag to warm up."

Scarborough grabbed two bottles of water and brought one over to PJ as the woman went to the changing room. PJ could only make out the back of her head. The short, boyish cut black hair seemed familiar to her, but she could not quite pin down where she'd seen it.

"I noticed that you haven't forgotten any of your best moves. Good girl." He took a slug of water. "Okay, let's get started."

He worked with her for an hour, took a ten-minute break, then had her go through some of the combination moves he'd taught her. She let her attention drift, and was taken down. "You lost focus, PJ."

"I did. Sorry," she said, wiping her brow with her sleeve.

"Where'd you go?"

"That woman you were working with. I saw her go to the changing room, but I didn't see her leave."

"Shame on you. You shouldn't have been thinking of anything else but survival."

"You're right. I've been so distracted lately."

"She probably went out the back door. A walk-in, wanting to take advantage of my free introductory training. She probably won't be back. So, what's distracting you?"

PJ was not in the mood to revisit all that was swirling around her, but had to ask. "Have you read the papers over the last few days?"

"I never read the papers…they pervert the facts, and only deliver bad news. Why?"

"Never mind, It's not important," she said, waving the question away. "I think I've had enough for today. See you next week?"

"You bet. You did well today."

PJ speed-walked home. She had stopped at the corner of Pearl and Broad Streets when it hit her. The woman at the gym matched Doug's description of the woman wanting to get into her apartment. But for the weird turns her life had taken over the past months, she would have thought little of the connection. At this stage, though, nothing was over the top. Anxious to speak with Doug again, she jogged the rest of the way. To her disappointment, Doug's shift had already ended, and Larry, his alternate, was standing at the door. Larry was much younger than Doug, and not nearly as diligent. He usually had his nose in his mobile device. Nonetheless, she asked the burning question.

"Hello, Larry."

He looked up. "Oh, hi, Ms. Hollinger."

"Have you seen a woman, around forty or so, with cropped, black hair come into the building today?"

He hesitated, as though he were considering the question. "I, um. I don't think so."

She closed her eyes in frustration. "Are you certain?"

"Yes, Ma'am," he answered a bit too vehemently. "You know, all sorts of people come and go through here, but I didn't see this particular woman. Maybe you should ask Doug when he's back on duty."

"I'll do that," she said, as he opened the door for her. "Thanks so much for your help."

When she got to her apartment, she unlocked the door and slammed it behind her, angry at herself for being snippy with the kid. Every little tick had become a major annoyance. Something was going on inside her that she did not like one bit. She checked her phone. Still no message from Reynolds. The familiar icy stab in her stomach spoke up as if to say, *face it, girl, you're about to be fucked.* She switched off the thought as best she could and took a long, hot shower. It dawned on her that she'd never taken so many showers in a day. They had become a significant part of her practice to stay calm and sane. She put on a pair of sleep shorts and a tee shirt. She was about to check the rest of her calls, when she heard a movement inside her apartment. She turned up the light in the far corner, and choked in air.

"Hello…Sis."

CHAPTER TWENTY-ONE

Propositions and Proposals

PJ steeled herself. The last thing she needed to do was to appear weak. She walked guardedly to the small sofa and sat, facing her nemesis. "How did you get in?"

"It's amazing what money can do, and the kid looked like he could use a few extra bucks."

"Whatever you gave him won't last long after he's fired."

"No one will know…unless of course you tell them."

"I have no choice. He's now a security risk."

Candace made a sour face. "Always goody-two-shoes." She glanced around the room. "Very cozy. But enough small talk. From recent headlines, it won't be long before your pretty little ass is behind bars." Her laughter held a sinister tone that sent an icy distress call through PJ's veins. She closed her eyes and blew out a long breath. "Why are you here, Candace?"

"Guess."

PJ had a flash of clarity. "It's you, isn't it? The anonymous eye-witness. Oh, my God, I should have known." PJ threw her head back and laughed. "Of course, the money. So what kind of deal did you make?"

"At this point, it's just a carrot, waiting for you to nip at."

"Look. I've considered giving you your share, despite your malicious acts. It's only fair. Peter Romano was your father, too."

"Well, well. Isn't that generous of you, Sis"

"But it's a complicated situation, Candace."

"So uncomplicate it. And I'm not settling for half. I want the entire two-million!"

"That's not going to happen. The money is in a trust."

Candace's face turned an angry red. She stood and pointed a Sig P365 at PJ's face. "What the fuck does that mean?"

"It means I can draw only so much per month until my 35th birthday. Those are the conditions of the bequest. So I guess you're just out of luck."

"What the fuck! Why wait until your 35, as if you're not already an adult? Is that some kind of magic number?"

"I have no idea. Maybe he was buying time for me. Trying to protect me against sociopaths like you."

Candace jabbed the gun in PJ's neck. "I know you have other money stashed away someplace. Money that your rich parents left you."

"Splitting our father's money is one thing. But you will not get a cent of my parents' hard-earned savings."

"I should shoot you right now."

"But you won't. You're obviously desperate for money. And I'm your only hope," she said, gently pushing the pistol away. "So why don't you put the gun away before I break your arm."

"That sure of yourself, are you?"

"I'm only one match away from a black belt."

A long silence fell over the room before Candace spoke. "Here's my proposition, and the only option you have, or you'll enjoy that special comradery a prison has to offer."

"I'm listening."

"I want two million by next week or I go to the police with my story; my eyewitness account of the murder of Cardinal Montini."

"I told you, I don't have access to the two million dollars. And if you think you can intimidate me, you haven't learned much. It's my word against yours…and you're obviously not a credible witness."

"You think so? Did I mention I have photos that prove you killed Montini? You have until Monday," Candace said, surprisingly calm. "If I don't hear from you, you can kiss your good life goodbye…one way or another." She stood, tucked the gun in her ratty jeans, and left.

***

PJ poured herself a shot of bourbon, her hands shaking. She was certain Candace was bluffing about the photos…but what if she wasn't? What if she really did have photographic proof of the murder? She needed to speak to Jeff in a hurry. She tossed down the drink then poured another. Not ten-minutes later, there was a loud knock on the door that made her spring from her chair. Apparently,

Doug was off duty, or he would have rung her up. She waited, holding her breath. Her jumpiness was something she thought she'd overcome years ago. The next knock was louder than the first. She went to the door and looked through the peephole, her fear immediately flipped into irritation. *Well, it's about time.* She opened the door. Jeff Reynolds stood there, that nausea-inducing half-smile on his face. "May I come in?"

PJ stepped aside to let him in. "You could have called first."

"I figured the security guy would ring you up, but he was fast asleep. Wasted, if you ask me."

Unbelievable. "I need to know what's happening, Jeff. I'm dangerously close to the precipice of a long and rocky drop."

Jeff put his arms around her in an attempted hug. She quickly pulled away and stepped toward the living area. "I really need to know what I'm up against. And what kind of defense you're planning"

A growl escaped his throat. "I think we should both have a drink first."

This is too much. "I don't want a drink, Jeff. I want you to be my attorney. If you can't do that and maintain the proper client-attorney posture, I'll find another."

To PJ's astonishment, he grabbed her and kissed her hard on the mouth. She struggled against his strength, but he had her arms locked around her. She could hardly move. She considered a knee to the groin, but held off. "Let me go, Jeff. I mean it."

He kissed her lips again, then her neck, whispering in her ear. "Don't you know there's not a day that goes by that I don't think of you. That I don't see your face, your lips, before me. I need you, PJ. And you need me."

"Let me go, Jeff. I can barely breathe."

He loosened his grip and took a step back, giving her just enough room to use a spinning back sweep, with a blow to the sternum. He fell back, winded. "Fuck! I can't breathe. You broke my ribs!"

"You'll be fine. I didn't break your ribs, but it will hurt you to breathe for a day or two. I told you to let me go. Now I'm telling you to get out. I don't need you, Jeff. I don't need anyone like you. Just leave."

He struggled to his knees, then to his feet, grabbing onto the edge of the sofa while pressing a hand to his chest. "You need to know something, PJ," he panted. "Think of it as a proposition. I'm not giving up. I want you as I've never wanted anyone. And I always get what I want. Always."

"Get out now, Jeff, and save us both a lot of trouble."

"That's just it, my love. You're already in a lot of trouble. And I'm your only ticket out."

PJ walked to the door and opened it half-way. "We're done here."

"My father and the AG's father just happen to be golf buddies." He continued between short, painful intakes of breath. "As thick as cement. That's one of the reasons I was able to get such a timely appointment."

"What are you getting at, Jeff."

"I can have this whole affair cling-wrapped and put on ice—for good—with just one phone call."

"And you're telling me this now, after all the twists and turns and wrangling. Why?"

"Ah. Glad you asked." He sat himself slowly on the sofa, wincing in pain. "Here's my proposition." He took a painful breath. "I want you to marry me." He smiled slyly, his lips snaking like the viper he was. "It's that, or spend the rest of your life in prison."

The incredulous look surfacing to her face spoke a thousand uncivil words. Had she heard right? Could he have the unmitigated audacity to propose to her? She could hardly believe it. But there was no imagining his gall, his arrogance. "That would make me wife number four."

"But who's counting?" he sniggered.

She opened the door as wide as it would go. "I'd rather spend the rest of my life in jail. Get out!"

CHAPTER TWENTY-TWO

On the Run

The familiar scent of lavender drifted from the lilac candle on the reception desk creating an aura of calmness, as it was intended to do.

"Good afternoon, stranger." Elena's silky voice had an extra measure of welcome to it. Having worked with Dr. Stoller for fifteen years, her persona took on the quality of her boss's affable manner. "Despite that serious face, you look absolutely wonderful."

"Thank you, Elena. It's good to see you." She managed a broad smile.

"That's better. How was Ireland?" PJ looked away, giving the question some thought.

"Interesting."

"Hmm. Sounds like you need to take that up further with Dr. Stoller." Elena pressed the intercom. "PJ is here."

PJ had made a double appointment. If she could have, she would have scheduled a triple session, needing so desperately to recap her abduction, all that had transpired in Frascati, and her memory loss so that she might better understand the true nature of the black hand manipulating her life. Stoller, however, focused the entire session on her childhood, and her periods of dissociative behavior. He reserved the last forty minutes for another hypnosis session.

***

Feeling a bit shaky after her visit, PJ took a cab downtown rather than risking passing out on the subway. When it pulled up to her apartment building, there were two cars illegally parked in front of the entrance. One, a black, unmarked Dodge, the other, a patrol car, its strobe lights pulsing. "Please drive around the block."

When they were safely out of sight, PJ had the driver pull over so she could think. After about ten minutes, she gave the driver her grandfather's address on Long Island.

"Why haven't you returned my calls?" He scowled, pulling her into the house. He closed the door, drew down the shade then put his arms around her as she wept on his shoulder.

"It's all right, baby."

"I'm so lost," she gasped between sobs.

"It'll be all right." He walked her to the sofa, sat her down and handed her a box of tissues. "Let me get you something to drink." He was back minutes later with two snifters of brandy.

"Here. This will help." He gave her time to compose herself as they sipped brandy.

"Better?"

"Yes."

"How's your fiancé?" PJ gave him a raised-brow stare. "You have this knavish way of intertwining subjects."

"Just making conversation."

"Val's off chasing some recalcitrant birth-mother in Texas."

"See. It works."

Deep sigh. "Not really."

"Talk to me, sweetheart."

She clasped her hands in her lap to keep them from trembling. "I…I'm sure I'm about to be arrested."

"Come on. You're jumping to conclusions a mile higher than warranted."

"I shot him, Sil. I pointed a gun to his head and shot him. In cold blood. How could I have done such a thing? Who am I? What kind of evil lives inside me?"

"Stop it, PJ." He took her hand. "Whatever happened, it was not your fault. Even if you did shoot him, you were in shock. Traumatized. Call it what you will. But it wasn't you who pulled that trigger."

She stood, raking her hands through her hair. "Then who was it?' Who committed such a horrific act?"

They both froze at the pounding on the door. "Don't say anything, PJ. Do you have a lawyer?"

She gave a scornful laugh. "Let me put it this way; what idiot fires her attorney when she's about to be arrested?"

He couldn't hold back a slight smile. "Sounds just like you." The hammering became more insistent. "Go into the bedroom and hang tight," he said, heading for the door.

Standing on the porch was a tall, portly man with salt-and-pepper hair that at best had been finger-combed, and a suit jacket in need of a pressing. To his left and slightly behind stood his partner…a stark contrast of orderliness.

"Took you long enough, Romano."

"I don't get around as quick as I used to, Murphy. To what do I owe the honor?"

"Don't play dumb with me, Sil. We're looking for your granddaughter."

"And why would you think she'd be here; she has a neat little apartment of her own."

Murphy blew out a long stream of air. "Is she inside, Sil?"

"No. Actually, I haven't heard from her in a couple of weeks. I've left several text messages. She must be busy."

"Don't bullshit me, Sil…we go back a-ways."

"So you should know I'm not bullshitting you," he shot back, sounding quite convincing.

"What do you want with her?"

"We just want to ask her a few questions."

"Try her apartment again. She'll go home eventually," he said, shutting the door.

"We'll come back with a warrant, if necessary," Murphy shouted at the closed door.

PJ came out of the bedroom wearing her coat.

"Where are you going?" he said, keeping his voice low. "If I know Murphy, he'll be watching the house."

"I will not have you implicated in this drama. It's my problem and I'll deal with it."

"Says the woman who claims not to know who she is."

"Please don't mock me, Sil. I'm not in the mood."

"Take your coat off and let's hash this out. If you walk out that door, chances are they'll take you in."

She slumped in the side chair, but kept her coat on. "Charlie called," she said. "Walden wants to get me on a charter flight to their place in England, until I have a decent attorney."

Romano smacked his thighs. "Jesus, PJ! You can't keep running from place to place, trying to stay one step ahead of the authorities. You will only be making it worse for yourself."

She leaned forward and glared at her grandfather. "Then what do you propose I do?" she shrieked, her voice cracking with a mix of anger and fear.

"I'll tell you exactly what you should do, but you won't like it."

Having run out of arguments fifteen or so minutes after trying to convince PJ to turn herself in for questioning—which she flatly refused to do—Romano paced the room, clearly frustrated by the stubborn streak that ran through their familial DNA. "Just as I thought."

No one spoke for what seemed an eternity. PJ's thoughts hurtled through her mind like a 747 spiraling out of control. "I need to get home."

Romano groaned, clearly giving up. "Take my car. The garage is in the back. There's an alley to the right as you pull out. That will take you to the main road without being seen." She buttoned her coat, put the hood over her head, and gave Romano a long hug.

"Thank you."

He could not help the moisture welling in his eyes from leaking out. "Be safe. And, please, call me. I'm here for you, sweetheart. Whatever you need."

She followed his instructions, continually checking the rear-view. When she was about a mile out on the highway, she relaxed a bit. But not for long.

CHAPTER TWENTY-THREE

A person of Interest

Despite not owning a car, the decision to maintain the monthly fee for a reserved parking space turned out to be a judicious one. She drove around the block making sure she'd not been followed, then pulled into her spot in the complex's underground garage. With a feeling of uneasiness, she walked quickly toward the elevator, scanning the area. A car door slammed. Seconds later, another. She froze, then slipped behind a pillar. Two people were making their way to the elevator, a man and a woman. They were arguing. The man was older than the woman, perhaps her father. She breathed a sigh of relief. She made sure they were completely out of sight before stepping back into the light. The area was deserted.

She took the back elevator, which took longer than a snail making its way up a drainpipe. When she at last reached her apartment, she locked the door behind her, finally able to take a full breath. She drew all the curtains, grabbed a bottle of water from the fridge, and slumped on the sofa.

The tears came. Quiet, simpering tears. This was her life now. She'd become a fugitive.

The house phone rang. Startled, she jumped up and moved quickly in the direction of the sound, knowing it would be Doug. By the time she got to it, he had hung up. Before she could ring him back, there was a knock on the door. She peeked through the eyehole, and muffled a gasp. It was the man and woman from the garage. The man knocked again, hard. PJ sprung back, immobilized, unable to think.

"Penelope Jane Hollinger. Lt. James Murphy and Detective Laura Fields, NYPD. Please open the door."

After a few deep breaths, she opened the door, but kept the latch on. "Yes?"

"May we come in, Ms. Hollinger." The woman spoke. "We'd like to ask you a few questions."

"What about?"

"I'm sure you know, why we're here," Murphy said. "So make it easy on both of us." Fields gave him an admonishing side glance.

"May I see your ID's?"

After stalling as long as she could, for what purpose she could not even explain to herself, she unlatched the door and motioned them inside. The two sat on the sofa facing PJ, who sat on the edge of the matching side chair.

"Can I offer you some water, or tea?"

"This is not a social call, Ms. Hollinger."

PJ was beginning to dislike the lieutenant, a stern-looking man in his fifties who did a good impression of Columbo. "I'll take that as a no."

Fields, apparently attempting to deflect Murphy's harshness, asked for water. Murphy took out a small black notepad and a pen. After handing Detective Fields a glass of water, PJ resumed her seat on the edge of the chair.

Murphy got right to the point. "Ms. Hollinger, tell me about your relationship with one, Cardinal Roberto Alphonse Montini."

PJ did not expect that to be the first question. She collected her thoughts, trying hard not to reveal her nervousness. "I had no relationship with the Cardinal," she said. "In fact, we'd never met."

"And yet you knew more about him than most, according to your scathing exposé."

"That's what I do, lieutenant, find and research the truth about people and events. Then report the facts."

"Facts or fake news?"

As a child, when PJ was not believed, or her honesty questioned, she would turn tomato red, stamp her feet, and cry bloody murder. As she matured, she developed a talent for converting anger and frustration into short, acerbic responses that left her antagonist on the foiled end of the conversation. This was one of those times. Enraged, she stood and calmly said, "If you have probable cause, arrest me, or leave. But don't malign my work. Clearly, you do not have the credentials for a literary critic."

"Our apologies, Ms. Hollinger," Fields once again interceded. "It is not our intention to alienate you. But you must understand, at this time you are a person of interest in our investigation of the Montini murder, and we would like your cooperation in answering a few questions that may clear up some of the confusion surrounding this case." She frosted her explanation with a slight smile. Murphy rolled his eyes.

PJ was not unmindful of the *good cop, bad cop* ploy. She decided she would cooperate, on her own terms, answering as circuitously as she could. She sat. "My answer stands. I did not have a relationship with Cardinal Montini."

"But you did have a relationship with Cardinal…or is it pope…Peter Romano."

She knew this was coming. "Yes."

"And?"

"And what?"

Obviously, forbearance was not Murphy's strong suit. He sighed again, more emphatically.

"What was your relationship to Peter Romano"?

PJ looked Murphy directly in his eyes. "His eminence, Cardinal Peter Romano, was my biological father." She glanced at Fields, then back at Murphy. But you already knew that."

"Just corroborating, Ms. Hollinger." He said. "Inspector, um…" He turned to Fields.

"Doyle," she reminded him.

"Yeah. Inspector Doyle was kind enough to forward us a transcript of the case file."

Annoyed, PJ got up, walked to the window, and drew the curtains aside to let the moonlight pour some brightness into the darkening room. "Why are you asking me questions you already know the answers to? Why not just get to the point, Lieutenant?"

Murphy said nothing. Instead, Detective Fields responded. "We are in possession of a written document by an as yet anonymous witness who claims to have seen you point a weapon at the Cardinal…and fire it."

Murphy cleared his throat. Clearly, by the glowering look he gave Fields, he had no intention of divulging this information.

Candace! She actually went through with it. "That's very interesting, detective," she said as calmly as she could. "And what makes you think this…anonymous claim is true?"

Fields was about to answer when Murphy cut her off. He stood. "We're in the process of substantiating the claim, and the next time we come back, it will be with a warrant for your arrest." He signaled Fields that they were leaving. "We'll let ourselves out."

Laura Fields was a dedicated cop with five year's experience in the Homicide Division, two years working with Murphy. She had done intense research on Penelope Jane Hollinger, and decided that if she did indeed kill Montini, she had a damned good reason. Murphy, for his part, had no doubt she was guilty of the crime. Aware of the soft spot he had for her grandfather, he compensated by being harder on her than was his customary approach. When they got back to the car, with the doors closed, he let Fields have it. Ranting and raving at her for "opening your big mouth." And "I was saving that piece of information for the right time…now was not the right time. Fuck!"

Fields took it without a word as she always did. She had gotten used to his rampages when things didn't go his way. She waited until he was done. "You didn't have to be so hard on her." They had nothing, and he knew it. Until the witness came forward, he could not arrest her. The DNA and fingerprint samples were not only inconclusive, but explainable. The transcripts indicated she had been abducted and held in the Frascati house. The fact that she was at the scene was not in question. But Murphy knew she did it. After eighteen years in the Homicide Division, his gut had never failed him. She did it. No question.

CHAPTER TWENTY-FOUR

The Text

Not fifteen minutes after her unwelcomed company left, Doug knocked on her door. "Sorry, Miss PJ, just wanted to make sure everything was okay before my shift ends."

"Thank you, Doug. I'm fine." She waited for him to continue as he did not seem to want to leave. "Would you like to come in for some tea before you go home?"

"That's awful kind of you, but I know you had a busy day. Just wanted to check in. Oh, and to tell you the new guy is first-rate, so you don't have to worry. I interviewed him myself. He's A-okay," he said, giving a thumbs-up for added emphasis.

"That's good to know. I do appreciate you, Doug. Be safe going home." By the concerned look on his face, she sensed there was something else he wanted to say. He shuffled his feet, then said, "Will do," and headed for the elevator.

Hmm. What was that all about? Having far more serious matters to consider, she let it go and checked her text messages, which were like NEON lights pulsing, CALL ME!! She had never felt such exhaustion from doing nothing. She thought about putting off the calls until morning, but knew she'd be awakened in the middle of the night by either Val or Charlie…or both. Sweet images of another hot shower and crawling into bed evaporated as she punched in Val's number. He answered before the second ring.

"Hey. I was waiting for your call. How are you?"

It was an effort trying to keep him from asking too many questions. "I'm well. You need to stop worrying about me."

"That'll be the day. You sound tired."

"I'm fine. It's just been a long day."

"Anything new with your case? Are things settling down at all?"

"Status quo. How is your hunt going?"

"I know you don't like talking about it," he said. "Especially to me. And I'm trying hard to abide by your crazy rules. But walking on eggshells hurts my feet, and I am well-attuned to your changing the subject tactic."

PJ chuckled. "Ah, you know me all too well."

"I miss you so much, Baby."

"Miss you, too. When are you coming home?"

"My client wants to go legal, and claim the right to know, forcing his biological mother to at least have a conversation with him. No telling how long that will take."

"So sorry. Speaking of legal, you'll be delighted to know that I fired my attorney."

"That's the best news I've had all month. I knew he was a worm from the get-go."

"I thought you'd be pleased."

"Pleased isn't the word. Such an arrogant weasel."

They spoke for another few minutes. PJ did not tell him she might be going away for a while. It would only create a situation she did not want to have to deal with. After saying their good-byes and I love you's, they hung up. PJ released a disconsolate sigh, and tapped in Charlie's number.

The call went to Charlie's voice mail box, but PJ did not want to leave a message. She had to speak to her friend personally. Five minutes later, Charlie called her back. "You rang, my sista, etc. etc.?"

"What's all that racket? I can barely hear you."

Charlie was at some fund-raising gala "Hold on, let me find a quiet space." When they were back on the line, Charlie could hear the despondency in PJ's voice.

"I'm fine," she insisted. But Charlie knew better.

"Talk to me."

"Let me call you tomorrow, you're obviously in the middle of something important…"

"If you don't tell me what's going on, I swear, I will catch the next flight to New York, and…and hug you until it squishes out of you!"

PJ chuckled. "Squishes? Adding to your vocabulary I see."

"You're skirting. And you called me, remember? Now let's have it."

There was no way Charlie would leave this alone until she knew all of it. So, PJ told her all of it. Charlie listened without saying a word for the lump in her throat.

"My grandfather is right," PJ admitted. "I can't keep running. Sooner or later everything's going to hit the fan…probably sooner."

"You cannot stay there! Please, PJ. Go to England. I will meet you in Knightsbridge. You need to be around people who love and support you."

"I just can't do this anymore, Charlie. I'm being sucked down a dark, abysmal shaft. I no longer recognize myself." The atmosphere in the room hung so heavy with silence, it was hard to breathe.

"I'm taking the next flight to New York," Charlie said flatly. Walden will get you the best lawyer on the East Coast. I promise."

Angry, PJ told Charlie in no uncertain terms, "if you disrupt your lives because of my mess, I'll never speak to you again!," And hung up.

PJ could not remember a time throughout their entire journey through life together, or apart, when either hung up on the other, or made such a declaration. She felt herself slip-sliding away. *Why is all this happening all at once? I'm being buried alive!* She tracked around the room mumbling to herself between sobs. There seemed no way out. No matter what she did, the end result would be the same…prison. But she couldn't just let them nail her to a tree. She knew how the Vatican operated. They protected their own while keeping their bloody hands pristine. She stopped suddenly and grabbed her phone. She didn't wait for a hello. "I need you to get me out of the country…quickly. Somewhere that has no extradition treaty with the US."

Surprisingly, Romano did not argue with her. He told her he would do everything possible. Truth be told, he would walk through fire for her. He did warn her that the odds of success were slim to none.

"You understand why I have to try."

"I do."

There was no way PJ would get a wink of sleep. She took that hot shower anyway. Tossing and turning made her even more weary. She got up, made some tea, and opened her laptop. She began researching criminal attorneys when her phone dinged an incoming text. It was from Jefferson Reynolds. She was about to delete it, but whether it was instinct, or just curiosity, she opened it.

My dearest. PJ. I knew you would not take my call. I forgive you. But I've decided to give you one last chance to accept my proposal (is that a pun?). Please read on before deleting as your situation has become critical. I've learned from a very reliable source that there is a major pow-wow about to take place in Albany, at the Executive Mansion of the governor of New York that will include the DA, the ADA, and big wigs from the Vatican and Italy's Department of Public Security. The subject of this tete-à-tete, my dearest, is YOU. The Vatican does not want to be in any way attached to this imbroglio (thus the reason you were not extradited to Rome), but their influence will prevail. The governor (and therefore the DA) is under duress to resolve the matter expeditiously. As I understand it, "Whatever it takes" was the phrase used. The Vatican has no interest in who or why; they want this case closed as of yesterday, and you're it! There's more, but I will save that for when we meet. Say yes, and your troubles, my sweet, will be over.

The blood-rush to her head left her spinning. She had to sit down. *Good God; the man is either Narcissus himself, or completely insane.* Before deleting the text, she typed, *Go to Hell*! Then threw the phone across the room into the fireplace. Fortunately, it was quite a warm night.

CHAPTER TWENTY-FIVE

The Witness

Candace had not enjoyed what one would call a tender relationship with her mother. They, in fact, bore a long-held resentment for each other. Their association was based on need. Lucinda Russell depended on Candace to help carry out her plan of revenge; Candace needed her mother's money to live on. Lucinda now dead, and the plan having gone awry, Candace found herself thirty thousand feet in the air without a parachute. She would either land softly into a field of cotton and financial freedom, or nosedive into a sea of impoverishment, and, likely, prison.

Sitting on the edge of a rotting pier in Sheepshead Bay, the question that kept popping up was, *How the fuck did I get here?* A squabble of seagulls flying overhead grabbed her attention. She brandished her middle finger. "Go on, shit on my head. That should complete my day." She lit a cigarette and took a long draw, dug into her pocket, and took out the note that had been left under the door of a rattrap she now shared with some do-gooder who volunteered at a shelter. Candace could sniff a sucker two miles away. She wrapped this one around her crafty finger and scrounged a place to stay after having been kicked out of the Little Italy loft for smoking. She unfolded and refolded the note several times before reading it for the third time. It was written on newsprint in black marker.

YOU'RE DEAD MEAT! LOOK FORWARD TO SEEING YOU SOON TO RIP OUT YOUR LYING TONGUE!

Sawyer! But how is that possible? She's in prison. Candace walked the eight blocks to the bus stop. Destination: library. She needed to find out if Sawyer had been arrested for Gino's murder. If not, her plan was reduced to a pile of manure, and her life was seriously on the line.

She spent the entire afternoon at the computer researching the Carlotti case, and found a column devoted to it on a police report listing local crimes in the Key West Weekly. Concetta Barone, it read, had been released. Her DNA did not match that found at the scene. She was being sent back to Italy to serve thirty-days for parole violation. Candace broke out into a cold sweat. She checked the dates. Sawyer would be released in seven days.

She went back to her apartment, and before slipping out of her backpack, downed a full tumbler of Vodka to calm her shakes. It was time to give it up. PJ was not going to come through with the money. *That bitch!* She had only one option, present herself as a witness in exchange for protection and immunity. Judging from the scuttlebutt surrounding the murder of Cardinal Montini, the State of New York was being pressured to nail the case shut. If that were true, Candace stood a good chance of getting what she wanted.

***

It was a chilly day in Albany for May. An overcast sky lent an additional air of somberness to an already gloomy state-of-affairs. For its level of confidentiality, the meeting was originally scheduled to be held in the governor's private office on the second floor of the

Executive Mansion. As the number of attendees was confirmed, it became apparent that the office would not do.

The governor had offered a flagged limo to accommodate the dignitaries representing the Vatican from the airport to the Mansion. They respectfully declined. Intent on keeping the *situation* as low-key as possible, they requested a Fiat SUV. As low-key as one could get given its high level occupants which included the Promoter of Justice for the Holy See, and Rome's Minister of Justice, who would be representing the Italian government. The Archbishop of New York would also be on hand, representing the archdiocese at the request of the pope.

The first to arrive were the New York District Attorney and the Assistant DA. They would report to the mayor, who was conveniently out of town. On the heels of their arrival, the archbishop, known for his practicality, drove up in his own Honda Accord.

When the Fiat was spotted by one of the state troopers posted at the Eagle Street gate some twenty minutes later, it was escorted around to a private entrance that was closed to the general public. The news media was, as had been prearranged, noticeably absent.

This entire proceeding was an immense hemorrhoid to the governor, from having to keep everything hush-hush, to playing second fiddle to an arrangement orchestrated by the Vatican. Other than transportation from the airport to the Executive Mansion, he would not be providing any of the pomp and circumstance these uppity clergy and justice officials were accustomed to. The meeting would be held in the Breakfast Room after a rather ordinary fare of scrambled eggs, sausage, and pastries. Even the cook questioned the meagerness of the menu.

For an additional nose-thumb, the governor kept his guests, who had already been seated, waiting for ten minutes, leaving the lieutenant governor holding the bag.

He strode into the room, voice booming. "My apologies, gentlemen…um…" He stopped mid-sentence, cleared his throat, and dipped his head toward the Promoter of Justice. "I beg your pardon. and lady." His mild chuckle fell flat.

Governor Tremont knew little about the Catholic faith. What he did know was that women were not a major part of its tradition. He was not even sure how to address her as he hadn't read the pre-meeting brief. He familiarized himself only with the documents concerning the murder case. The room fell quiet. The governor nodded to the wait staff to begin serving.

Wasting little time, the current Promoter of Justice for the Vatican, a statuesque woman of a certain age—the first woman to hold the position—ignored protocol, and in impeccable English with a lilting, Italian accent, opened the meeting.

"Governor Tremont," she began, hands folded demurely in her lap, her posture unyieldingly straight. "On behalf of the Vatican, we wish to thank you for hosting this critical meeting." She did not wait for a response, but continued seamlessly, making it clear to everyone present exactly who was in charge. "We've come all this way to solidify, if you will, our agreement concerning the unfortunate circumstances surrounding the murder of His Eminence, Cardinal Roberto Montini which, coming directly on the heels of the assassination of our former, albeit short-lived pope, Peter Francesco Romano, Pope Xavier, it is imperative that the Vatican's involvement in this transpiration remain…unnoticed." She took a breath and was about to continue, when the governor called for a note-taker.

"I beg your pardon, Governor." She placed her hands flat on the table and leaned forward, her eyes flashing darts at Tremont. "There will be no note-taking! It had been formally agreed upon by all concerned that this would be a closed meeting, the occasion for which will be swept from our memories the moment this case is resolved." She looked directly at the DA. "Which will be quite soon."

The woman took a sip of her tea, neatly wiped her lips, and resumed her straight-backed, hands-folded position. "Carlo Sabatino, Rome's minister of Justice, who would ordinarily be conducting this investigation and trial…"

Having had enough of this imperiousness, Tremont, clearly vexed, interjected. "One moment, Madam Promoter of Justice. There has not even been an arrest. Don't you think you're jumping the gun. After all, there may not even be a trial if the evidence is found to be insufficient."

The woman stared incredulously at Tremont. It was Sabatino who responded. "With all due respect, Governor, you do not seem to grasp the weight of this situation. We, all of us, given our respective responsibilities, have a major stake in resolving this matter as quickly and quietly as possible. Which can mean expediting certain procedures and processes."

There was no mistaking the disapproving frown casting a shadow over Tremont's face. "I'm not sure what you're suggesting, Minister, but we operate by protocol based on due process and justice. If bending the rules is your intent, I am not comfortable with that."

Everyone looked at each other in astonishment. The lieutenant governor leaned over and whispered something in Tremont's ear. Tremont turned a blazing shade of crimson having been reminded of a phone conversation in which he agreed, in his customary disinterested style, to whatever the Vatican proposed. "Apparently," he said, "I did not get the memo. Let's take a break." With that Tremont rose and left the room.

The Promoter of Justice looked directly into the DA's eyes. "I suggest that whenever Governor Tremont decides to return, he be given the full details of what is going to transpire regarding this case."

Several minutes later, Tremont returned and the Minister of Justice, along with the DA, laid out the plan. He sat and listened. His eyes closed. He said not a word.

The DA took the initiative to explain the "arrangement" that had been agreed upon. Sabatino, while taking a back seat to the proceedings, would remain on deck as advisor. In this extrajudicial process, Rome, in accordance with the Vatican's wishes, had deferred the prosecution of the case to the New York District Attorney—with the governor's approval.

"A witness has come forward with a laundry list of demands to which the governor has agreed in order to guarantee her testimony," the ADA explained. "We also have motive, and a partial print." According to the DA, the arrest of PJ Hollinger was imminent. There would be a Grand Jury rather than a preliminary hearing, which is always in the prosecutor's favor. The charge was murder in the first degree. They would ask for life imprisonment without parole.

"This is what the Vatican demands," the Promoter of Justice added, "and rightfully so."

Following an uncomfortable silence during which the ambient weight in the room hung heavier than a wet wool blanket.

"It sounds like a setup…one person's word against another's. Not enough to convict on reasonable doubt."

"It will happen," the woman said. "It *must* happen."

"I don't know if I can support such a move. It doesn't feel like justice to me."

"I am certain," she said, "that it will feel a good deal worse, governor, if you are removed from office."

There was a muffled gasp from the lieutenant governor in a room turned suddenly hostile.

"Do I make myself clear, Governor Tremont?"

Tremont glared at her. "Crystal."

CHAPTER TWENTY-SIX

The Arrest

Miserable over the wrangle with Charlie, PJ needed to expend her nervous energy. Pacing the small apartment did not cut it. She grabbed her shades and put on her go-to Yankees cap. Using the service door that opened onto Bleeker Street, she went for a run. Creating her own maze, she cut through buildings and shops that had rear entrances and exits, hoping to avoid recognition. When she returned to her apartment, she had clocked six miles without incident. She breathed a sigh of relief and jumped into the shower…her now favorite sanctuary. Hot showers apparently worked far better for her than drugs.

After a settling cup of herbal tea, she sat at the counter and opened her laptop to check her correspondence…and her financial state. She had spoken directly with Jefferson Reynolds, Sr. and had him transfer all her files and account information to Walden Thurgood, who turned PJ's financial affairs over to his own financial advisor/accountant. It was a difficult decision after Reynolds' many years of service to her parents as well as herself, but there was no way she would have any of her personal information anywhere in the vicinity of Jefferson Reynolds, the younger.

Startled by a sudden hammering on her door, she vaulted from her chair as her heart began to race. No one— other than police or emergency crew could get to an apartment without the resident being notified. She went to the door and looked into the peephole. Nothing. Someone had their finger over the viewer. Then a familiar voice rang through the hall. "Open the freaking door before I huff and puff, etc., etc."

Before she could take another breath, with tears rushing to her eyes, she flung the door open. "What took you so long?"

Watery-eyed as well, Charlie pulled her into a suffocating hug. "Don't you ever hang up on me again!"

By the time Doug reached them he was swiping the sweat from his face and panting. "Miss PJ…Miss PJ. I could not stop her. She, she got away from me."

"It's all right, Doug. No problem. She's my…sista."

Doug looked from one to the other, a question mark stamped on his face.

"Sorry, sweetie," Charlie said, patting his shoulder. "Didn't mean to rattle you."

PJ invited him inside. "Let me get you some water."

Having caught up on the events of the past couple of weeks, the two women were sitting at the island that divided the kitchen from the living area, snacking on smoked Gouda, sliced apples, and flatbread cracker bites, along with a bottle of Bourgogne Pinot Noir. PJ's mobile hummed.

"It's Val."

"Oooh. Put it on speaker so I can listen in."

PJ rolled her eyes and swiped the green icon. "Hi."

"PJ."

A chill ran through her. Judging by the tone of his voice, it was not good news.

"Val. What's wrong?

"It's my dad. He's been rushed to the hospital."

"Oh, no. What happened?"

"We don't know yet. I'm at the airport now, waiting for my flight to board."

"When do you land? I'll pick you up."

"Sometime around five. Dad's driver is picking me up. Meet me at the hospital. He's at Mt. Sinai West. I love you, PJ."

"I love you, too. I'll be there."

Charlie put her arms around PJ. "My God, what else?"

PJ suppressed a sob. "There's always something else."

"I'll go with you."

"No. You get some rest before your trip back. I will keep you posted."

As they argued the staying or going issue, the door to the apartment swung open, nearly coming off its hinges. The two women jumped out of their seats, stopped cold by the tall, wrestler type policeman in a ruffled suit who pulled a creased index card out of his pocket and began rattling off the Miranda rights.

"Penelope Jane Hollinger, you are under arrest for the murder of Cardinal Roberto Alphonse Montini." He took a deep breath as Detective Fields handcuffed PJ, then continued.

"You have the right to remain silent. Anything you say can and will be used against you in a court of law. You have the right to an attorney. If you cannot afford an attorney, one will be appointed for you. Do you understand the rights I have just read to you?"

Charlie grabbed Fields' arm screaming at the top of her lungs. "Don't you dare put those handcuffs on her. You can't just walk in and arrest someone. What are you, the Gestapo?"

Murphy pulled her off Fields. "If you don't calm down, Ma'am, I will cuff you, too."

"Fuck you!"

"Charlie, please," PJ said. "It'll be fine. They have nothing to hold me on."

"Don't you worry, honey, I'll be right behind you," Charlie sniveled. "Wally will get you the best lawyer there is. You'll be out of there before dinner."

"You have to contact Val. He mustn't know. Tell him…tell him I had to settle something with my contract. Tell him anything but do not tell him I've been arrested!"

"Seriously, PJ?

"Promise me."

"You know he will fume for keeping this from him."

"Promise!"

"Okay, okay. I promise. But it's not the right thing to do. Besides, Wally will fix this."

"I don't want Walden involved either. This is my mess."

"Uh, uh. You have no agency with Wally. He's my domain."

PJ looked at Murphy, her eyes welling. "Must you really take me out in handcuffs, Lieutenant?"

He stuffed his hands into his pockets and looked down at the floor. When his eyes again met PJ's he said, "Out of respect for your grandfather," and nodded to Fields to take off the cuffs.

***

Charlie was denied access to PJ once they arrived at the First Precinct. She waited in the lobby, paced, inquired at the desk every ten minutes, and made a general nuisance of herself until asked to leave. "Fine by me." She lifted the sleeve of her suit jacket and checked her Christian Dior Pearl and Diamond wristwatch. It was time she left.

Uber dropped her off at the entrance to Mt. Sinai at seven. They would not let her up, despite her vociferous objection. She was told that "Only family is permitted in the ICU, and just two at a time." In the end, she texted Val: *This is Charlie. Could you please come down. They will not let me up.* He texted back not three seconds later. *Be right down. Where is PJ?* Charlie ignored the question and turned off her phone.

He walked into the waiting area, eyes red and swollen, and offered his hand. Charlie brushed it away and gave him one of her vise-like hugs. "I'm sorry about your father. How is he."

Val sidestepped the query. "Thanks for coming, Charlie, but where is PJ. She said she'd be here."

After stumbling over her words, she finally assembled a plausible lie. "Contract issues."

"Contract issues?" His jaw tightened. "Of all the times I've given her the space she needed. Of all the dates she cancelled, or just didn't show up. Of all the 'I love you's' she didn't say. This is…this is…" His shoulders shaking, he turned away, unable to look at Charlie. She gave him a moment then gently turned him around and held him close while he buried his sobs in the crook of her neck.

When he was able to settle himself, he suggested they go down to the cafeteria, which was open 24/7. They sat quietly, Charlie sipping tea, and Val downing his fifth cup of coffee.

"They don't expect my dad to make it through the night," he said, his voice quivering. He was finally able to say the words out loud. "He's had a brain aneurysm, and is on life support." He slammed his hands down hard on the table. "Doesn't she know I need her with me now?"

"She knows, Val. Believe me, she knows."

"Then where is she?" he shouted.

Charlie could only stare into her tea. She did not like the image frowning back at her.

"Look, Val. I can only tell you she had no choice in the matter."

He looked at her, his face burning with anger. "We always have a choice."

She wanted to say, *not when you're in handcuffs.* But, of course, held her tongue.

Val stood. "Thank you for coming, Charlie," he said, and walked away.

***

A typical box-like space with a six-foot rectangular table in the center, and three strategically placed chairs—two quite serviceable on one side for the interrogators, and a hard backed metal chair, obviously meant to enhance the discomfort of the detainee—served as *Interrogation Room One* as noted by the metal plate on the door. PJ was escorted into the room, given a bottle of water, and left there, fighting the nausea, and mouthing affirmations, desperately trying to dredge up the grit and dauntlessness that had callously abandoned her.

Murphy and Fields were called into the captain's office minutes before PJ's interrogation.

"With all due respect, Captain, that is not standard procedure in felony cases."

The captain opened the bottom drawer of his desk, and took out a flask and tumbler. He filled a glass with as much scotch as he could without it spilling over, and took a long swig. "Consider this an exception to the rule, Murphy. And you're sitting on the wrong side of the desk to lecture me on procedure."

"We really don't have enough to hold her, only the word of a so-called *witness.*

"Listen, Murphy. And this goes for you, too, Fields. This is not up for debate. The word came down from both the mayor and the governor…"

"But, captain…"

He pounded the desk. "God dammit, Murphy, there's a lot on the line here. Just do what you're told. We don't want to come away from this looking like the assholes who created a national embarrassment for the Italian Government! Now get out of here and do your jobs."

Murphy stood. He took out his handkerchief and wiped his face. He looked at Fields' unapologetic frown. "Let's go 'do our jobs.'"

CHAPTER TWENTY-SEVEN

The Interrogation

Told to wait a couple of hours before questioning PJ, Lt. Murphy went back to his office and reviewed the file on this case once again. What he was looking for, he did not know. Something, he supposed, that would support keeping her over for arraignment. He waited only an hour.

Lieutenant Jim Murphy with Laura Fields at his heels entered the interrogation room to find PJ in a deep slumber. Exhausted from lack of sleep, and hours of pacing and thinking, she had sat down, laid her head over her arms, and fell into a state of reduced consciousness. The grating sound of metal scraping across concrete as Murphy pulled out a chair caused PJ to start. Blinking a few times at the harsh lighting, she focused on Murphy and asked for coffee. He glanced at the guard standing beside the door, who picked up the cue and left the room.

The questions came, but went unanswered. Murphy ran out of steam. He pushed back his chair and stretched his legs, crossing them at the ankles.

After two cups of black coffee and about thirty minutes of silence, PJ spoke. "I'm aware of your…misogynistic history, Lieutenant."

Fields' eyebrows climbed. She shot a quick look at Murphy then lowered her head to hide a satisfied smile.

"I graduated Summa Cum Laude from Stanford University and I hold two master's degrees," PJ said. "One in Journalism, the other in Communications. I am not an *airheaded female,* as you have been known to iterate. You're wasting your time if you expect me to answer any questions without my attorney present."

Murphy turned a deep pink. "I've read your bio, Ms. Hollinger. Your level of education is not in question here…and I am not a mis…whatever. It's just my way. An occupational hazard so to speak."

"Right," Fields chimed in, which awarded her a grizzly look from the Lieutenant. "What? I'm agreeing with you."

Murphy returned his attention to PJ. "I've known your grandfather for many years. I have a great deal of respect and admiration for him." He sat forward and clasped his hands on the table. "He's received more awards as an NYPD detective than I have fingers and toes. And I'm not ashamed to admit that he saved my ass more than once when I was a rookie."

"I appreciate that, Lieutenant. Using my grandfather to influence me. however, will not work."

Murphy breathed a sigh of exasperation. "I want to help you, Ms. Hollinger. I really do, but I need you to be totally truthful with me."

"I want to be totally truthful with you, and I will tell you everything as I remember it, but not without…"

"Yeah, I know, not without your suit." Murphy stood. "Well, I hope he gets here soon. Your arraignment is tomorrow morning." With that he grabbed his jacket from the back of the chair and walked out. Fields hesitated a moment, about to say something, then turned abruptly and left. Her one permitted phone call was to Charlie.

"My heart aches for you, my sista. How are you doing?"

"I'm doing my best to stay sane. This is surreal."

"Sit tight. Wally is in Taiwan for another few days, but he's sending you the best attorney in New York."

"Have you seen Val? How's his dad?"

"Not doing well. Val, of course, is livid. Honestly, PJ, I felt like a piece of shit lying to him."

"He cannot be part of this, Charlie. He just cannot!"

"I understand where you're coming from, but…"

"I'm sorry I put you in this position. I will text him as soon as I have a phone available."

"I think you're making a fatal mistake. It would be better hearing about this…situation...from you, rather than on CNN."

PJ could not hold back the tears much longer. "I can't talk long," she said, her voice cracking. "My arraignment is tomorrow morning. I have no idea what to expect. It's as if I were blind, feeling my way around in an unfamiliar room, bumping into objects I can't see."

"Have they questioned you yet?"

"Yes. I told them it was a waste of time, and that I would not say anything without a lawyer." She cupped her hand over her mouth to hold back a sob. "They've already booked me, photographed me, taken my fingerprints. They make you feel like you're a criminal before you even enter a courtroom. This is due process?"

"Don't focus on that, PJ. Please. It will all work out. Stay strong."

"Of all the difficulties I've faced in my life, I've never felt so…dreadfully hopeless."

"I don't know anyone as resilient and courageous as you, my sista…never have. You will come through this, like you've come through everything else. Wally won't let us down."

PJ flopped on her bunk, dripping wet after having done a series of crunches, push-ups, and jumping jacks to intentionally drown out the defeatist thoughts jangling in her head. A guard appeared with keys clanging, and opened the cell door. He stood aside, allowing a wisp of a woman to enter. Her startling white hair was pulled back into a French twist. The woman had deep, Caribbean blue eyes, and dimples that drew one immediately to her well-cared for, tanned face when she smiled.

"Good afternoon, Ms. Hollinger. I'm Victoria Abbott. I will be representing you." She stretched out her hand toward PJ, who took it gladly.

"I'm so pleased to meet you. Thank you for coming."

"Ah, well, you can thank Walden Thurgood for that…and his lovely wife, who's already run up a three-thousand-dollar service fee in phone calls, texts, and emails she insisted I return personally."

"Sounds like Charlie."

Abbott sat at the edge of the bunk bed, took out her recorder, and cut to the chase. "We do not have much time. Walden…and Charlotte…filled me in as best they could, but I need you to tell me straight out, in detail, the events that have culminated in your arrest—without embellishing or editorializing. Go!"

PJ took a few moments to gather her thoughts and adjust herself to Abbott's direct, authoritative persona. She told her about the flashes of memory. "I don't remember anything from the time I felt a wet, clinical-smelling mask pressing against my nose and mouth, until the time I woke up on the plane about to land at Teterboro."

"All right. Tell me about your life, from your childhood onward to the abduction."

PJ sat on the floor in the Lotus position, facing Abbott. She closed her eyes and sighed deeply. "My biological mother, who was only fifteen, was brutally murdered. I was taken from her by caesarian section and sent to a convent in California to be cared for…so I was told later."

PJ narrated her story as she experienced it. Basically, everything she had told Jeff Reynolds, whom Victoria Abbott was familiar with. "Hmm. Excellent criminal attorney," she remarked. "If you ignore the fact that he's as slimy as a slug."

"That describes him nicely." Her chronicle ended, PJ looked expectantly at Abbott, who had not blinked once during her narrative. She had not taken her eyes off PJ the entire time. *Irritating.*

"Aren't you going to say something, Ms. Abbott?"

"I'm processing."

"I see." But, of course, she did not. "Why are you staring at me?"

"Dear girl. I am processing. Understand that surpassingly beautiful women such as yourself experience life differently than the average woman. And that must be taken into consideration."

"What on earth do you mean?"

"Depending on the jury pool," Abbott explained, "you will either be acquitted or judged guilty. We need a jury consisting of a majority of men…preferably middle-aged men."

"Are you saying that spending the rest of my life in prison is a probability?"

"I am saying, PJ, that I will be laser-focused on contouring the right jury pool."

"It seems to me that the case they are building against me is completely bogus."

"Yes, well, the prosecutor is a self-serving ass. He'll do his best to see that you go to prison." She cleared her throat. "I have it on good word that the Vatican has put you on their *burn her at the stake* list."

PJ sprung up like a Joey out of its mother's pouch. "Ms. Abbott, you are my only hope. But your cavalier attitude is not comforting."

Ignoring PJ's concern, Abbott turned off the recorder and returned it to her briefcase. "The Vatican, as well as the Italian government, can go to Hell." She smiled at PJ. "They don't know who they are dealing with. And please, call me Victoria. We are going to get uncomfortably close to each other; using first names will ease the awkwardness."

PJ did not know what to make of this woman. She took a long breath and let it out slowly. "Wadlen thinks highly of you," she said. "I suppose that's good enough for me."

"Good to know. Here's what's going to happen. We'll be going into the interrogation room shortly. They will throw more of the same questions at you. Do not show any emotion. Say nothing unless I nod that it's okay to answer. Understood?"

PJ's eyebrows went up. "Perfectly well."

"Good. At the arraignment tomorrow morning, "you will be asked to plead guilty or not guilty. You will plead not-guilty."

"But…"

"There are no buts. You will plead not guilty. Is that clear?"

PJ's jaw locked. The color to her cheeks blossomed from a soft rose to a deep cherry, but she managed a "quite clear" in response.

Suddenly, PJ began hyperventilating. She could not catch her breath. Abbott pulled out a paper bag from her case. "Here, put this over your nose and mouth, and breathe in and out…that's it. You're having a panic attack. Try to relax your muscles."

The panic attack was an old friend. PJ knew exactly what to do and after several minutes, her breathing returned to normal. "Do you always keep a paper bag with you?"

"Always. This happens often with clients…although this is an unusual case on several levels. But we'll discuss that later," she said, cutting off the question about to spring from PJ's mouth.

"I will do my best to get you released on bail, but it's going to be a hard sell. You have already been booked, which is unusual without disclosure. And the DA flatly refuses to discuss a plea bargain. Unfortunately, you will have to spend the night here."

"What? No! I…I can't."

"There is nothing I can do about that at this point."

"Why? I don't understand. I have no criminal record…not even a driving ticket, not one!"

Abbott snapped her briefcase shut. "PJ, allow me to argue your defense. That's what I'm here for."

PJ was having her doubts about the *incomparable* (according to Walden) Victoria Abbott. But what choice did she have? It was as though she had to choose between burning to a crisp in a fire, or jumping out a ten-story window.

"Look," Abbott said. "I understand your angst. I promise, I will do everything in my power to get you through this. Not only because I have a deep respect for Walden, but…" Abbott stood, lowering her head to avoid the protruding edge of the bunk above. "but because I sense there is something going on behind the scenes that does not feel right, something I promise to look into. In the meantime, be your usual self-assured, assertive, but respectful self." She called for the guard then turned to PJ. "Ready?"

***

The interrogation went exactly as Abbott said it would. After another two hours and no headway, Murphy called it a night. "I have one final question, Ms. Hollinger…Why did you murder Cardinal Montini?"

PJ stiffened and was about to react. Abbott put her hand on PJ's arm. "We're done here, Lieutenant. We will see you in court."

Murphy and Fields left the room. Abbott handed PJ her card. "Get some sleep. You need to be fresh and at the top of your game in the morning. I will be here at seven-thirty a.m. sharp. That will give us time to armor up. See you then."

PJ was up and pacing at 5:30 the next morning. Seven-thirty came and went. No Victoria Abbott. Eight, eight-thirty. Still no sign of Abbott. The arraignment was at ten. Trembling with panic, she called for the guard. "I need to contact my attorney. She was supposed to be here at 7:30. My arraignment is at…"

"No phone calls until after the arraignment."

"But I…" The guard had already walked away. *Asshole!* She sat on the edge of the bed and scraped her mind for possibilities: stuck in traffic, a last-minute appointment, a change of heart. No. Abbott would have contacted her to say so. She wrapped the blanket around her shoulders and rubbed her arms to quell the icy fear that chilled her inside and out. Her thoughts swam from the past to the present without settling on either. *Am I losing my mind?* Recalling Abbott's advice, she shook off whatever was directing her wayward thoughts and inhaled deeply, relying on her standard breathing technique, she held each breath to the count of four, then released it through her mouth in short spurts. She grasped for calm, but yielded blazing anger…the very prod she needed to override her fears. She would walk into that courtroom calm and clear-headed—lawyer or no lawyer.

The prison bus arrived at 9:35. At 9:50, PJ was escorted into an over-crowded courtroom, hoping to see the sleek, stoic face of Victoria Abbott. There was no one at the defense table. So much for hope. Nonetheless, she would follow Abbott's instructions. *Not guilty.*

About forty minutes later, PJ was called up. The judge scanned the front of the room. "Do you have an attorney, Ms. Hollinger?"

She said the only thing she could. "My attorney has been delayed, Your Honor." Just then, a forty-something, rather lanky man with rimless glasses and a retro crew cut rushed through the courtroom door. "I am Ms. Hollinger's attorney," he said breathlessly, taking long strides to the table. "Excuse my tardiness, Your Honor. May I have a moment to confer with my client?"

The judge blew out an impatient breath. "A moment."

He turned to PJ. "I'm Henry Weiner, Victoria Abbott's associate," he whispered. Sorry to say I haven't had a chance to go through your file. We'll have to play it by ear. Any questions?"

Play it by ear? Is he joking? "If we're 'playing it by ear' I don't think we have time for questions," was her snippy response.

PJ was advised of her constitutional rights, and the charges against her. "How do you wish to plead, Ms. Hollinger?"

She took a deep breath and in a clear, sure voice said, "Not guilty." A woman in the last row, closest to the door and wearing a black, wide-brimmed hat that hid most of her face cried out. "Liar!" She ran from the room in a blur, leaving the courtroom buzzing. The judge had to hammer his gavel several times to restore order.

Weiner turned to PJ. "Who was that?"

"I have no idea," she said, but she had, in fact, a very good idea. "What happens now? You can get me released on bail, can't you? And where is Victoria Abbott?" Before Weiner could answer, the DA stood.

"Your Honor, due to the heinous nature of this crime, and the fact that Ms. Hollinger has proven to be a flight risk, the prosecution requests bail be denied."

The judge looked at Weiner expecting a response. "Mr. Weiner, have you anything to say on behalf of your client?"

Weiner took a few seconds to gather his thoughts, during which time the Court Clerk handed the judge a note. Weiner rose slowly. "The crime was indeed heinous. However, my client has not yet been judged guilty of this crime; therefore, the level of the crime has no bearing on bail. Also, as you can tell by this overcrowded room, Ms. Hollinger is a respected public figure, unlikely to get around without being recognized. Additionally, my client has no previous record of any kind."

The judge put the note in his pocket, removed his glasses, and ran a hand over his face. He shot a quick look at the DA. "Bail denied." PJ jumped up. "No! Why?"

"Mr. Weiner, restrain your client."

"Your Honor, I respectfully ask on what basis is bail being denied? Clearly the prosecution has not presented sufficient probable cause."

"I doubt that we would be here, Mr. Weiner if there weren't sufficient probable cause. However, the prosecution has opted for a Grand Jury. We will let them decide. Bail denied." He slammed the gavel unnecessarily forceful, concluding the arraignment.

PJ dropped into her chair, stunned. She was given some water before being taken to the facility. Weiner gave

PJ what was meant to be a reassuring pat on her shoulder as she was led out of the courtroom in handcuffs.

CHAPTER TWENTY-EIGHT

The Accident

Romano had hit a brick wall in his efforts to get PJ out of the country. Those contacts he could trust were either *out-of-town*, or never returned his urgent messages. He knew he was being stonewalled. Something was going on. Even Murphy, who over the years would consult with Romano from time-to-time, even he was talking in riddles. The word was that both the mayor and governor were muzzling department heads. Precinct captains were being reassigned. But no one was talking. Romano was certain that it was all connected to the murder investigation, or the lack thereof. Getting her out of the country would take a miracle.

Murphy contacted Romano to advise him that PJ had been arrested, charged, and arraigned, that bail had been denied and she was on her way to Rikers.

After running out of expletives and quieting down, Romano told Murphy in no uncertain terms that he was leaving for Rikers and that Murphy had better arrange for him to see PJ if he didn't want to "lose your manhood."

***

The largest penal colony in the world, known as Rikers Island, sits in the East River in the Bronx. The only way on and off Rikers is by way of the Francis R. Buono Memorial Bridge, simply referred to as the Rikers Island

Bridge. The reputation of every one of the ten correctional facilities there, and their history of violence and maltreatment had become a cliché. There was an ongoing political battle to close the facility entirely, but given various hotly debated issues, nothing was moving forward.

When PJ heard the judge dispatch her to the women's facility on Rikers Island, she PJ thought her heart had stopped. Assuming she'd be released on bail, she was not prepared for such a shock. She declined the one phone call offered her. She sat in a cereal box of a room with bright lights and yellow walls, unmoved by the intended effect of warm sunshine. For hours she alternately paced and sat. She tried some Yoga positions. Nothing worked to unwind her tangled nerves. They offered her dinner, but she refused knowing her stomach would not hold it. Finally, after hours of not knowing what was going to happen next, she was taken to processing, then to the showers. After being perfunctorily examined by the prison physician, she was given her orange jumpsuit and a *Welcome Tote* containing underwear, pajamas, bedding, a plastic plate, fork, and knife; toothpaste and toothbrush, and some paper and golf pencils. She was then taken to her cell.

Minimalistic is an understatement, she thought, as she entered the crude four-walls and a barred entrance and exit that would be her home until the trial…and thereafter until her conviction. NO! *Acquittal! Until my acquittal!* She rebuked herself, doing her damnedest to stay positive. The door had a narrow rectangular window in it with bars so close together a fly could barely get through. The cell was a single with a cot-like bed, a sink, toilet, desk, and chair. There was also a bench opposite the bed. She wondered how she would ever survive in this suffocating, oppressive space?

The Women's Correctional Center, although not without its share of harshness and abuse, is a notch or two above the other correctional facilities on the Island, thanks to the current warden, an ardent advocate for prison reform. She had upgraded the cells, toilets, and showers. Enhanced security by adding more than one-hundred cameras in locations subject to drug passing and violence. She installed a library and a gym, and instituted educational programs. Many on the Commission of Corrections opposed this as a "waste of state funds," but the warden had one or two political backers with influence. After two years, the *new* women's center was heralded as a major improvement for Rikers. Its positive impact rose and fell as most of the women there, like PJ, were awaiting trial, and so they came and they went...and they came.

***

The visitation room was virtually empty. Romano stood as PJ was brought in, uncuffed, Murphy a step behind her. "You owe me, Romano," he said, leaving them to visit.

Romano ignored him and put his arms around his granddaughter. "I am so sorry, sweetheart. I've tried every bleepin' avenue I know…"

"It's okay. Really. This, this…whatever it is…will at some point be yesterday's news," she said, trying to believe her words. He held her away and looked at her. "You look tired. But otherwise, none the worse for wear. As a matter of fact," he said "you look like you're sixteen in that ponytail. I love it."

She smiled. The first in days. "How are you, Sil?"

He put up his hand. "We're not going to talk about me. I'm convinced there is some funny business going on, and I promise you I will get to the bottom of it."

"No. I don't want anyone involved. I've been doing a lot of thinking…meditating. We need to let the justice system work."

"But, sweetheart, the justice system doesn't work. I've dealt with it for a lifetime. Trust me, it's broken, and those who deign to fix it, eventually get sucked into the muddy swamp."

She took his hand in both of hers. "Don't take this the wrong way, but you're not getting any younger. You need to take better care of yourself."

He brought her hands up to his mouth and kissed them. "Who is your attorney?"

"Well, my attorney is Victoria Abbott, but…"

"Who?"

"Victoria Abbott, but she never showed at my arraignment. Her associate…"

"PJ, Victoria Abbott was in a horrible auto accident early this morning. She is in a coma at New York Presbyterian. No one told you?"

PJ's hand flew to her mouth, muffling a horrified shriek. It took a long minute for her to slow her racing heart. "I somehow feel responsible. That poor woman."

"Good God, PJ. Give yourself a break! Please don't add guilt to your already overtaxed sense of responsibility."

"I can't help thinking she would not be in a coma were she not representing me. This is just too coincidental," she said. "Something smells of treachery. How did it happen?"

"T-boned at Broadway and Fulton. Driver's side. Perp is in the wind."

"Hit and run. Of course."

Romano sat back and stretched his legs. "You're right. Given the circumstances and the fact that the perp scrammed makes it look like a deliberate act—I can't believe they would stoop to this level.

The question hanging in the air was, who are they? PJ jolted at the clanging of the heavy steel door being unlocked.

"Times up, Detective Romano."

They looked at each other. "Time flies when you're having fun," she said, with a sardonic smile.

"How's your Italian?" Romano asked.

"Hmm. Not too bad, why?"

"Non lasciare che i bastardi ti raggiungano."

She chuckled. "'Don't let the Bastards get to you.' I will keep that in mind." She hugged him again. "I love you, Granddad."

Romano turned his head as tears began to surface. "I love you more, granddaughter."

***

After a sleepless night of distressing dreams, PJ awoke in a cold sweat. She sat on the edge of the bunk and wrapped herself in the blanket. But it was more than the cold that made her teeth chatter. As hard as she tried to resist, a disquieting foreboding and sense of hopelessness was boring its way in. If the Vatican had the power to leverage its influence to the degree they had in the past, life imprisonment would be the likely outcome. Her decision was made. She had to tell Val. It was the right thing to do.

She was allowed fifteen minutes for the most regrettable phone call of her life. After four rings, the call went to voicemail. She hung up. She figured either he is not available, or is so angry he will not take her call. But that was not Val. More likely, he'd been trying to get in touch with her. But, of course, her mobile phone had been confiscated.

Later that day, the guard came to open her cell. "You have a visitor," he said. This time, there was no special treatment, he cuffed her before escorting her to the visitation room. She assumed it was her lawyer, but when she saw Val standing at one of the tables, she had a sudden urge to ask the guard to take her back to her cell. She did not think she could face him. *Coward!* She lifted her hands to her cheek to brush away the wetness, and walked to him. He looked awful; hair askew, eyes red and weary. The guard removed the cuffs. Before he could tell them to be seated, Val stepped forward and pulled her into his arms, burying his face in her neck. "Oh, God, PJ" he moaned, his voice gritty with emotion. "Why? Why didn't you tell me? Why won't you let me help you? Take care of you?" He kissed her forehead, her cheek, her lips. "I can forgive you anything, but please don't shut me out."

The guard inserted his baton between them. "No touching. Sit!" Val was about to react, but PJ put a gentle hand on his arm. They sat, facing each other.

"How did you find out?"

He explained that he'd checked his missed calls and was curious about the unfamiliar number. He tapped in the number and was informed that he had reached the Women's Correctional Facility on Rikers Island. "It took me a while of head-shaking before I figured it out."

"I'm sorry you had to find out that way," she said. "Admittedly, I've been cowardly about telling you."

"I wish you understood, at long last, that you are not in this alone. I want to help you. I need to help you."

"I don't want to talk about it."

"You're the most incorrigible, stubborn female I've ever known."

"I was so sorry to hear about your dad," she said. "You know I wanted to be there for you.

"Stop. I know you would have if you could. It's a devastating loss. But he kept his illness to himself. He'd been battling heart disease for years."

"How is your mom?"

"As you can imagine, she is heartsick, but handling it like the trouper she is. Grieving and angry at the same time."

PJ lowered her eyes and looked away. "Does she know?"

"About your…arrest? No. I didn't want to add to her grief."

"She must be wondering why I wasn't there."

"That's not your worry. I will tell her when the time is right."

PJ clasped her hands on the table. *The time is right now. I must tell him. This cannot go on indefinitely. What kind of a life could he possibly have picking up the pieces as they fall off me? He had to move on.* "Val, listen to me. I don't want you coming here. I don't want you involved. I don't want you in court."

He took her hands in his and squeezed. "A nuclear bomb couldn't keep me away."

"I'm not saying this lightly, Val. You need to stay away, or there will be collateral consequences for you. You need to think of your reputation, your mother's standing in the community."

His face turned gray. "You can't be serious. People who love each other support each other. Do you think for a moment I'm worried about my reputation? Come on, PJ."

Before she could stop herself, she took his face in her hands and kissed him hard on the lips. "I'm so sorry, Val. I won't let you throw your life away."

"There is no life without you," he said, irritated. "And it's my decision to make, not yours."

"I can't do this. Everything is in limbo right now. Please understand." She stood and signaled the guard that the visit was over. "You have to move on to the wonderful life that you deserve." The guard put the handcuffs on her and walked her out of the room. Val just stood there, unable to move as he watched the heavy steel door slide shut behind her. *Move on? How?*

CHAPTER TWENTY-NINE

No Escape

Romano had been waiting thirty-five minutes for Murphy to show. In the meantime, McGarin's grew incrementally noisier as the after-work crowd piled in as though it were Black Friday at Macy's. He couldn't blame Murphy if he had second thoughts about meeting. The favor he was asking was crossing a line. He'd give him another ten minutes, then move to Plan B—which he hadn't figured out yet.

Murphy slid into the booth as Romano was signing the check. He put the pen down and leaned back watching the detective loosen his tie then snap open the collar button of a too-tight dress-shirt that made him look like he'd swallowed a balloon. Neither of them said a word until the waiter came over and asked Murphy what he'd like. "Just water, please, with lemon."

"On the wagon, Murph?"

Murphy gave him a look that was part irritation and part frustration. "I came because I consider you a friend," he said. "You're the best cop I've ever known, and I've learned a lot from you. All the good stuff I've done is because of your influence."

"I hear a *but* coming."

"But…there is no way I can help you implement an escape without putting my career and my pension on the line. Not to mention incarceration."

The waiter placed Murphy's water in front of him. "Will there be anything else, sir?"

"We're good. Thanks." Murphy looked down into his glass, absently stirring his water with the straw. The silence between them drowned out the Happy Hour chatter in the bar.

After thinking on it, there was only one thing Romano could say. "I understand, Murphy. It was a stab in the dark. I should not have put you on the spot like that. I know in six months you're up for full retirement and out of all the bullshit that keeps being shoveled into the face of a continually *repurposed* justice system. Enjoy your retirement, my friend."

Surprised by Romano's passive acceptance, Murphy teased, "Giving up so easily? You really are getting old, Sil"

"You noticed."

Murphy relaxed a bit, wiped the sweat off his face with a napkin and leaned back. "I had a meeting with the DA before coming here," he said. "Truth be told, that's the reason I showed up."

Romano's brows met in a puzzled frown. Murphy leaned in and spoke in a whisper. "I did some underground research on this chick who claims to be a witness. She has a rather shady past, including some mental health information that has been redacted from her file."

"And?"

"And I told the DA that she was not a credible witness, and we really had nothing legit to hold PJ Hollinger in pretrial detention."

"Good man."

Murphy gave in to his poorer judgment, signaled the waiter over, and ordered a scotch and soda." "There's more, Sil…and it's not good."

***

Dressed discreetly in cheap, navy-blue pants suit she'd picked up at Walmart, and a ruffled at-the-collar white blouse—not her customary style—Candace waited in the outer office, eyeing the young officer guarding the area. The desk clerk nodded to the officer then addressed Candace.

"The ADA will see you now, Ms. Baker."

The guard opened the door for her and escorted her into the room. The ADA remained seated behind his desk, leafing through some papers. Without looking up, he told her to have a seat. "That will be all, Keagan." The officer, who usually stayed in the room unless otherwise instructed, had just been otherwise instructed.

As far as she could imagine, this was her final option. If they did not agree to it, well, they had better agree to it. She opened her purse and dug out a pack of Newports.

"You cannot smoke in here, Miss," he said, finally looking up. Candace twinged. Not so much for the cigarettes, but for not being addressed by name, as if she were of no importance. Without her they had no case. *Dirtbag!* Her smoothed over façade was beginning to crimp.

The ADA pulled back from his desk, giving his paunch some breathing room. He slid his glasses up to the ridge of his nose with his index finger. "So, Ms. Barker."

"It's Baker."

"Right. So, what have you got for us?"

His attitude was annoying. They should be pandering to her like a queen. They needed her. Her testimony would make or break their case. Maybe she had been too mysterious, too unbelievable. Maybe she was deluding herself as to the extent of their need as opposed to the extent of her own.

"Are you going to answer my question, or continue to stare at the framed Constitution on the wall? I can get you a copy of the full text if you'd like."

Candace's face turned a hot pink. *Fuck this.* She stood and headed toward the door.

"I could detain you for making a false statement," he threatened. She stopped, turned, and with characteristic flippancy said, "I don't feel quite welcome here. You certainly don't seem overly interested in your star witness. You have my number." She again turned to leave, this time more slowly.

"My apologies, Ms. Baker. Please sit down. You've given us a great deal to think about. So, let's discuss."

Candace now felt she had the upper hand. "I hear from reliable sources that the only argument the DA has for probable cause is an eye-witness…me."

"And who are these 'reliable sources,' Ms. Baker?"

She smiled. "I think you know as well as I do that the streets have eyes and ears."

"I would hardly call that reliable. And your demands are extremely…excessive."

"Well, then, you have a decision to make, don't you?"

The expression on the ADA's face had been irritatingly neutral throughout their conversation. He said nothing for a good many intense minutes, then blew out a breath of stale tobacco and bourbon. Candace had to turn her face away.

"We can offer security from now until the trial ends. Then you have a choice, either be on your way, or be placed in the witness protection program." He had been instructed by the DA to do whatever it took to secure her testimony in court. He waited for her response before continuing.

"What about immunity…and recompense?"

"It appears you left Italy without permission while an investigation was still in play. That investigation has been shut down and no charges have been filed against you. However, there is an arrest warrant here in the U.S. for falsifying identification documents, which can be a felony, depending on the situation, and incur a sentence of up to five years."

"That cannot happen. I won't spend another day in jail!"

"We may very well be able to take care of it…with your cooperation."

"You had better take care of it," she growled, "or there won't be any *cooperation.*"

The ADA's eyes nearly popped out of his at such brashness, but he knew Baker had the trump card…and would not hesitate to play it. He also knew he must not give in too easily. "I don't appreciate being threatened, Ms. Baker. I will do what I can. That's all for now. I'll be in touch."

Several days later, Candace was taken to a *safe house* where she would stay with a rotation of female officers throughout necessary court appearances and the trial. She would have to appear before the grand jury. The ADA did not seem to think there was any doubt that PJ Hollinger would be indicted. Having experienced the *system* first-hand, Candace thought he was a little too sure of himself. The important thing was that they had agreed to all the terms of their *star witness*. She smiled inwardly. Things were looking up.

***

"Okay, Murphy, tell me what I probably already know."

"I need some reinforcement first."

Romano ordered another round. They exchanged small talk while waiting for their drinks. Romano kept thrumming his fingers on the table.

"Stop. The rat-a-tat-tatting is driving me nuts."

"Nerves."

When the drinks finally came, Murphy took a long slug before speaking. "The Staff of God being wielded by the Vatican holds a formidable power," he said. "Even to the extent of having the Roman Government do its bidding."

"How deep does this go, Jim?"

"Deep and wide. From the IO at the federal level, down to the governor, mayor, and DA's office. They've all been given orders not to compromise international relations with Italy."

"Jesus!"

"Word is that Montini was a blackguard the Vatican wants buried for good. They've been covering up for him from one pope to another."

"Seems like his murder sprung open Pandora's Box." Romano said.

Murphy sighed. "Your girl has gotten herself into an inextricable situation, especially now that Victoria Abbott is out of the picture."

Romano put his elbows on the table and covered his face with his hands.

Lt. James Murphy felt a tug on his heart he could not ignore. "I can give you a name, but that's all I can do."

Romano looked up, eyes red. "I can't let you do that. There are too many spokes in this wheel. Someone's likely to find out."

"It's just a name. A long shot, even. No one will find out. He's one of my old CI's. Anyone could find his name on the department's list of confidential informants."

While Romano signed the merchant copy of the bill and pocketed his credit card, Murphy grabbed the customer copy and wrote something on the back. He scrunched it in his hand and tossed it to Romano as he slid out of the booth. "Good luck, Sil."

***

The prison walls could not keep out the oppressive grayness of the day. The skies opened like a burst dam. It was a hard, cold rain. Few prisoners braved the weather, and those who badly needed a smoke sought refuge under a small canopy overhanging the steel exit and entrance doors. With eyes closed, lifting her head to the heavens as though in prayer, PJ stood in the open under the full deluge of a relentless rainfall. But she was not praying. She was having a meltdown. The old demons pouring over her.

She dropped her head and began walking slowly toward the chain link fence. The few prisoners remaining under the canopy watched her, elbowing each other. Without missing a step, she took hold of the fence and began to climb. The jeers and shouts egging her on alerted the guards, who got to her before she reached the electrified circular mesh wires welded to the top of the fencing. Babbling about needing to go to a funeral, she was taken to the infirmary, where she was heavily medicated and put on suicide watch in an eight-by-eight isolation room with a ten-foot ceiling and two video cameras.

When PJ awoke, two days later, she was back in her own cell and Lieutenant James Murphy was sitting on the bench facing her bunk. She sat up, rubbed her eyes, then ran her fingers through her long, tangled hair, tucking the runaway strands behind her ears. She took a few minutes to focus, and in a voice grizzly from dryness asked why he was there.

"Well, for one, I promised your granddad I'd look in on you." She gave him a wry smile. "And for two?"

He did not answer immediately. She needed to go back to sleep. But her parched mouth felt as if it were coated with sand. She got up, staggered across to the sink, and ran the water until it was cold. She filled her cup several times, and drank three full cups, one after the other, as though she'd just trudged across the Mojave Desert. "Why am I so thirsty?"

"Maybe because you haven't had an ounce of water in over two days?

"That doesn't make sense. I drink at least two quarts a day."

Murphy rubbed his forehead.

"You didn't answer my question," she said.

He looked up. "Two, you need to know what's going on."

"I thought my lawyer was supposed to do that."

"Abbott's still in a coma. It doesn't look good."

PJ sighed deeply. "Dear God. What about the associate, Weiner? Or was he killed off as well?"

Murphy frowned. "What are you implying?"

"I'm not implying. It just seems a bit too coincidental that Victoria Abbott, a respected and successful women's advocate attorney, is put out of commission shortly after agreeing to defend me."

Murphy looked down at the floor. "That's a strong accusation."

PJ closed her eyes, trying to ignore the throbbing in her head. "Given my years of education and experience as an investigative journalist, I don't think I would reduce it to an accusation."

Murphy rubbed his bristled chin. "Between you, me, and the wall, I'm inclined to agree."

"Good to know. That and three bucks will get me a ride on the subway, should I ever climb out of this abyss."

Murphy let the snide remark slide. "It's unheard of that anyone is released so quick from suicide watch," he said.

"Quickly."

"What?"

"Never mind."

Murphy put both hands on top of his head. "Jesus Christ!"

"And what does suicide have to do with any of this?"

He narrowed his eyes. "Ms. Hollinger. Can you tell me what day it is?"

"Oh, for heaven's sake."

"Please. Humor me."

"The last I checked it was Tuesday."

He shook his head. "You don't remember do you?"

"Remember what? Will you stop playing word games, Lieutenant!"

Her legs began to buckle. She moved to lie down and barely made it to the cot.

"Today is Thursday, Ms. Hollinger."

As though she hadn't heard him, she lay on the cot and placed an arm over her eyes.

Murphy went on to explain that she had been put on suicide watch two days ago. When he finished talking, he waited patiently for PJ to say something. Silence. His patience having been spent, he got up and paced. "Do you remember standing in the middle of the yard in a downpour? Or climbing the fence soaking wet?"

Again, no response.

"Ms. Hollinger!"

"No. I have no memory of what you've described."

TWENTY-FOUR HOURS EARLIER

Governor Tremont was not one to be easily intimidated. But when his political career depended on walking a tightrope that traversed the rough seas from the Vatican, to the Italian government, to the U.S. State Department, well…

His unannounced arrival at the prison entrance startled the guard, who became tongue tied until the governor stuck his head out the window of his limo. "Open the gate you fool, I'm in a hurry."

The guard immediately did so, followed by an urgent call directly to the warden's office. One would think that the President of the United States himself had arrived for all the confusion and scuttling this news created. The warden, though surprised, remained unruffled.

"This is an unexpected honor, Governor," she smiled, extending a hand.

"You may not feel that way after our visit," he said with a Texas Hold 'Em poker-face. Tremont was more than bitter. He was angry. After only seconds of a banal exchange, he came directly to the reason for his visit. "You have a prisoner on suicide watch."

"We have two on suicide watch."

"I'm referring to Penelope Jane Hollinger—PJ Hollinger. She must be taken off the watch, and the…incident must be treated as if it never happened."

The warden squirmed in her chair. "That's not possible, Governor. It is legal procedure pending a psychiatric eval. And the Commission of…"

"I've already addressed the members of the commission. I'm here to eliminate the middleman, as it were. They understand the gravity of the situation involving Ms. Hollinger. We want to keep this case as low profile as possible. And I'm holding you personally responsible for the safety of this detainee. No headlines."

"But, Governor…"

Tremont stood. "Let me put it plainly, Cynthia. If you want to keep your cushy job, you will delete the record and put the lady back in her cell. Nothing happened! Isn't that right?"

Tremont did not wait for an answer. He rose to go. "Oh, by the way, Ms. Hollinger will be sharing a cell with another inmate." The warden glared at him. Seized by a moment of charity, Tremont softened his voice. "Look. I don't like this any more than you do. We both have our jobs to do." He took out a small index card from his breast pocket and handed it to her. "This is the inmate who will bunk with Hollinger. Socialization is important." He said, and walked out, leaving the warden with a job to do.

CHAPTER THIRTY

No visitors!

Still feeling guilty about the deception, Charlie would not dare contact Val. She reached out to Sil Romano. She'd only met Romano once, and thought him a lovely man, sensing immediately his deep concern for PJ. Frantic by the time she finally got him on the phone, she garbled her words before her brain could catch up to her tongue. Romano did not have the opportunity to get to know Charlie well, but from what PJ had told him, they'd had a close, long-term relationship.

"Please, Mrs. Thurgood, calm down. I'm only catching every third word," he said. "Take a breath." Romano had been unsuccessful in reaching the CI Murphy had referred. It seemed he'd been picked up on a drug charge and, sadly, was unavailable. But he was not giving up.

"They won't let me see her, Mr. Romano. I flew in yesterday and went directly to the facility, but they said she cannot have visitors. I don't know what's going on," she shrieked, hiccupping sobs.

He was at a loss for consoling words. "I understand you're upset. Let me find out what's going on."

"I need to see her," she said, blowing her nose into a linen, lace handkerchief PJ had brought back from Ireland.

"Please, call me Sil."

"Only if you call me Charlie," she sniffled.

He agreed to meet her at the Pierre later that evening after he'd gotten some information. That seemed to calm her…somewhat. *It had been a long time since he'd last experienced a hysterical woman.* He immediately called Jim Murphy for an update. And after a rather intense conversation with the detective, Romano took a cab to East Sixty-first Street.

Charlie waited at the bar in Perrine at the Pierre hotel where she was staying. She greeted Romano with one of her crushing hugs. "Thank you so much for coming."

"How could I not? I know how special you are to each other." Romano was not one for compliments. In a former life he would have described Charlie—wearing a Donatella Versace teal blue blazer and jeans—as *fetching.*

"What would you like to drink, Mr. Rom…Sil?"

"I would ordinarily have a beer, but a glass of wine seems more appropriate for these surroundings."

"Not at all. Their Guinness is excellent," she offered, nervously tapping her foot. "If you like dark beer."

Romano ordered a Miller Lite on tap, and Charlie, a Cabernet.

"When can I see PJ?" she blurted, giving up all efforts to subdue her anxiety.

The dreaded reply hung in the air for the time it took Romano to sip and swallow…and think of a better answer than the one he had prepared. Either way, it was not consoling news. He took another quick sip and cleared his throat. "It sounds much worse than it is, and there are numerous options." *There had to be.*

He did not tell her about the suicide watch incident as he had been informed that officially, it never happened.

He did say that she is refusing visitors. "She's had…an emotional setback and is keeping to herself for a time." What could he say? That she had gone bonkers and had no memory of it? "She just needs some time to recoup."

"Well, that's just bullshit! She can refuse anyone she wishes, but there's no way she will not see me…or I will wring her neck!"

"I can see why you and my granddaughter are bosom buddies," Romano laughed. "Your mutual intransigence has bonded you." When Romano left her at the bar, she was on her cell phone, in tears, placing a call to her husband. *He'll be home in a day.* She told herself. *He will take care of this.*

***

Following Murphy's visit, PJ fell into a deep sleep, missing the four o'clock stand-up count. The warden, still steaming over the governor's *orders*, could not shake the feeling that this prisoner was a pawn in a rigged game of chess. She fired up her computer and searched the database for Penelope Jane Hollinger. She scanned her profile and any history of priors. When about half-way through the file, she punched the intercom. "Collins, bring me DIN 24-A-0006, Penelope Jane Hollinger, ASAP." She sat back and stared at the ceiling, shaking her head.

The grinding of the cell door sliding open made PJ jump to her feet. A forty-something prison guard stood aside the opening. "The Warden wants to see you."

Momentarily dazed, PJ just stared at her.

"Now!"

Each clockwork movement of the cell doors noisily opening before her and closing after her as the two made their way to the warden's office grew more and more abrasive. Her stomach muscles began to contract like a coiling spring. She knew she would not make it very far before the spring sprung. She turned to the prison guard to warn her, but it was too late. The projectile required the clean-up crew to be notified while PJ was taken to the washroom to get herself together.

"Excitement seems to follow you, Ms. Hollinger," the warden said, waving PJ to the seat across from her desk. "You have not been here two weeks, and already have managed to collect three incident reports." She let the airless void between them settle.

"I've read your file," she said, causing waves of sound to vibrate through PJ's body like a tuning fork. Caught in a vortex of non-reality, PJ could only hear the echo of cell doors opening and closing. The out-of-body phases were becoming more frequent, as were the nightmares, which had returned with a vengeance. Time seemed to have slowed to a crawl, like scenes from a movie drilled down to slow motion. One moment was no different from the next. Whatever she did was robotic. She feared her brain would eventually atrophy. Maybe that wouldn't be so bad, she thought. The inability to think could be a blessing. Despite the yellow pads and golf pencils she was given, she had lost all motivation to write. they languished on the small writing table in her cell. She was living someone else's life. At the end of week two; she'd stopped her kick-boxing practice, and daily jogging became a quick walk around the Yard.

"I'm moving you to a different block, Ms. Hollinger."

PJ looked up. A question in her eyes if not on her tongue.

"It's for your own protection. Maximum security, affording less of a chance for any…unwanted incidents." The warden tapped her fingers nervously on the desk. "You'll be sharing a room with another inmate," She added, absent-mindedly fingering the index card Tremont had left her. "Socializing is important."

PJ closed her eyes and dropped her shoulders as if to say *go ahead, do with me what you will.*

"It will take a few days for the paperwork to be completed," the warden said. "In the meantime, I am recommending you for group sessions with the clinical psychologist who meets with some of our ladies once a month."

"No!"

"I beg your pardon."

"You can beg all you want. Unless on suicide watch, I'm not required to see anyone I don't wish to see."

The warden pursed her lips and took a deep breath. "Look, Ms. Hollinger. I'm trying to help you here. The *incident* you cannot seem to recall is very concerning. By all accounts, you are slipping into a state of depression that is common among new detainees."

"I understand. May I go now?"

The warden stood and leaned in toward PJ, hands flat on her desk. "You are smarter than this, Penelope. If you do not get hold of yourself, you will not get through this…or what's ahead of you." She told PJ that she needed some outdoor time, and assigned her to grounds duty. "The schedule will be given to you when you report to the grounds supervisor tomorrow morning." She nodded to the guard. "Now you may go."

***

He came at me in the night. His devil eyes nailing me to the wall. I wanted to fight back. But I was frozen in fear. I knew he was coming for my soul. I was dead, yet I felt the gun in my hand. Someone was raising my arm. Higher, higher. From somewhere in the distance a shot rang out. And then another. A spray of blood covered my face, shocking me back to life. I looked down. My shoes were covered with blood and brain matter. I wanted to scream, but had no voice. I could hear someone calling my name...

"Hollinger. Hollinger. Wake up. You have a visitor."

Slowly, PJ threw her legs over the bunk and dropped her face in her hands trying to orient herself in real time. She walked over to the sink and splashed cold water on her face, grabbed a towel from the rack, and patted her face dry. When she'd gotten herself together, she turned toward the guard. "I am not accepting visitors."

"Well, you're accepting this one. Warden's orders." She waved PJ toward the door. "Let's go."

Still a bit out of it and not willing to expend the energy to resist, she tied her hair back and followed the guard.

Behind a column with chipping, sickly pale-green paint, PJ could see a pair of shapely legs sticking out from one of the tables in a room otherwise deserted. It was not, she realized, the customary visitor's day. But she'd know those legs anywhere.

Charlie didn't wait for PJ to reach the table; she jumped up and ran to her. Before enveloping her in the *jaws of life*, she grabbed PJ by the shoulders and shook her.

"Why are you doing this?" she squealed. "Shutting out those who love you. Why!" She could not hold back the tears, neither could PJ. They stood this way, gripped in each other's arms, until the guard, sitting in a corner chair, warned them about touching.

"I can't do this much longer, Charlie," PJ moaned as they sat next to each other, their intertwined hands hidden under the table. "It's like a bad dream. I click my heels, but instead of Kansas I wake up on a bunk in a tomb. If I stay here another day, I will curl up and die."

Charlie gave PJ a *Mr. Freeze* glare. "Who are you? And what have you done with my sista?"

"I'm tired of fighting. Wherever I turn, a disaster awaits. Everything has become a battle for survival."

"Listen to me!" Charlie squeezed PJ's hands. If Wally can get me in here with their myriad restrictions, he will get you out. You cannot give up," she pleaded, a stream of tears cascading down her cheeks. "Val is half out of his mind because you won't see him. And your grandfather. He doesn't know which way to turn to try to help you because you're so Goddamned stubborn!"

"Hey!" This from the chair in the corner. "Keep it down."

She lowered her voice. "Penelope Jane Hollinger, I will not let you do this to yourself. You know I can match your stubbornness. Even top it."

PJ relinquished a half-smile. "I know you can. But why would you?"

"How could you even ask that when you know you would do the same for me?"

Whatever dam holding back the swell of emotions that had built over time, broke. PJ could no longer contain the torrent now erupting in uncontrolled sobs. Charlie took her in her arms. "It's all right, my darling. Let it all out. This is just what you need." She clasped PJ's face in her hands and bored into her eyes. "Now you will take charge of your life, and come out fighting like you've never fought before."

CHAPTER THIRTY-ONE

The Mole

Charlie's visit was just what PJ needed; the flint to ignite her fire. She felt a surge of…something. Not quite optimism, but a jolt of energy. An eagerness to get on with the battle. But she did not kid herself; this would be nothing less than war, and as in war, only one side would come away victorious.

Determined more than ever to fight back, she settled into the mind-body practice that had been her normal routine for years. A grueling physical regimen, and daily meditation. She grew stronger every day, and kept her mind on survival. She even gained back six of the ten pounds she'd lost. She was driven. Striving to be at her mental and physical peak. She could do no less if she hoped to come through this conflagration on the right side of victory. Suddenly she was nine years old, and could hear Brett Hollinger's voice. *Show them what you're made of, my girl!*

After her daily five-mile run around the perimeter of the yard, PJ headed for the showers. There were usually four prison guards on duty. Two along the corridor to the bathrooms, and two inside the showers. The women's bathroom area also included lockers and a changing area…all in open view. The CCTV cameras throughout the area precluded any chance of privacy.

As she queued up on line to wait her turn, she did not notice that two of the guards were not at their respective posts, and the green light on the overhead camera at the entrance to the shower stalls was blinking red. Distracted by her thoughts on the up-coming meeting with her annoyingly indifferent attorney, she paid no attention to several women who left the line and walked out. It had been weeks since her last meeting with Weiner, and she was anxious to see him. Turning over in her mind the concerns and questions she needed to discuss with him, she ignored the first commandment of prison life: *Always be aware of your surroundings.*

PJ was third in line with one woman behind her when she felt an intense sting on the left side of her ribcage. Instinctively, she spun around in the direction of the hit with a Muay Thai kick, knocking the Shiv out of her assailant's hand. The attacker doubled over in pain, clutching her now broken wrist. Two of her minions fell on PJ, but they were not quick enough to trap her arms.

PJ concentrated all her weight on a palm thrust into one of her attacker's nose, just below the nostrils, effectively putting her out of commission. She sprung to her feet and executed a rear kick to the head of the third attacker, knocking her out cold.

***

"This does not help your cause, Ms. Hollinger."

She trained her piercing emerald eyes on him, darting fiery sparks. "Are you saying that it would have helped my cause better had I been killed?"

"You are misconstruing my words," Weiner said, irritated. "I am merely stating a fact. There is no question that you had to defend yourself. Be thankful it was only a flesh wound," he added more gently. "The problem is every word, act, or lapse in judgment, all of it. These things will be scrutinized by the prosecution, and wherever even remotely possible, they will paint a very dark picture of you."

"Good to know. Maybe I should just shoot myself now and save the state…"

"Please, Ms. Hollinger, be careful what you say. You never know who is listening, and I'm sure you do not want to be put on suicide watch again." Weiner sat on the bench opposite PJ.

PJ brushed back the strands of hair that had fallen over her eyes. It had been quite some time since she'd had a trim. While the prison provided such services from outside professionals, she would never position her head in or around anyone holding a scissors inside this denizen of evil. Her throat, emitting a groan, agreed. "Do you have any good news for me?"

"I wish there were something positive to tell you, but anything that Victoria collected supporting your defense is on an encrypted drive that only she can access. I'm working from ground minus zero here," he lied.

With a weighty sigh, PJ stared down at the floor. "Is she still in a coma?"

"Sadly, yes." Neither spoke. "There are people who may be able to decode the encryption," he offered after a moment. "We're working on it. But time is against us." He pulled a document from his briefcase.

Her already knotted stomach, cinched tighter. *I will get through this. For as long as I have breath, I will fight.* "Like it or not," she said. "You are my attorney, Mr. Weiner, and you have an obligation to put together a strong defense."

He handed her the document. "I will do my best."

She glanced over the paper then looked at Weiner. "A Grand Jury?"

"Afraid so."

"But we can't present a defense at a Grand Jury hearing."

"Unfortunately, no, we cannot. Most prosecutors in a criminal case of this import opt for a Grand Jury. This is no surprise."

"It is possible, though," she said, aware of the slight quiver in her voice, "that the jury will not find probable cause for a trial." Weiner snapped his briefcase shut and called for the guard. "Hold onto that hope, Ms. Hollinger. I'll be in touch."

Disheartened, particularly by Weiner's *that's life* attitude, but unwavering in her resolve to hack off each obstacle that sprouted its beastly head, she sat at her desk, pulled the yellow pad toward her, and began to write. *The only thing I can do right now,* she reasoned, *is get it all on paper.*

The following morning, PJ was moved to a different block. She was pleased to see that it was larger and had a window, albeit barred. She wasn't thrilled about the roommate. She'd barely entered the room when the young woman excitedly introduced herself.

"I'm Kami. I'm so happy we're going to be roommates," she gushed. "You're practically a celebrity here." PJ was not in the mood for friendly. She just wanted to be left alone with her thoughts. She all but ignored the girl.

"I waited to give you dibs on upper or lower bunk."

"Thanks" she said, and threw her things on the lower bunk. She set up her personal items and organized her writing tools on a wide shelf attached to the wall that split at the corner forming two desks. Each side contained a lamp and a storage compartment. Two chairs were also provided. The commode in the corner of the cell, separated from the bunks by a plastic floor-to-ceiling room divider, afforded a scintilla of privacy. The woman chattered away until she struck PJ's last nerve.

"Look," PJ scowled, "I don't mean to be rude, but would you just shut up for ten minutes!"

"Oh, sorry. It's a nervous habit. Sorry."

Sensing that the environment was rubbing off on her, PJ sat on the edge of her bunk and took a deep breath, containing her impatience. "What did you say your name was?"

"Kami. Kami Bryant"

"How old are you, Kami?"

"Almost twenty."

"You're much too young to be in this dismal cage."

"I shot my boyfriend," Kami volunteered casually.

"I see." PJ was entirely willing to drop the subject, in fact, she could have kicked herself for starting this *not-where-she-wanted-to-go* conversation. But, of course, Kami, whose mouth was turbo charged, continued.

"I'm just sorry I didn't kill him," she giggled.

The three short, quick blasts of a siren indicating lights out did not deter Kami from asking the question. "So, did you really kill that priest?"

PJ walked over to the desk, turned off the lamp, and got into bed. "I wish I knew."

Another two weeks were coming to a close and no word from Weiner. Her brain was about to explode with Kami's constant blathering. She asked far too many questions and showed more interest in PJ's issues than her own serious charges of assault and battery, and attempted murder. Her skin was thicker than Pluff Mud. Regardless of how sarcastically or directly PJ made it known that she did not want to discuss the matter, nothing seemed to stop Kami's questions. PJ could not help wondering if she was a plant. She seemed overly intent on trying to get PJ to talk about Montini's. Ignoring Kami, she turned her thoughts to Weiner. He was less than enthusiastic, to say the least, about defending her. She thought about changing lawyers...again, but it was just too late, and Charlie promised that Walden would talk to him, make sure he wasn't shirking his responsibility in filling in for Abbott. The feeling of helplessness and having to depend on others to get through this calamity was dragging her down like a hundred-pound albatross around her neck.

She thought about Val as she does at the beginning and end of each day...and in-between. If she allowed herself, she would daydream about him to fill the loneliness and pacify her guilt.

She was doing the right thing. She'd ruined her own life, and was not about to ruin his. The fire of hope was at best glowing ashes, the calm and serenity of her daily hour of meditation, increasingly shattered by *what ifs*. She had to work hard at impounding such thoughts. As painfully tempting as it was to see him, she declined Val's visits—

usually two to three times a week. She would not take his calls. He wrote her, asked friends to intercede. He clung to the hope that she would soon give in after having had enough of his relentless pursuit.

But she never read his letters. If she did, she would not be able to walk away from the profound love she had for him. But she did not throw them away. She saved them in a shoebox.

The sound of jingling keys heralded a visit from the friendly neighborhood prison guard. "Hollinger! Your mouthpiece is here. And Bryant…uh, oh…the warden wants to see you," the guard winked. "Have you been a bad girl?"

"What, no!"

***

PJ was hard-pressed to withhold her irritation, but neither did she want to antagonize her only hope of a defense. She nearly choked on the words. "Thank you for coming, Mr. Weiner."

"We're all working around the clock, literally, to cover Victoria's cases," he said. "But I do have news."

She felt the spike of a cold sweat breaking out. She could never read his unchanging, vapid expression, giving credence to her conclusion that his limbic system was unserviceable. Weiner unbuttoned his suit jacket and took a seat. He cleared his throat. "The prosecution has completed its jury selection and the grand jury hearing has been docketed two weeks from today."

"That's crazy. These things generally take months."

"As I mentioned, all parties are anxious to have this case behind them, if for no other reason than to assuage

Rome, which is under pressure from the Vatican." Weiner was cautious about how much he told PJ, but he thought she should be aware of the outlying pressures being put upon those involved…even if what he told her only scratched the surface.

PJ stood, paced around the table, and sat down again. "This feels disturbingly like scapegoating. Is that what I've been set up to be?" she said, her throat dry and her voice wavering. "A scapegoat?"

"Shoddier things have happened."

Well, that's helpful.

"It does not look like they are continuing their investigation, other than gathering evidence against you," he added, noting the look of astonishment on PJ's face.

"You can use that, can't you? As part of my defense." Weiner was silent. "Mr. Weiner?"

He blew out a shaft of air as if he were blowing out candles on a birthday cake. But this was no party. "I'm afraid, Ms. Hollinger, that won't be enough."

***

Kami Bryant's eyes widened at the sight of the man sitting on a corner chair in the warden's office.

"I understand, Ms. Bryant, that you've met ADA Michaels."

Byant seemed flustered. "You're not taking back your promise, Mr. Michaels, are you?"

"Why don't you sit down, Kami," the warden said gently, gesturing to the chair opposite her desk. "ADA Michaels would just like to speak with you."

CHAPTER THIRTY-TWO

Retribution

Born at the short end of the umbilical cord, Concetta (Sawyer) Barone's existence was one of abuse and violence. Her destiny—preordained by a mother who abandoned her directly from the womb to an empty locker at Rome's train station—irrevocably cutting the cord—was about to be realized. She anticipated no less. Bounced from one foster home to another under Italy's *l'affido familiare*, her moral compass, if ever she possessed one, had long since been replaced by animal instinct; survival at any cost. When she ran away from her last foster home, she was found and arrested for stabbing her foster father. She was fifteen. But her life of crime had only just begun. She was incarcerated at the Juvenile Detention Center for eighteen months, and as her luck would have it, shared a cell with a psycho who was serving a life sentence for the gruesome murder of her entire family; a miscreant from whom she had learned much.

Sawyer eventually hooked up with a stoner, but never used the stuff. She had subsequently been arrested several times for possessing and selling coke. She made the mistake of marrying the loser believing he could support both his habit, and her wished-for lifestyle. But life is messy and some outcomes are inescapably transparent. When Sawyer, predictively, had had enough of her husband, she sawed off his head as perfunctorily as slicing a rib roast. She would face a conviction of twenty-five years in prison. And the rest, as they say, is history.

Sawyer rallied every last one of her *gratuities*, and after serving thirty days for breaking her parole, she left the prison with a new identity, passport, American Express credit card, and two hundred dollars in cash. She was flush. On the down side, she had been betrothed to her parole officer by virtue of a bracelet that would adorn her ankle for the length of her parole. She would, of course, cleverly circumvent this small inconvenience with a homemade *Faraday shield,* which would give her the head start she needed to get to New York.

***

On her way back from her *visit* with the ADA, Bryant was mumbling to herself, rehearsing what she was told to say. When she got to her cell, PJ was doing push-ups. "Don't you ever get tired?" she chortled nervously. "You already have a body to die for."

"Exercise is good for the soul."

Bryant climbed on her bunk and plopped down eliciting a strangled squeak from the springs. Her nervousness vaporized most of what she had practiced. She was clearly not a suitable candidate for undercover work. But she had to do it if she ever again were to breathe the air of freedom. "Why did you shoot the priest?" She blurted.

PJ stopped dead, mid push-up, and squeezed her eyes impermeably shut until the pain reached the back of her head. "What did you say?"

"Everyone knows you did it…but why?"

She jumped to her feet and pulled Bryant from her bunk to the floor in one seamless movement. She straddled her and pinned her shoulders. "What's your game, little miss dumb blonde? You haven't ceased asking questions since day one. Are you trying to get me to confess?" she gnarled through a locked jaw. "Is that it. Did they plant you here?"

"N, no." She began to cry. "I, I'm just…curious. Please don't hurt me."

PJ stood, grabbed Bryant's hand, and pulled her to her feet. "Will you stop that blubbering? I'm not going to hurt you." She looked around the room for a camera or other electronic device. "This is for whoever is listening." And in a clear, loud voice she said. "I did not kill anyone. Or if I did, I have no memory of such an act. Furthermore," raising her tone another notch, "a coerced confession is not admissible in court, you dumbasses!"

By the time PJ had gotten her anger under control, it was past two a.m. But sleep was like catching an air bubble without having it evaporate. Pointless. She sat at the desk and began to write. *My dearest Val.* She crossed it out and started over. *Val.* No. that didn't work either. She tried several times more, but could not get passed the salutation. She crumpled the paper and tossed it in the trash can. Maybe tomorrow.

Tomorrow brought disheartening, albeit not surprising, news from Weiner. "The Grand Jury found enough probable cause to vote for a jury trial," he told her bluntly. "The decision hinged on the testimony of one, Candace Russell Baker, as we knew would be the case."

She buckled up and dug deep for the steadying optimism that fought against burrowing itself into the nebulae. "So, what's next?"

Weiner had other devastating news, but he withheld it from her for the time being. "Jury selection begins on the sixteenth." He paused. "Someone seems to be subverting the plan to keep the media at bay. Expect lots of media coverage and protesters"

"Protesting what?"

"Just be prepared. We will be surrounded by guards and thereby protected."

She could no longer hold back the spindles vigorously agitating her stomach, and without warning chucked up her breakfast, little as it was. Weiner jumped back to avoid the spray, but could not save his shoes.

Four a.m. and PJ lay awake on her bunk trying to wrap her brain around the fact that she is hated. People are saying awful things about her, protesting, calling her witch and devil. *I've tried to do good my entire life,* she sobbed, *only to become a pariah.*

SEVEN DAYS EARLIER

Candace had been feeling the effects of confinement in a suffocating environment with an uncommunicative female NYPD officer charged with protecting her. Her only in-take of fresh air was going and coming from the Grand Jury hearing. She looked for an opportunity during these trips to make her move. Following her testimony, the judge called a recess. Candace turned toward the officer. "I need to use the toilet."

"I'm right behind you."

"Jesus. Give me a break. Can't I have some privacy for once!"

Her bodyguard jeered at her, but gave in and escorted her to a private lavatory used by court personnel. She unlocked the door. "You have ten minutes." A woman in a clerk's uniform approached.

"Someone's in there," the guard advised. "She won't be long."

"No problem." The clerk did a quick survey of the area and when she was satisfied it was safe, executed a choke-hold on the guard, who was late going for her gun, and stuffed a rag in her mouth. She dragged the woman into the restroom and locked the door. The gun fell from the guard's hand and the attacker kicked it away. She then jammed the woman into a stall and finished the job with a knife through her heart.

Having heard the commotion, Candace held her breath and remained behind the door...until it was ripped off its hinges with one kick.

Bewildered, Candace did not believe what her eyes were seeing. "Sawyer? What the fu..." Before Candace could complete the question, Sawyer slashed her arm to the bone. Candace released an agonizing scream but somehow found the strength to kick Sawyer out of the stall and onto the floor.

"You double-crossing, bitch," Sawyer thundered as she got to her feet. "I'm gonna cut you to ribbons."

Candace fell to her knees, gushing blood as she tried to hold her arm together. She spied the gun on the floor about two feet away and wrapped her good hand around it just before Sawyer thrust the knife into her chest, pulled it out, and thrust it again into her abdomen. Candace went down, but not before she got off three consecutive shots into Sawyer's back as she groped for the door.

THE PRESENT

Weiner broke the news to PJ about the deaths of Candace and a felon named Concetta Barone. She knew nothing of Barone, and had mixed emotions over

Candace's final ending. A part of her felt relief, another part, deep sadness. *A wasted life,* she thought, *like mine is turning out to be.* "How will this impact my case?"

"Little to no impact. Their argument hinges on Candace Baker's testimony, which was taped at the Grand Jury hearing and, since she cannot appear, is admissible at trial." He did not tell her that he made no effort to argue the judge's decision under the hearsay rule.

"But she's dead! Doesn't that negate…something?"

"No. It will stand. Our defense hinges on discrediting the witness, which is often seen as a non-defense. But it's all we have."

PJ took a sip of her bottled water, got up, and paced in a small square. Moving helped delay the onset of an emotional reaction.

"Hollinger!" warned the guard posted at the entrance to the visitation area. She gave him a smoldering look, and sat.

"That is not very encouraging, Mr. Weiner."

He began packing his papers. "To be honest, I've had an uphill climb trying to delay the process, which usually takes months. We are talking weeks," he said.

I wonder why, she mumbled under her breath.

"Remember," he said, "We only have to plant a doubt in the mind of one juror."

Right.

"I will see you in court."

PJ was escorted back to her cell, thankful for the silence since Kami Bryant had been sent back to her former block. She sat on the edge of the bunk and buried her head in her hands. The signal sounded for lights out, but she knew she wouldn't be able to sleep. She turned on the desk lamp and began going through the week's mail hiding under the paperweight. She tossed out the unknowns—no doubt the usual hate mail—and kept the last two; a letter from Val, and one from Charlie. She put Val's aside for later filing in her shoebox, and opened Charlie's.

Hey, my sista. I know you're on pins and needles as am I, waiting for this spurious trial to begin and end…and it will…and you will be back in your home state of California living the good life you so very much deserve—along with me—ha, ha. Wally says they have nary a thread holding their argument together. We will be there with you all the way. Love you!

CHAPTER THIRTY-THREE

Valdur Kendall

"Welcome back, Mr. Kendall." Caught as he tried to slip unnoticed into his office at Kendall and Son, Val grumbled a "Thank you" and continued walking. The change in his temperament was palpable, his thoughtful and gracious demeanor noticeably absent. Having stayed on as admin assistant at Val's behest after Martin Kendall's death, Mrs. Cummings understood the reason behind this transformation. She followed him into his office and handed him the stack of messages.

"Anything urgent?"

"Mrs. Thurgood called several times after trying to reach you on your personal line, which for some *cracked up reason*—and I am quoting verbatim—you did not return her calls." Her heart jumped a half-beat at Val's almost-smile.

"I'll take care of it."

"And, of course," she said, "the implacable Mr. Wellington left his usual one-hundred and-one messages."

The hint of a smile abruptly disappeared.

"May I get you some coffee?"

"I'm fine." Cummings was about to leave when he stopped her. "Mrs. Cummings," he said. And left her name hanging in the disquieting atmosphere.

"Is something wrong, Mr. Kendall?"

He took a beat or two before answering. "Everything is wrong, Mrs. Cummings." He was well into addressing his stack of messages when his phone buzzed.

"Mr. Wellington is on line four. He must be ill…he is actually polite today."

"Small miracles." *No point putting off the inevitable.* "Put him through to my private line." Val took a long breath before pressing the blinking red light. "Lester."

"That would be me. How are you, my boy."

Val stiffened. *I'm not your freaking boy.* "Doing just fine. And you?"

"Good, good, good. Listen, I know you're a busy man, but let's schedule a dinner meeting to wrap up our agreement."

Great. "I'm going to need some time, Lester. I literally just walked in the door."

"Understood, but time waits for no man."

How original. "Give me a couple of days."

"You got it. My driver will pick you up at five on Thursday." Wellington hung up before Val could protest.

Shit and double shit. Without thinking, PJ's favorite expletive rolled off his tongue. He swept the papers from his desk and threw the paperweight against the glass wall, missing Mrs. Cummings' feet by inches.

"Oh, my."

"Sorry." Val loosened his tie and began picking up the strewn papers. "Mr. Wellington has that sort of effect on people. Fortunately, the glass is shatterproof," he said, tossing the papers haphazardly onto his desk. "I'll need you to call a board meeting as soon as possible."

She stood there, a question burning her tongue, but said nothing.

Val took off his jacket and tossed it onto the side chair. He sat back down. "Was there something else, Mrs. Cummings?"

"Oh. Oh, yes." She stepped up to his desk and handed him an envelope. "This just came for you by courier. Rather pungent." She turned and walked out, her finger to her nose, restraining a sneeze.

The note was addressed to Valdur Kendall, Esq. in gold leaf, and wax-sealed. *How baroque.* He didn't have to bring his nose to the envelope to know who had sent it. *She must have used the entire bottle of Notorious.* Its strong scent hung heavily. The note contained few, unambiguous words:

Hope you had a good trip. Looking forward to seeing you soon. Fondly, Patricia.

He tossed it into the pending tray. *Shit and doub…*He rolled his eyes and pressed the intercom. "Would you to come to my office, Mrs. Cummings?"

He waved her to the soft chair. "Please, sit down. There's something we need to discuss."

While he was a financial whiz kid from an early age, his passion belonged to *Parent Trace,* a non-profit he'd founded several years prior, which located and connected biological children and parents. The time he devoted to Kendall and Son, although quite productive, he considered part-time, although Kendall, Sr. would vehemently disagree. He saw his son's dedication to *Parent Trace* as a passing interest. Because of the love and respect he had for his dad, Val did not argue the point.

It was through *Parent Trace* that he had met PJ Hollinger when she actively began searching out her past, the first step of which was to find her biological parents. He knew instinctively that he had found the woman he would marry.

***

Wellington's influence covered a vast demesne, a world handed down from his grandfather, to his father, to him. A visionary in his own right, Wellington's interests ranged from real estate development, to oil and gas, to AI technology. Industries in which he increased his dynastic fortunes tenfold, making him one of the wealthiest men in the world. Money—notwithstanding the prosaic adage that it cannot provide happiness—can buy a great deal of other things. As promised, Wellington's driver picked up Val at the stroke of five. The drive seemed longer than usual. Finishing off some notes on his MacBook, Val hadn't been paying attention to his surroundings. He felt a bit disoriented when he looked out the window to find the driver pulling up to Wellington's Cessna Citation 680 standing by on the tarmac. "What's going on? Why are we here?"

"Mr. Wellington's last-minute surprise, sir. He's waiting for you on board."

God help me.

"There you are, my boy." Wellington rose and threw his arms around Val in an unwelcomed bear hug.

Val frowned. "Lester, where are you taking me? I have appointments to keep, and…"

"No worries, my boy," he assured Val, pounding him on the back. "We'll be back in a flash. Grab a seat and buckle up."

They landed in Naples, Florida at approximately eight p.m., and were seated at Baleen by nine-twenty, the proprietor having agreed to stay open until midnight. "Why here, Lester?"

"I love this place! What could be more favorable to a friendly agreement than a charming and picturesque view of the harbor on the Gulf of Mexico, further improved by the chef's *Seafood Platter Royale*. Trust me, you'll eat it up," he chortled, enjoying his own pun.

"I'm meeting with the Board tomorrow."

"Indeed you are, my dear boy. But not to worry. I'll have you home before the sun overtakes the moon."

The thought swung through Val's mind that there was only one thing he hated more than being called *my boy*, and that was being called *my dear boy*.

They ordered dinner and a bottle of Chateau Mouton. Val did enjoy the seafood platter, but he managed only half, his digestive tract not cooperating with the intervening discussion. At exactly eleven-thirty, they shook on a verbal agreement with some contentious elements remaining unsettled. Wellington appeared satisfied, but undoubtedly not delighted. "We can work out the details to our mutual benefit, I'm sure."

On the flight back to Tenafly, the men were quiet, both apparently reflecting on their discussion and its possible ramifications.

"I'm going to get personal here for a minute, son," Wellington said in a hushed tone. "I'd really like you to get to know my Patricia better. She's quite a gal."

Uh, oh. Here it comes. "I'm sure she is."

"She is an integral part of my business operations. And is presently running our commercial real estate division."

Val perked up. "I didn't know that."

"Oh, yes. She has a civil engineering degree from Columbia, and an MBA from DeVry."

"Impressive."

"I run many of my decisions by her. We don't always agree, but it's a beautiful thing to have someone you can absolutely trust to be honest with you. Am I right?"

"It's a blessing," he said, and meant it.

"She also holds my heart in the palm of her hand. Anything that makes her happy is a done deal."

"Are you trying to tell me something, Lester?"

"You know me, I say it like it is."

"And you know, of course," Val made it clear, "that I'm engaged to PJ Hollinger."

Wellington was not one to mince words. He was inclined, however, to reach for diplomacy when dealing with Val Kendall. But not always. "I understand she's in prison."

Val shut him down in no uncertain terms. "That is not your concern, Lester."

"But…"

"There are no buts. The subject is closed."

CHAPTER THIRTY-FOUR

The Acquisition

Val was ready to get out of a responsibility he never wanted. There were no misgivings about Wellington taking over the company, provided that his requirements were met—and therein lay the rub. Wellington's offer was more than acceptable. The corporate structure, which would be built on Lester Wellington as President and Patricia Wellington filling Val's position as Vice President and CFO, was agreeable. The timeline was reasonable, and the new location did not present a problem. The points of contention, however, were conditions that Wellington had thus far rejected.

Val knew that the announcement he was about to make to the Board would be met with much grumbling and opposition. He misjudged, however, the brouhaha that erupted at his declaration to the shareholders that he had begun negotiations with Wellington Industries to acquire Kendall and Son. His decision was met with as much enthusiasm as a snake bite. Since he held the majority of voting rights, the meeting was a formality. But Val detested conflict within an organization that had consistently been able to resolve differences peacefully and respectfully. He explained that the transfer of ownership hinged on immutable requirements.

Wellington insisted Kendall and Son be absorbed into Wellington Industries under the corporate name of Wellington Financial Services.

"No deal, Lester," Val snapped. "My father would turn over in his grave for such disrespect."

Wellington swiped his hand over his face. "No disrespect intended, son."

"Please don't call me son."

Wellington's face turned the color and texture of cranberry sauce.

"If you truly want this to happen, Lester, you know my stipulations. The corporate name will be Kendall-Wellington Investments. All staff and personnel will remain, with the exception of those who choose to leave. This includes members of the board. Of course, you can always add new members at your discretion." Wellington kept swirling his wine. He said not a word.

"Additionally," Val continued. "Mrs. Cummings, should she agree, will stay on as Patricia's administrative director."

Wellington's face registered his disapproval.

"These requirements are non-negotiable, Lester."

Wellington pushed back his chair, stood, and buttoned his suit jacket. "I'll think about it," he said, and left the table.

***

The visitation room was swarming with bodies. It was *Family Day* at the Women's Detention Center. The room was charged with energy and voices talking over each other. Charlie had to speak close to PJ's ear to be heard.

"Wally spoke to Henry Weiner," Charlie yelled over the din. "He said he is thinking about a diminished capacity defense."

"You know more than I do," PJ shouted back. "He doesn't speak to me. What is he so afraid of? If he'd rather not represent me, why doesn't he simply recuse himself?"

"He cannot do that, PJ. If he did, he knows that if...when...Victoria Abbott comes out of her coma, he would be toast."

"How is she?"

"I hear she may be improving. The brain swelling is going down."

"Well, that's some good news."

"PJ?"

"It's so easy to see, Charlie, when you have something on your mind that's bouncing on the tip of your tongue. What is it."

"Won't you at least talk to Val? He comes out every weekend hoping you'll see him."

PJ turned away and closed her eyes. When she opened them, the room was a blur and her heart pumping bloody tears.

"He's not going away."

"Please, Charlie. You know I can't. I ache to see him. To hold him. But he deserves so much better than a felon who will probably spend the rest of her life in prison. He has his whole life ahead of him. I will not allow myself to get in the way of that. I love him too much."

Charlie, frustrated by the stone wall, slammed her palm on the table. "You are so goddamned stubborn!"

"You've told me that at least a thousand times."

"You have no right to make that decision for him." She looked squarely into PJ's watery eyes. "Did you know he is selling Kendall and Son to Lester Wellington?"

PJ could not believe her ears. "What?"

"He's good with it. Tells me he never really wanted to get involved with running the corporation."

"Why Wellington? And what about *Parent Trace*? That's his brainchild."

"He didn't go into it. But he'll now be devoting all his time to *Parent Trace*. The company is burgeoning. He had to hire an additional investigator."

PJ brushed the tears from her cheeks. "That's wonderful. It's all he ever wanted to do."

People began filing out as the lights blinked on and off. Charlie grabbed PJ's hands. "I don't want to leave you." They embraced for an eternity before Charlie had to leave. "See you again soon, my sista. And think about seeing Val."

***

"May I ask what you have decided, Mr. Kendall…about the acquisition?" Mrs. Cummings inquired after stepping into Val's office.

Val, his jacket off and shirt sleeves rolled up, put down his pen and sat back. "We're at an impasse, Mrs. Cummings. But I assure you, your position will not be in jeopardy."

"Thank you. Whatever happens, I will be fine. Your father, rest his soul, built a very comfortable retirement package for me."

"Yes. I know. And well deserved."

Cummings stood there, hands dangling at her sides, staring through the floor to ceiling window at the towering buildings jutting into the sky.

"You all right, Mrs. Cummings?"

"It was not the same after your father's passing, and it will not be the same without you." She said, as stoically as her heart would allow.

"It will be fine. I promise you."

"Oh, my goodness. I almost forgot. Ms. Wellington has asked to see you. She's waiting outside."

"Ah, yes. The closer."

"I beg your pardon?"

"Oh, nothing. Give me five minutes then send her in."

Patricia Wellington's demure persona obscured a woman of intelligence, charm, and determination. Having met her several times in the company of her father, and once when she invited him to dinner, Val paid only the requisite attention to her. He could not deny, though, that his interest in her had been sparked by the revelation of her accomplishments. Obviously, she was not just another attractive female on the hunt for a well-healed partner. She was probably worth double of any of the eligible bachelors in New York…including himself.

He rolled down his sleeves, put on his suit jacket, and straightened his tie. He walked around his desk to shake her hand as she entered the room. "Good to see you, Patricia." She ignored the extended hand and gave him a warm hug.

"Good to see you as well, Valdur."

He winced inwardly at the formality. "Please, sit."

"Thank you." She sat on the five-thousand-dollar chestnut Audo Copenhagen loveseat his mother had picked out for him. It was meant to give the office a warm, welcoming aura. Nonetheless, Val felt a certain tension as though a heavy mist followed Patricia into the room.

"I'm not much for small talk," she said after some moments of awkward silence.

"Well, you've got company there," he smiled.

"I came to apologize…for my father."

"No need, Patricia."

"My friends call me Patti."

"And mine call me Val."

"Valdur is a Nordic name," she said.

"The name was my mother's idea. She's Scandinavian. She thought it was a strong name."

"It is," Patti agreed. "It means *ruler*."

The red button on his desk phone blinked. "Excuse me." He pressed it and brought the phone to his ear. "Yes?"

"Mr. Wellington is on line two."

"Tell him I'll call him back." He put the receiver back onto its cradle and grinned. "Does your father know you're here?"

She sighed. "He's not supposed to. But my father has a sixth sense I've been trying to elude forever."

"The two of you seem close."

"We are. He holds onto me for dear life. After my mother's death, he felt angry, confused, completely off-course. I've become his anchor, a preventative from getting lost at sea."

"Pardon me for asking, but doesn't that make you feel kind of…chained?"

"Not so much chained as claustrophobic. I've had to learn to set boundaries."

"No doubt."

"My father is not a bad person. Impatient and blustery at times, and often has difficulty controlling his tongue."

"No kidding."

She half-smiled. "He's basically a good man, an honorable man, Valdur…Val."

"If you say he is, I believe you. I really don't know him all that well."

"I…I'm hoping that will change."

"That depends on him."

"He told me he walked out of your meeting because he became angry. He does not want to be angry with you, nor you to be angry with him."

Val was seeing a part of Patricia he had not noticed before. He had casually dismissed her as a tag-along, softening her father's presence. He realized, with a twinge of guilt, that he was beginning to like her. He cleared his throat. "I've given your father my stipulations and they are non-negotiable." He got up and joined her on the loveseat, sat at the opposite end, and angled himself to face her. He crossed his legs. "I don't mean to be implacable, Patti, but these conditions are both professionally and personally important to me, and to this firm."

Patricia focused on her hands, clasped and settled in her lap, thinking over what Val said. After a lengthy moment, she looked directly into his eyes. "I don't find anything unfeasible about your conditions," she said with a lovely smile that showcased perfectly straight, white teeth. "Perhaps we could have dinner soon," she said.

"I'll be leaving for Colorado next week on business."

"Well, then. How is Friday, around seven?"

CHAPTER THIRTY-FIVE

The Trial

Weiner bemoaned the fact that his hands were tied. The judge blocked every motion he requested. He would not reconsider bail, and the DA's office refused a plea bargain. PJ doubted that Weiner had put his back into her defense. And she was right. His reports to her were nine-parts hyperbole, and one-part truth.

"I asked for a reduced sentence for a plea of guilty in consideration of the fact that you were under duress at the time," he explained to her during their trial prep meeting."

"Duress?" she screeched. "I was out of my fucking mind!"

Weiner loosened his tie and sat, his hands fumbling with the lock on his briefcase. It was the first time PJ could recall the phlegmatic attorney appearing nervous.

"It was by all standards a perfectly reasonable request," he said. "But the DA patently refused. The upshot is that you will be tried for premeditated, first-degree murder, which carries a life sentence without parole. I've had several meetings with the DA's office, and even one with the governor. The State is adamant." Weiner was lying outright about meeting with the governor. And he only had one tete-a-tete with the DA, just to appear as though he were doing his job.

PJ was no longer hearing him. She closed her eyes against the rising alarm that was gripping every part of her. *I will get through this. I will not give up or give in.* She repeated these affirmations over and over until the tuffet of knots garroting her stomach loosened, and her pulse slowed. "What is your plan, Mr. Weiner?" she asked after having calmed herself.

"The trial is in six days. I've done my best to attempt the impossible in the short time I've been given to prepare a defense."

Another excuse, each more feeble than the last.

"I'm depending on reasonable doubt," he said, adjusting his glasses. "As I've said, all we need is to win over one juror."

The little confidence she had in Weiner from the outset had gradually crumbled to none at all. But there was nothing she could do about it at this stage. She'd survived much in her short life. And she would survive this. But the brain-twitch suggesting that this drive, this determination to overcome was meaningless self-talk, distressed her. She kicked the thought to the curb in a hurry. Getting bogged down in pessimistic what-ifs was not helpful. Thoughts of Val cropped up as they usually did when her resistance was low. She kicked those thoughts away as well. How on God's earth, she questioned, had she slid into this fathomless rabbit hole?

Walden had arranged for himself, Charlie, and Sil Romano to spend the day before trial with PJ. Charlie had brought her several changes of clothing…all of them business suits in subdued shades of midnight blue and charcoal gray.

"Since when have you become so conservative? I'll look like I'm attending a funeral."

"You'll draw enough attention without your favorite creams and greens and teal blues."

As they were leaving, Charlie slipped PJ a couple of Ativan. "Take one tonight. It will help you sleep."

"Sleep? What's that?"

"Make sure you take one tomorrow morning before you leave for court."

"Yes, Mama." They hugged until Walden had to pull them apart.

"It will all work out, PJ," Walden said, trying to sound reassuring.

The Ativan was useless. PJ's ungoverned mind vaulted from one depressing thought to another, disrupting any chance of sleep. After several rounds of tossing and turning she sat up. The clock read two a.m. She tried meditating. When that didn't work, she did a series of push-ups and crunches. She lay down at about four. Slept until five or so. The trial was scheduled to begin at ten. She chose the dark blue suit over a heather tank top, applied a few strokes of mascara and a dab of blush. She took a sip of water with the Ativan just as the guard appeared to cuff and escort her to the prison van. Weiner would meet her outside the courtroom at nine to go over procedure.

She was given no warning of the minacious crowd of protesters, the majority Catholic, that awaited her with their invidious taunts and placards as though she had nailed Jesus to the cross herself. Neither the Italian Government nor the Vatican was pleased with the media circus. They amped up the pressure to have this trial over and done with.

To avoid possible violence, the van drove around the back of the courthouse and rushed PJ through the private entrance used by the judge and courthouse staff, narrowly avoiding the onslaught of a group of protesters as the heavy steel door closed noisily against their offensive. Weiner was waiting in the prisoner's room with the standard pep-talk; *stay calm, keep your head up, no outbursts.*

The Ativan was kicking in. The tightness she felt from the ends of her hair follicles to her toenails was beginning to slacken. She said something to Weiner. He turned and asked the guard if she would take the cuffs off before walking into court. The guard looked at PJ with genuine regret, "I'm sorry. I'm not permitted to do that."

PJ closed her eyes to center herself, took a deep breath and followed Weiner into the courtroom, the guard at her side clasping her arm.

There was the anticipated buzz in the standing-room-only courtroom as she walked in. An imposing presence under any circumstance, PJ labored to maintain her usual poise and self-possessed demeanor. Her eyes focused ahead, she stepped behind the attorney's table followed by Weiner. The officer removed the cuffs, and PJ sat, somewhat out-of-it.

She trusted Charlie's promise to make certain Val would not be in court. She flipped the thought to more pressing matters parading through her mind like rows of tin soldiers. As she was reciting her standard calming affirmations, her ears picked up a soft whisper from behind. "I love you, my sista." PJ felt tears well, even before she turned. Charlie reached over and hugged her shoulders. "You've got this!" she said. Walden, sitting beside his wife, caught PJ's eye and gave her a wink.

In the very last row, at the far left of the courtroom, Val Kendall stood behind a pillar, virtually invisible, his heart unable to stop racing as his eyes fell on PJ. After she was seated, he could see only part of her beautiful face. It was all he held in his sights, as if his peripheral vision were blacked out, a veil of darkness shrouding his despondency. He was losing her, and ultimately, an immeasurable part of himself. He could not let that happen. She would be acquitted, and retrieve all the lost pieces. He would make sure of it.

Val shot up from his reverie at the bailiff's booming voice. "All rise. This Court with the Honorable Judge Harrison Davis presiding, is now in session. Please be seated and come to order."

Davis looked out over the courtroom. And then directly at the defendant. *How unfortunate,* he thought to himself, then proceeded with his instructions to the jury.

"Ladies and gentlemen. Your task, your obligation and responsibility, is to decide the facts of this case from the evidence presented, and only from the evidence. The defendant, having declared herself *not guilty,* is thereby presumed innocent until proven otherwise beyond a reasonable doubt." He hesitated, excluding the part where he explained reasonable doubt to the jurors. "You may take notes and extend any questions you have through the bailiff. Thank you." He looked to the prosecution. "Mr. Michaels?"

Michaels stood, buttoned his suit jacket, and walked toward the jury box. "Your honor, counselor," he faced the jurors, smiled, and placed his hands on the railing. "Ladies and gentlemen of the jury." He deftly replaced the smiling mask with a solemn frown. "On the fifth of September 2019, His Eminence, Cardinal Roberto Alphonse Montini, while tied to a chair unable to defend himself, was shot and killed in cold blood. The perpetrator of this crime is sitting demurely in this courtroom." He made a quarter turn and waved an arm toward PJ. "Penelope Jane Hollinger, more widely known as PJ Hollinger. Be prepared," he admonished, raising his voice a notch. "The defense will attempt to convince you that Ms. Hollinger has no memory of the event, doubts, in fact, that she was there in the Frascati house at all. But don't be fooled by appearances or the pretense of amnesia. The prosecution will show, beyond a shadow of a doubt, that Ms. Hollinger, premeditatedly and with malice, murdered Cardinal Roberto Montini. It is your duty, ladies and gentlemen of the jury, to ensure that justice prevails, and thus have no other option than to find the defendant guilty of premeditated murder in the first degree. Thank you."

Charlie could sense the sickening sensation that matched her own emanating from PJ. She leaned forward and placed a hand on her back, feeling the apprehension pulsating through PJ's skin.

Unsmiling, hands in his pockets, Weiner casually walked to the center of the room, presenting a veneer of teeming indifference rather than that assurance of innocence a defense attorney brings to the opening statement. Charlie and Walden looked at each other, mirroring frowns.

"PJ Hollinger is not a murderer," Weiner began. "As an investigative reporter, and more recently, a prominent TV newscaster, many of you in this courtroom have no doubt heard of her many achievements in the world of journalism. It has been her lifelong commitment to research and report only the facts, a commitment that makes her stand out in today's world of fake news and biased reporting, as fair, truthful, and above reproach. When she declared herself 'not guilty' she was being honest. The prosecution will parade what they perceive as evidence…evidence which is groundless at least and circumstantial at best. It is your responsibility, as Judge

Davis has pointed out, to base your decision on facts proven beyond a reasonable doubt, a decision that could only lead to a resounding, not guilty!"

The first week of trial, Michaels funneled in a series of witnesses who basically repeated the same damning statements: *PJ Hollinger seen running from the Frascati home, her DNA found in the residence, and a partial print on the murder weapon.* He was saving the video testimony of the now deceased eye-witness, Candace Baker, for the final blow.

Michaels introduced the gun that was used to murder Montini as exhibit A. PJ expected Weiner to object, but he said nothing. She shook her head and whispered into his ear.

"Why are you not taking exception? Partial prints are unreliable as solid proof. Surely you can have an expert witness attest to their imprecision."

Weiner puffed up his cheeks and exhaled noisily. "It doesn't work like that, Ms. Hollinger. I will address the gun at the appropriate time."

"Time is running out, Mr. Weiner."

Michaels was on a roll. The following Monday would see the prosecution strike a disastrous blow to the defense with a surprise witness.

CHAPTER THIRTY-SIX

Lies

Night fell with a thud, closing the lid on a week so hellish PJ was only too willing to return to her cell. She craved sleep, but it would not come. Hiding within the recesses of a mind in desperation, as the world around her spinned out of its orbit, the usual questions—*why and how*—came to the forefront of her thoughts, subverting every effort to rise above circumstances. So recently bathing in the euphoria of a promising career, now drowning in a sea of gloom and dashed hopes, her eyes rested on a copy of the Bible, courtesy of the State. She opened it and the Book of Job popped up. *How appropriate,* she thought. *The Lord gave, and the Lord hath taken away.* She returned the Bible to its place on the shelf, and took out her journal.

Weiner sits there, she wrote, *as if he were a spectator, coughing up an occasional objection, but showing few indications of a viable defense. It seems obvious to me that he is taking a dive, being threatened in some way—or paid off—to throw this case. I feel so helpless.* She stopped writing, the words blurred by unfettered tears.

When Weiner received an addendum to the prosecution's witness list, he was surprised, but did not question it, and cavalierly neglected to inform his client.

The protestors had not given up. The courtroom was packed with a mix of die-hard supporters. Friends, colleagues, acquaintances, as well as those who wanted to see her hang, and, as always in high-profile events, curiosity seekers. All were about to get an earful.

The perpetual darkness of her courtroom wardrobe further weighed down PJ's sinking spirits. She needed brightness, if only in the color of her apparel. She asked Charlie to bring her favorite Gabriela Hearst cream, single-breasted suit which she wore with a peach silk blouse. She walked into the courtroom to the barely suppressed gasps escaping the mouths of the spectators.

With several raps of the gavel, the judge directed the assemblage to quiet down. "Are we ready, Mr. Michaels?"

Michaels stood. "Ready, Your Honor. The State calls Jefferson Reynolds to the stand."

The buzzing of a thousand bees zizzed inside her head as her insides gathered in a crush of crystalized bile. She swallowed, tried for a deep breath, and flung an angry glare at Weiner. "What the hell, Henry?"

He frowned at her. "Is there something I should know, Ms. Hollinger?"

"Why didn't you tell me he was a witness for the prosecution?" she said, trying to keep her voice low. "If you would rather not defend me, please, recuse yourself. I'd do better with a State appointed attorney."

Reynolds sauntered up to the witness chair and was sworn in. He sat, scanned the jury, and smiled. Michaels stepped around the table and stood in front of it. "Mr. Reynolds, would you tell the court how you came to know the defendant, PJ Hollinger?"

"Ah, the Devil wears Prada."

"Just answer the questions asked, Mr. Reynolds. No editorializing, please," the Judge said.

"Of course, Your Honor. PJ—Ms. Hollinger—came to me for help. She was wanted for questioning by the Italian police for the Montini murder and was slated to be extradited to Italy. She told me she could not go to Italy, and begged me to help her. Which I did." He harpooned a contemptuous look straight at PJ. "For which, incidentally, I have not yet been paid." The room crackled with laughter.

PJ was making copious notes, intermittently drawing Weiner's attention to what she had written. He read her notes without comment.

"Obviously, Mr. Reynolds, you no longer represent Ms. Hollinger," Michaels continued, "or it would be you at that table." He nodded toward the defense table. "Can you tell us to the best of your knowledge what happened?"

"Be happy to. "Ms. Hollinger began stalking me."

"What?" PJ, half out of her seat, screamed.

Judge Davis pounded his gavel. "There will be no further outbursts," he thundered. "Is that clear, counselor?"

"Yes, Your Honor. My apologies."

"Apologies?" she pounced on Weiner, squelching her voice. "He's lying through his teeth!"

"Continue, Mr. Reynolds."

Reynolds inhaled his annoyance. "Yes, Your Honor. The defendant would not let up. She even went so far as to offer herself to me."

With that, PJ lost every ounce of self-restraint she had left. She jumped up, nearly toppling the table. "You lying son-of-a-bitch. You…" Weiner grabbed her with both arms and forced her into the chair.

"Your honor, if it please the court," Weiner had to shout over the raucous outburst that had erupted in the courtroom. "I need a private word with my client."

"Indeed, you do," Davis said while trying to maintain order. His arthritic wrist began to act up with every blow of the gavel. He stood, his anger unhidden by pulsing temples and a crimson flush to his cheeks. "I will clear this courtroom if you do not come to order," he shouted, and waited for quiet to prevail. "We will take a fifteen-minute recess." Bang!

Val had left his hidden corner of the courtroom just before recess was called. He found the men's restroom and kicked open the stall door. He closed the lid and sat, running his hands over his face and through his hair in unrestrained weeping. He understood now why she insisted so vehemently that he not be present. He felt the sting of her humiliation as though it was his. He would not go back in. He needed to get some air untainted by the stench of lies and treachery. He threw cold water on his face, loosened his tie, and straightened up. He headed for the exit when someone grabbed his arm. She turned him around and took him in her arms.

"Oh, Val. What are you doing here?" Charlie whimpered.

He unclasped himself from her grip. "I'm going to kill the bastard!"

She brushed away the wetness settling on her cheeks. "Well, that will certainly help."

"I've been so angry with her, Charlie. Closing me out, refusing to see me. But if the situation were reversed, I would not want her to witness my degradation and dishonor from that bottom feeder," he said, his fists curling tighter with every word. "He's going to feel the pain he's caused…and then some." He kissed her on the cheek and left the building.

****

PJ laced into her attorney as the door closed behind them. "What kind of a defense attorney are you," she shrieked. "How can you allow him to denigrate me like that knowing, as I'm sure you do, his iniquitous reputation?"

"Please, Ms. Hollinger. Calm down."

"If you tell me to calm down one more time, I will throw something at you."

"I am doing my best given…"

"Oh, please, not another excuse. If this is your best, I can barely imagine your worst!" Her eyes drilled into Weiner's, their faces only inches apart. "Tell me truthfully, Henry. Are you purposefully losing this case, because sure as hell, you're not doing very much not to."

Weiner paled. "Wha..what are you implying," he stammered."

"I'm not implying anything. I'm telling you. You had better set the record straight on cross. Everything Jefferson Reynolds said was a lie to feed his narcissism. Read my notes. The truth is all there."

"All rise." As Judge Davis took his seat, Weiner had finished reading the last sentence of PJ's three-page notes. His racing heart was thudding in his ears. Whatever conspiratorial agreement he had made with the cabal seeking the speedy and incontestable disposal of PJ Hollinger and the Montini case was about to bite him in the ass. He had no choice but to sound convincing at this point.

Judge Davis instructed the court reporter to read back Michaels' questioning of Jefferson Reynolds. PJ dug her nails so deeply into her skin, her palms began to bleed. After the reading, Davis asked Michaels if he had any further questions for the witness.

"Absolutely, Your Honor." He stood, but remained at his seat as Reynolds took the stand again.

"Mr. Reynolds. You are still under oath," Davis advised.

Michaels proceeded. "Mr. Reynolds, under what circumstances, did you decide to no longer represent PJ Hollinger?"

"After she threatened to take me before the bar with some fantastic accusation."

"And what did she accuse you of?"

"She told me she would say that I made untoward advances."

"And did you?"

"I already told you what happened."

The judge instructed Reynolds to answer the question.

"Of course not."

"No further questions."

Henry Weiner strode over to the witness box, notes in hand. He knew he had to present a semblance of a reasonable defense, or it would be much too obvious that he was allowing the prosecution to overshadow him. He adjusted his glasses and made a quarter-turn toward the jury.

"Speaking of fantastic, Mr. Reynolds, is it not true that it was you who propositioned Ms. Hollinger, and when she rejected you, it was you who threatened her, on more than one occasion? On the evening that PJ Hollinger refused your advances, for example, you told her, and I quote." He read directly from PJ's notes. "It's in your best interest to stay on the good side of me, my sweet." He looked at Reynolds, whose scornful grimace spoke volumes about the man. "And when she rejected your proposal in no uncertain terms, you told her that either she marry you, or—and again I quote—'you will spend the rest of your life in prison."

"And the jury is supposed to believe that tripe because she says so?" Reynolds growled.

"And the jury is supposed to believe you, Mr. Reynolds," Weiner returned the jab, "A barefaced womanizer, married four times, and currently fighting a paternity suit?"

"Objection!"

"Sustained!" Davis used the gavel once again, as the courtroom hissed with reaction. He faced the jurors. "The jury will disregard Mr. Weiner's remarks as to the character of the witness. It will be stricken from the record." He looked at Weiner. "You know better, counselor."

Weiner walked back to his table. "No further questions, Your Honor."

The *fresh* air did little to simmer Val's boiling rage. He sat on the courtroom steps thinking reckless thoughts. He called Romano, who had come down with Covid the day before the trial, and was in quarantine. "How are you feeling?"

"Grumpy. How are things going?"

"I need a favor."

"I guess no answer is a good answer."

"I can't talk about it right now, Sil. I need some information. Right now."

Romano called back within fifteen minutes with the name of the hotel where Jefferson Reynolds was staying.

CHAPTER THIRTY-SEVEN

A New Best Friend

The Four Seasons was a short cab ride from the courthouse. Val figured walking would get him there sooner. It would also help expend some of the voltage spawned by his anger.

When he reached Barclay Street, he walked through the alley adjacent to the hotel's employee entrance, and waited. Twenty minutes had gone by when a tall young man, most of his dreads bunched inside a pendulous, multicolored knitted cap, came out for a smoke. Val walked up to him and waved a one-hundred-dollar bill under his nose. "I lost my swipe card and need to get into my room."

The kid stared at Val, then looked around. He stomped out his cigarette and pulled the bill out of Val's hand.

Val checked out Reynolds' suite, making certain no one was there. When satisfied, he grabbed a beer from the mini-bar and made himself comfortable. His fury rose with each passing hour. He paced. Had two more beers. Paced. Another two hours passed.

The stately grandfather clock in the corner of the suite gonged twelve times when Jefferson Reynolds staggered into the room and headed for the bed. Val pulled off his tie and slung it around Reynolds' neck, twisting it tighter than he'd intended. He let it slacken when Reynolds nearly passed out. He opened his eyes and choked out the words. "I…I can't breathe. What the fuck."

"What a wasted trip," Val said. "You're so drunk you won't even remember me beating the shit out of you. I should kill you while I have the chance." He rolled up his tie and put it in his pocket before inflicting a kidney punch that sent Reynolds to his knees. "But why go to prison for a lowly slug like you." He felt some measure of relief as he leveled a kick to the ribs of the now prone Reynolds, hearing them crack. "I'll take some hot sauce with my ribs, thank you," he faux-laughed.

Pulling Reynolds up off the floor, Val laid a solid right hook to his face, breaking his nose. "If you remember anything, remember this, you piece of dung. This is for PJ." With a final blow to his face, Val let go of Reynolds, who folded to the floor, unconscious.

As a dimming moon receded under the dusty peach glow of twilight, Val found himself at the First Precinct in the interrogation room. He sat back, resting his hands in his lap, and closed his eyes. Two breaths away from falling asleep, he heard the door open. A stocky, middle-aged man walked in, took off his rumpled suit jacket and hung it over the back of the chair. He sat.

"I'm Lt. James Murphy. And you're in a bit of a jam."

Val smiled at Murphy. "It was so worth it."

Murphy opened the freshly constructed case file. "I see where Mr. Jefferson Reynolds claims you put him in the hospital."

"He's lucky he's still breathing."

Murphy did his best to hold back a faint smile. "So, you don't deny it?"

"Deny it? I want the entire world to know I beat the shit out of that slimy eel."

"Look, Mr. Kendall. I've known Sil Romano for a long time. He filled me in on what happened. And I certainly understand your anger. Do you have a lawyer?"

"I don't need a lawyer. I can use some time alone with nothing to do."

"Might be longer than you'd like."

Murphy stood and collected his jacket. "I'm afraid you're stuck here for the night. Your arraignment is tomorrow morning. The court will appoint a lawyer if you don't have one." Murphy turned to leave, then turned back. "Plead guilty and explain to the judge that Reynolds threw the first punch. You'll be out on bail before the end of the day. Good luck, Mr. Kendall."

The following afternoon, Val was sitting across from Lester Wellington at Piccola Cucina, Wellington's favorite Italian restaurant in SoHo. "I'm more than a little embarrassed, Lester. Thank you for bailing me out."

"No need to feel embarrassed, son. I understand a man's compulsion to defend those he cares about," he said in earnest. "Particularly, the women in his life. But I didn't bail you out."

"I don't understand."

He rested his back against the large throw pillow and took a sip of Chianti. "I took the liberty of having a friendly chat with our Mr. Reynolds. I managed to convince him that it would be best for all concerned if this hoo-hah went away."

Val looked dumbfounded. "I've gotten the impression that convincing Jeff Reynolds of anything that doesn't match *his* intentions is like climbing Mt. Everest backwards."

Wellington's mild chuckle showed an appreciation for the analogy. "That notwithstanding," he said, "humans are known to have a change of heart at one time or another. Case in point: Reynolds has dropped all charges. No bail, no record, no nothing."

"I'm almost afraid to ask how you were able to get him to agree to dropping the charges?

The waiter arrived with their dinners as Wellington drained the last of his Chianti.

"To quote a renowned piece of dialogue from one of my favorite Brando films, 'I made him an offer he couldn't refuse.'"

Val lifted his glass to Wellington, something he had never imagined doing. "I will leave it at that." Clink!

Hard-pressed to admit it, that single gesture touched Wellington's heart, opening an avenue to a relationship he was determined to see materialize. "By the way," he said, "I spoke to Patti, that is, she spoke to me. " He sat forward and clasped his hands. I will meet your contractual demands. I trust my daughter's instincts. And I trust you, son."

Curiously, Val did not mind the familiarity.

"Even though you stood up my daughter," Wellington added with a wink.

"What? When?"

"You do have a good excuse."

Val smacked his forehead. "Oh my God. I completely forgot. I…I must apologize."

"Send her some roses."

***

When Wellington handed Kendall a million dollars of his money to manage nearly a year earlier, it was not an arbitrary decision. Valdur Kendall's reputation as a financial expert was taking off. And Wellington spent a good deal of time and expense on an in-depth profile of the impressive young magnate. After having met Val, he became obsessed with bringing him into the Wellington fold, a vision of the son he never had. Often described as tough and coarse, perhaps even crude, his reputation rose before him as an extraordinarily brilliant businessman, evidenced by his wealth and overwhelming success. Ostensibly, Valdur Kendall was nothing like him. Yet he saw Val as the better part of himself; his values, ethics, and honesty, as Wellington discovered, defined the boy and the man. He also believed Val to be the perfect match for his beloved daughter.

***

Weiner spent an entire week calling character witnesses to the stand. Friends, acquaintances, colleagues, even the doorman where PJ lived. Finally exasperated by Weiner's never-ending caravan of witnesses extolling the many virtues of PJ Hollinger, ADA Michael's complained to the judge. "Your honor, how many more witnesses must we sit through describing Ms. Hollinger as the ultimate paragon of virtue."

"Your point is well taken." Judge Davis, reminding himself of the importance of relegating this case to the archives, chided Weiner. "Mr. Weiner, I think you've made your point. Let's move on."

Michaels called his next witness. "Would you kindly state your name and profession for the court."

"Dr. Adam Colletti. I am a forensic scientist specializing in fingerprint identification."

Michaels walked back to his table and returned to the witness holding a plastic bag containing a .45 caliber pistol. "Dr. Colletti, can you identify this .45—Exhibit A— as the weapon used to kill Cardinal Roberto Montini?"

"Yes. That is the gun I examined."

"And were you able to identify any fingerprints thereon?"

"Yes. No question. The partial print belonged to the defendant, Penelope Jane Hollinger."

The collective murmurings filled the courtroom as if one voice. Once again, the gavel came down.

"No further questions."

PJ glared at Weiner. He stood and approached. "Dr. Colletti, would you please describe the method you used in identifying the print…a partial, latent print."

Colletti looked at Michaels, perplexed. "It…it's rather complex."

"Are you implying that the members of this jury would not understand?"

"Objection."

"Sustained."

"I will rephrase, your honor."

"Please do."

"Is it not true, Doctor, that there are a number of different methods used to identify fingerprints?"

"Yes. That is true."

"Would you then, briefly describe the method you used."

"How is this relevant, Your Honor?" Michaels intervened.

Annoyed by these constant interruptions, Davis allowed the question.

Colletti took a deep breath and explained the process.

"Would you agree, Dr. Colletti, that any process that relied on human experience and judgment, including human error, by definition, includes a certain error rate."

Colletti hesitated, gathering his thoughts. "If you are questioning my expertise, I have been doing this for over twenty years, and with increasing knowledge and technological advances, the error rate is virtually zero!"

"Virtually?"

"Objection!"

Judge Davis had his fill. "Sustained. I believe Dr. Colletti has fully answered your question, counselor."

Weiner turned on his heels and walked back to the table, where PJ was shaking her head.

That night, desperation forced PJ to take two Ativan. But each time she dozed off, sleep would sprint away like a deer at the sound of a twig snap. Her mind was not so much on the trial, or her possible fate. She could not stop thinking of Val. Did she make the right decision, sacrificing herself in so achingly painful a way, so he could live? The thorn in her heart bled visceral pain. Michaels was about to close the lid on the coffin with his final witness. PJ would soon have her answer.

CHAPTER THIRTY-EIGHT

Patti

The flowers arrived just as Patricia Wellington was about to leave their townhouse in midtown. The enclosed card made her eyes mist. *At last*, she thought, *I'm being seen.*

So very sorry to have missed dinner.

It will not happen again.

Val.

The apology was followed by a text asking Patti to dinner the following evening. She accepted, gleefully. He told her he reserved a table at Aquavit, a Scandinavian restaurant, and that since she lived on the East side, he would meet her there.

She had taken Val for a romantic. Certainly, for a first *date*, he would have picked her up, regardless of where she lived. She hoped she had not misunderstood his intent. She preferred to think she hadn't.

She wore a V-neck, Fit & Flare Armani mini dress in camel; a good match for her deep brown eyes and chestnut hair. She was shown to a table for four, but did not question it. When she spotted Val, after twenty minutes and a glass of Merlot, he was carrying a couple of swollen briefcases and his never-without laptop.

He dropped his paraphernalia into the vacant seats, and smiled. "So sorry I'm late. I wanted to make sure I brought everything we would need for our first transition meeting."

She had anticipated a peck on the cheek. Her broad smile turned chilly as her assumption, it seemed, had been entirely off.

"I didn't know this was a business dinner," she ventured. "I thought…"

The waiter brought over a tasting platter. "Some tidbits to consider before ordering," he said.

"Thank you, Alrick. Would you bring us a bottle of Dom Perignon." He looked at Patti. "You look lovely. You were about to say something?"

"Not important."

"Everything you say is important, Patti. This transition, it's like…it's like giving up a child for adoption. You want to make sure the child is brought up in a safe and loving environment."

She tried on a smile. "That's an interesting analogy. But you have nothing to worry about. I will take good care of your baby." While not admitting it, Patti had never had Nordic food before, but she could not stop raving about it. "Absolutely wonderful!" The evening was spent enjoying a sumptuous dinner, two bottles of Dom Perignon, and reviewing portfolios and financial sheets that Val needed Patricia Wellington, as the new CFO of Kendall & Wellington Investments, to sign off on.

As they were about to wrap things up, Patti raised her glass. "Here's to a new relationship." They clinked glasses, Patti's meaning very much dissimilar to Val's understanding of it.

He saw her to the door, delighting her with a peck on the cheek. "I will see you before I leave for Colorado."

A wide smile returned to her lips. "I'd like that."

He looked at her questioningly. "At the contract signing."

"Oh, of course."

***

A sort of melancholy hovered over Val all morning, mounting in intensity as he walked the entire floor of Kendall and Son. He had not expected the sting of nostalgia that was pinching his heart. More surprising were the tears that filled his eyes as he thought about his father and the love and attention he had given to this company, its staff and clientele. Until that moment, he had not realized the attachment he had to the firm. He ended up in his father's old office, peering out the window.

"Valdur?"

He discretely wiped his eyes. "Mom. You're early." He gave her a hug. "Tea?"

"Not just yet, dear. How are you?"

They small-talked their way to the conference room. He'd invited her to be present out of respect for her shareholder position with the firm, which would remain at five per cent under the new corporation, and because he thought she would want to be there.

The Kendall's corporate lawyer arrived at the same time as Lester and Patricia Wellington. Mrs. Cummings showed them into the conference room, which was nicely set up with pitchers of ice water, juice, pastries, coffee, and tea.

Val stood, greeted the Wellingtons, and introduced his mother. Wellington, who had not expected to meet her at such a venue, was somewhat taken-aback. She held out her hand to shake his. He instead took her hand, bent slightly, and kissed it. "I am honored, Mrs. Kendall. I can see where your son gets his good looks."

Val and Patricia glanced at each other, stifling a giggle.

Wellington was a man of exceptional good taste. He'd always taken pride in his appearance, although if pushed he'd admit he would do well to lose ten pounds. His suits were personally tailored. His ties, scarves, and shoes imported from Italy. At nearly seventy, he maintained a smooth, ruddy complexion, and still sported a fairly dense crop of gray-to-white hair and an always well-manicured goatee. Sparkling ocean-blue eyes that looked out on the world with an inborn skepticism, were the first things one noticed about Lester Wellington...and a key feature that held the attention of Val's mother.

Other than a few minor points that needed to be ironed out, the signing went without a hitch. At twelve-thirty, Mrs. Cummings wheeled in a cart with several bottles of champagne on ice and six Waterford crystal goblets engraved with the letters *KW,* per Wellington's instructions. She poured the champagne and handed each person a glass, leaving one empty. She was about to leave the room, when Wellington stopped her. "Mrs. Cummings, you neglected to pour yourself a glass." She remained with her mouth open. "Please," he extended his hand to her. "You are part of the Kendall-Wellington family. You must join us."

Val poured her a glass and handed it to her, his eyes beaming.

Wellington raised his glass. "I'd like to make a pledge."

"Of course you would," Patricia laughed. "A simple toast would be the norm."

"Ah, you know me too well, daughter. But a pledge in this instance I believe is more appropriate. I pledge I will devote myself, and I know Patti will certainly agree. We will devote ourselves to bringing Kendall-Wellington Investments from the top dozen to the top five wealth management companies in the country.

"Hear, hear," Val piped up. And they all clinked glasses.

"Patti," her father said. "Why don't you shadow Val today…get a feel for things"

Val, rolling his eyes as he walked his mother to the door, looked back at Wellington, thinking of ways to avoid it. Not willing to upset the apple cart so soon after *happy hour,* he acquiesced. "Of course. Mrs. Cummings will arrange to have you taken home, mom." He kissed her and told her he'd stop by before leaving for his trip.

"Nonsense," Wellington interrupted. It would be my pleasure to see the charming lady home."

Val had not anticipated the sweet smile his mother gave Wellington.

"In fact," Wellington continued. "I would be honored, Mrs. Kendall, if you would allow me to take you to lunch."

Oh, my God. No, Val groaned inwardly. Her response made his eyes pop out.

"That would be lovely," Mr. Wellington.

He took her arm. "Please, call me Lester."

Mrs. Cummings cleared the room and Val walked back to his office in a daze, Patricia following. He flopped in his chair and looked at her. "What just happened?"

She laughed. "I think my father is smitten."

Annoyed by her flippant response, he lost his cool. "This wasn't part of the deal. It will never work. I won't allow it."

"You won't allow it?" she said, hurt. "You do not have that power, Valdur."

They said nothing further to each other. Patti got up to leave. "My father is a good man. An honorable man. He has a kind and generous heart he allows few, if anyone, other than myself, to see," she said. "Yes, he can be gruff and impatient. These are just shields protecting fears and vulnerabilities from being exposed…the same way in which a pelt protects an animal."

"My apologies. I just cannot see them together."

"Firstly. I think you're jumping the gun. They're just having lunch, for heaven's sake. And secondly, if you make even a slight effort to get to know Lester Wellington, perhaps extend him some grace, it might alter whatever it is you think of him." And she left.

CHAPTER THIRTY-NINE

The Crack of Doom

Val's world had become a Kafkaesque landscape, pressed down as he was by a dark oppressive foreboding. Distracted by all that was going on around him, he reluctantly turned over his caseload to one of his minions, and headed back to New York. He spoke to Charlie daily. She kept him up to speed on courtroom events—which so far had not been encouraging—but that wasn't enough. He had to be there. One way or another, he would find a way to get PJ to see him.

Because his flight was delayed, Val was late getting to court. He took his usual stance behind the pillar as ADA Michaels was finishing up introducing his star witness.

"Although, unfortunately deceased, the recorded testimony of Candace Russell Baker, before and during deposition, will serve as viable testimony." Michaels directed the jury's attention to the screen. The video immediately panned in on Candace's face. It depicted Candace being sworn in, and the microphone turned on before Michaels began questioning.

With every muscle in spasm, PJ could not stop shivering as she watched.

"Ms. Baker. Please state your full name, and the events as you witnessed them on September fifth, 2019."

"Candace Russell Baker," she responded in a soft, wavering voice. Continuing her *eyewitness* account, she employed her complete storehouse of thespian artifice acquired during her brief acting career; the wet tears staining her mascara, her wringing hands, nervously mauling a handkerchief. She employed her entire repertoire. From the clearly visible reaction of the jurors—and PJ's rising blood-boil—it had served her well. Michaels devised the questions strategically, and the lies came one after another. The entire deposition took one hour and ten minutes. Done and done.

Beyond herself, PJ whispered in Weiner's ear. "Do something."

Weiner stood, cleared his throat. "Your honor, in view of the fact that the witness cannot be cross examined, I would like to remind the jury that she, Candace Russell Baker, had been given immunity from a number of crimes, including a felony, for her testimony. Secondly, as the only eye-witness, her testimony is simply her word against my client's, and thus questionable, prompting reasonable doubt."

Michaels jumped out of his seat. "Objection!"

"Sustained." Davis scowled at Weiner. "Counselor, I will remind you, though I trust you are well aware, that the direct suggestion of reasonable doubt is well outside your sphere of influence." He turned to the jury box. "The jurors will discount Mr. Weiner's second remark as it pertains to reasonable doubt."

***

Val prevailed upon Charlie to talk to PJ. "I must see her, Charlie. This is killing me."

"Believe me, love, my pleadings have become a mantra. It's almost as though she's punishing herself."

He raked his hair with both hands and stomped around the room. He slogged back to Charlie, his moist, red eyes betraying him. "Doesn't she know it's me she's punishing?"

Charlie put her arms around him, but there was no consoling the man. "She believes she's saving you."

"Saving me?"

"Don't you see, she's lost all hope. She's sunk into the pit of resignation, and she will not bring you down with her. This is her response each time I try to talk some sense into her."

Val sighed heavily. "It's clear to me that this thing can go either way. I'm worried."

"Aren't we all. Walden is meeting with Weiner to talk to him about having PJ's psychologist testify about what it means to be in a dissociative state."

"Why does her defense attorney need someone to tell him this?" Val shouted. "Stoller should have been on the witness list from the get-go."

"I know. This whole thing is mystifying. Trials take forever. This one seems to be on steroids. It's going much too quickly. There is so much being kicked to the curb, I don't know what to think anymore."

Other than Charlie's parting words—"I will sit on her until she agrees"—the two left it at that.

Val returned to his brownstone to go over messages, mail, and to arrange his calendar so he would be able to attend court every day. For now, just seeing her lifted the color of his day from black to gray.

Pinned down by the continual yammerings from Val's and the Thurgood's disapproval of how he was handling the defense, Weiner finally subpoenaed Dr. Stoler as an expert witness.

Of course, charged with wrapping up this case in record time, ADA Michaels reacted poorly. He ultimately lined up several *expert* witnesses to refute Stoler's testimony.

After two weeks of the prosecution's witnesses battering Stoler's testimony that an individual in a dissociative state could indeed commit an act or acts they would not normally do, Michaels was ready to rest his case.

Weiner had to be careful in presenting a plausible defense while not tipping the scales too much in PJ's favor. He had more plates in the air than he could balance, and if any crashed to the ground, he could kiss his comfy life in the Cayman Islands goodbye.

The attorneys gave their closing arguments to the rapt attention of an overflowing courtroom. PJ, her eyes closed the entire time, appeared to be in a trance-like state. Even Weiner asked if she were all right. She did not respond.

Judge Davis instructed the jury about the guidelines for deliberation in a case of first-degree homicide, reminding them that they must apply the standard of proof—"beyond a reasonable doubt"—to this criminal case, and base their decision, which must be unanimous, on the facts, evidence, and credibility of the witnesses. Following these rather brief instructions, the jury was dismissed to deliberate.

***

Walden flew in from Germany to be with Charlie, who was well-passed the worry stage and approaching hysteria. "They said nothing about the abduction, the trauma, Lucinda Russell's vendetta. And Weiner…he actually seemed afraid to oppose the ADA. The trial is rigged, I tell you!"

"Please, sweetheart, calm yourself. It is not helping anyone. We will all get through this."

"How?"

"Charlotte, your anxiety is permeating the atmosphere with negativity. Good vibes, my darling, good vibes. PJ will be acquitted!"

Charlie put her arms around her husband and wept on his shoulder.

There was no sleeping that night. Romano, out of quarantine, but still feeling the effects of Covid, was on the phone with Val every hour on the hour. Val walked the floors, swirling a tumbler of bourbon, which he never drank, for the better part of the night.

Late spring brought record rainfall bursting from clouds that transformed day into night, bringing with it a sense of foreboding that was becoming all too familiar. Over the weekend break, PJ sat in the Lotus position on the floor of her cell, meditating, but thoughts of happier times with the Hollingers, Charlie, her days at Stanford with her roomies…and Val…kept interjecting themselves. She conjured his face before her. *Man of my dreams, love of my life, it seems our love song has hit a flat note.* Steeling herself for the worst, she took two Ativan, courtesy of her much-loved supplier, and slept for a few hours.

The lights clicked on at 5:30 a.m. and the sounds of jangling keys and heavy metal doors opening and closing ushered in the morning, its heaviness like a bag of rocks slung over her shoulder as she attempted to climb this craggy, steep mountain, shoeless.

Thirty-six hours. And twenty-five minutes later, it was announced that the jury had reached a decision. The rushing and clambering to get back into the courtroom resembled a high-speed car chase. PJ was brought into the sound of dust settling. For all her meditating and calmness, she had to work at controlling her shaking hands and chattering teeth. She took her seat next to Weiner, and clasped her hands tightly in her lap.

"All stand."

The judge waved everyone to be seated and addressed the jury. "Has the jury reached a decision?"

The foreperson stood. "Yes, we have, Your Honor."

"Would the defendant please stand."

PJ was forced to grip Weiner's arm to steady herself, her knees shaking, but head up and shoulders back.

"Please state your verdict."

The foreman read from his notes, never looking up. "On the charge of premeditated murder in the first degree, we the jury find the defendant, Penelope Jane Hollinger...*Guilty.*"

The word *guilty* reverberated in Charlie's brain like the church bells of *Notre Dame*. Not realizing she'd been holding her breath, she slipped quietly to the floor as though her bones had disintegrated. Walden grabbed her around the waist and took her outside, despite her protests.

"I have to see her, talk to her. This cannot be. How could Weiner let this happen?"

"This was a butchering of justice for certain," Walden said, smoldering as he marched her out the door. "We will appeal!"

The uproar in the courtroom could be heard through the halls. The judge's pounding gavel had little impact. PJ was handcuffed and escorted from the room, tears streaming down her face.

Pushing his way through the mass of reporters and bystanders, Val's anguished cry, "PJ!" echoed off the walls. He stretched out his arm to her, but was a second too late as the guard pushed her through the side door nearly closing it on Val's hand.

By the time Charlie found her legs and raced back to the courtroom, Weiner was heading for the exit. They slammed into each other. It took every bit of her remaining strength not to slap him across his face. "You're nothing but a hack," she told him, daggers firing from her eyes. "I will see to it that you are disbarred!"

"I could care less," he smirked, and left the courthouse for the last time. Or so he thought.

CHAPTER FORTY

The Caged Bird

The breaking news of the Hollinger verdict spread faster and wider than *The Big Burn* of 1910. Patricia Wellington was sitting across from her father in the breakfast room of their Scarsdale home, both on laptops. When the *Breaking News* banner about the trial popped up on their respective screens, they looked at each other.

"What are you thinking, sweetheart?"

Putting her coffee cup down, she took in a deep breath and let it out slowly. "I'm thinking Val must be grief-stricken…and I feel helpless to console him."

Wellington took out his cell phone and scrolled his contacts. Patricia reached over and put her hand over his. "Let him be, dad. He needs time to process."

"He needs you, is what he needs!"

She gave her father a half-smile. "I don't know if he'll ever come to that conclusion," she said, tears clouding her vision.

***

"She promised she would see me after the verdict," Val groaned.

"She hasn't broken her promise, Val," Charlie assured him. She just needs time to adjust. She's not accepting any visitors, not even me. Although when I do see her I'm going to smack her silly." Charlie could hear the strain in Val's voice. Trying to lighten things up was pointless.

"It's been two weeks."

It was a rare moment when Charlie remained wordless.

"Charlie? You still there?"

"I'm here. There's something off about this whole affair," she said, suddenly. "Who was involved and how it was handled—or mishandled—from the outset, including Victoria Abbott's *accident.*"

"I know. There's no doubt that the system is corrupt. But why PJ?"

"Wrong time, wrong place. Politics is a nasty business," Charlie said, stating the obvious.

"So what happens next? We've got to get her out of there." Val's voice cracked.

"We will! Wally found an ace lawyer in LA who will be filing a notice of appeal."

"And how long will that take?"

She hoped Val hadn't heard the quiet moan that escaped on the edge of her breath. "A while."

***

Despite his daughter's advice, Wellington reached out to Val several days later. As she had warned, Val was not receptive. Wellington backed off. For the next several weeks, Val drove up to the Bedford Hills Correctional Facility for Women in Westchester every weekend feeling positive that she would see him. He was resigned to never giving up, but driving back after his most recent disappointment, he felt a little less resolved, and not in the best of moods. He had not eaten all day. He was hungry. He stopped at The Inn at Pound Ridge, and slipped the maître d' a fifty-dollar bill to seat him without a reservation. Val had known that Lester Wellington lived in Westchester County, Scarsdale, as he remembered, but the thought that he'd run into him never entered his mind.

"Val, my boy!" Wellington boomed, arms outstretched. "Fancy meeting you here!" Val stood, feigning a smile, and accepted Wellington's bear hug. "Hello, Lester."

Never one to duck an opportunity to speak his mind, regardless of how graceless it might be, Wellington jumped right in. "Are you avoiding us, son? We haven't seen or spoken to you in some time."

Val shrugged. "Busy."

"May I join you?"

What could he say? "Sure." He motioned to the chair opposite.

"What brings you up this way?"

Val poured himself a glass of water from the Carafe wondering how Wellington knew he was at The Inn. He thought about delivering some snarky response, but was just too tired and downcast to be clever. "I've been coming up every weekend since…"

"Of course!" Wellington ran his thumb and forefinger over his goatee, as was his habit when he pretended not to know something he very well knew. "Visiting Ms. Hollinger. How stupid of me."

"I'm not having much luck with that," he said spontaneously, his tongue loosened by the ache in his heart. "She says she's not ready to see me."

"I understand, son," Wellington said truthfully. "When I lost my wife, the thought that I would never see her again, never..." He looked away for a moment. "It nearly crushed me."

Not really understanding why he wanted to know, he asked Wellington how long he and his wife were married.

"Thirty-four wonderful years."

Val was suddenly overcome with jealousy. "At least you had her for thirty-four years," he said sharply, unable to hold back the tears. Wellington did what was unprecedented for him. He put his hand over Val's and squeezed. "I feel your pain," he said, and gave Val a moment. "I think we could use a drink, son." He signaled the server. "Bring us a bottle of Catena Zapata Malbec."

After a satisfying Lobster dinner and a bottle of wine, Val asked after Patricia. Wellington smiled. He'd been waiting for the right time to bring her into the conversation. "She's worried about you," he said, honestly. "And so am I."

Val said very little as Wellington discussed the acquisition and what remained to be done for the successful transference of executive responsibilities. He also missed no opportunity to extol the virtues of his "brilliant and beautiful daughter."

Not being much of a drinker, after sharing a bottle of Malbec Val was approaching three sheets and heard only half of what Wellington was pushing. After the second bottle had been drained, he was in the best mood he'd been in for months, referring to Patricia as Patti, and revealing that he really liked and respected her. That's all Wellington needed to hear. He drew dangerously close to badgering Val to date his daughter. "You have your whole life ahead of you, son. It's up to you to make it a meaningful and satisfying one." And the final pitch. "And you will not be able to do that without a loving and loyal partner."

Apparently, Wellington went too far. Val would not be ready to consider such an arrangement for some time to come. His ears perked up at the man's audacity. He leaned in toward Wellington, his eyes narrowed slits. "I *have* a loving and loyal partner." He got up from the table, steadied himself before taking a step, and teetered toward the exit, leaving Wellington with a red face, and the check.

***

The Bedford, as it was known locally, was a measurable improvement over Rikers. But other than a fragment of its population who were utterly determined to rise above the many ways prison tore down the fabric of a human being, layer-by-layer, the harshness and loneliness of prison life afforded little room for hope.

For the first few weeks, PJ allowed herself to drift in a haze of self-pity thickly laced with rage. She kept to herself, made no attempt to socialize, and outrightly refused all visitors. She, in effect, collapsed inside herself, a necessary implosion from which she would emerge victorious and renewed…that was the hope.

Indulging in a pity-party of one became tiresome. What remained following her self-induced shutdown was a fiery anger that sparked her mission to turn the *system* on its head. She had the power of the written word. But she could not get it done alone.

The phone call Charlie waited for with bated breath finally came, lifting the smog that had settled over her life, enabling her to exhale. "Damn it, PJ," she howled, unable to hold back her sobs.

"I'm sorry, my sista. I'm so sorry. Please forgive me. I just…"

"There's nothing to forgive," she said, sniffling. "I know you. I know you needed time to regroup. You and Wally are my only family. Never close me off like that again!"

"Never!"

"I'm flying out to see you tomorrow."

Tomorrow seemed like a month. Sitting at the visitation table, Charlie looked around. "I know we're not supposed to touch. Oh, fuck it!" She practically leaped over the table and wrapped her arms around PJ's shoulders until the guard yelled through his mini-megaphone. "No physical touching!"

Charlie held on a second or two longer. Squinching her face, she mimicked the guard as she sat down. "*No physical touching.* Moron. Is there another kind?" PJ eased out a smile.

"So, my sista, what's the plan?"

"Well, to start with, I'm back to my routine, building stamina for the fight ahead, because fight I will!"

"Now you're talking!"

"The trial was nothing but a three-ring circus for the entertainment of 'the people.'" She closed her eyes and regaled Charlie with their favorite, and most appropriate, poem. "*I know why the caged bird sings. A bird that stalks down his narrow cage can seldom see through his bars of rage."*

"His wings are clipped and his feet are tied." Charlie continued, *"So he opens his throat to sing."*

PJ swiped a tear away and leaned across the table. "This caged bird is going to sing all right, with another expose that will turn the justice system on its head!"

***

Despite the fragile thread of hope, Val expected to be turned away once again. When the guard gave him the visitor form to fill out, he thought his feet had left the ground.

The visiting room trilled with multiple conversations. PJ, her hair pulled back into a ponytail, with those runaway tendrils framing her face, strode to an empty table and sat, folding her hands in her lap and training her eyes on the visitors' entrance. She had prepared well for this visit, but her heart literally fluttered at the sight of him standing in the entranceway, skimming the room. She watched him, tears brimming and heart heavy. When their eyes met, Val momentarily froze before abandoning the rules he had agreed to, and ran into her arms. One of the guards was about to walk over to disentangle them, but was held back by her shift partner who had taken a liking to PJ. "Let them have their moment."

Val kissed every part of her face and neck until he found her lips. Those in the room began to stare. The guards had no choice but to break them apart and order them to sit down.

He took out a handkerchief and blotted the tears from her face, then wiped his own. "Tell me this is not a dream,"

"It's so good to see you, Val."

"You look amazing, sweetheart. Healthy," he said. "I am so relieved that you're taking care of yourself. I've had nightmares of you beaten down by this depressing hell-hole. But I know you're so much stronger than that. We'll get you out of here. I promise."

It was time to say what she must say. While the guards were focused elsewhere, PJ put her hand over Val's and squeezed. "We both know that will never happen. The Vatican is a very powerful influencer."

"We know no such thing, PJ. An appeal is being filed as we speak."

"Val. We must be realistic. Almost ninety per-cent of appeals are denied."

"Well then, yours will be among the ten per-cent. It will happen. I know it will. It has to!"

"Hollinger!"

She pulled her hand out of Val's and gave the guard a deadly stare.

"We don't have much time," she said. "I'm only allowed four hours a month visitation, and Charlie is scheduled for next week."

"Four hours a month! Who makes these rules?"

"In case you've forgotten, this is a maximum security prison. They barely allow us to breathe."

"You cannot stay here," he said, as if he hadn't heard her.

Frustration and anger at her situation surfaced with a vengeance. "Dammit!" she stormed. "You're not hearing me, Val. I'm here for life. You're not. You need to leave here, forget the past, and move on. You have your whole life ahead of you. I will not allow you to waste it."

"I thought we were partners, PJ," he said, keeping his own anger in check. "Since when do you make decisions for me?"

"Since I heard the words *life without parole*." She looked at him, her fear, frustration, and longing taking a back seat to the crushing pain in her heart. How she loved him. But love was not enough. The prospect of spending the rest of her life in prison did not extend to a happy ever-after life with the partner she had chosen. The break was inevitable. This would be the last time they would see each other. He had to accept that. There was simply no other way for either of them. They were helpless against the capriciousness of fate.

CHAPTER FORTY-ONE

Life Goes On

On a balmy morning in October, blazing with the colors of autumn—fourteen months after PJ Hollinger's conviction—Victoria Abbott opened her eyes. Surrounded by the Chief of Neurology, the resident physician, and the ICU nursing staff, Abbott's face registered a mental fog of confusion. In a barely audible rasp, she managed to speak. "Where the fuck am I?"

While her first words in eleven months drew a chuckle from her audience, clearly Abbott had not meant to amuse.

The word spread throughout the legal community faster than the *McLaren Speedtail*. Within hours, ADA Michaels was called to the governor's office. He sat opposite Governor William Tremont for ten straight minutes watching him click his Lazlo pen—a gift from his wife on his election. *Click, click; click, click.* "I am so fucking tired of these foreign pinheads inserting themselves into our justice system," he burst out suddenly. *Click, click; click, click.* "Assholes!"

"For assholes," Michaels said, "they apparently know what's happening before we do"

"This whole mess with Abbott was their lamebrained idea," Tremont howled, flipping the pen across his desk. "But we'll be the ones on the rack in a congressional hearing."

Michaels jolted forward. "Wait. What are you talking about? What congressional hearing?"

"It's only a matter of time before Abbott shifts her brain into fifth gear and finds that truck driver with the heavy foot."

Michaels just stared at him, trying to process what he was hearing.

"The guy was paid in US currency!" Tremont wailed. "Who do you think is going to be jabbed with the accusing finger?"

Michaels covered his face. "The Justice Department," he moaned. He looked up at Tremont. "And they'll drag us into damnation with them."

"I'm done with this. They can have my job," he said, loosening his silk tie and undoing the top button of his custom-tailored shirt.

"I don't think you mean that, Bill."

ONE YEAR EARLIER

Val left the prison in a state of desolation. But he was not about to give up on the seemingly shattered dream of growing old with the love of his life. He promised himself he would do everything and anything to change PJ's mind. She was in a dark place. He understood that. It would take time and effort to walk through this fire. But he knew no one else as strong-willed and determined as PJ Hollinger. She would not capitulate to the vagaries of life. He was counting on it. She just needed time—and some good news—to grow and strengthen her resolve to fight her way through this. He convinced himself that she would be granted an appeal at the very least.

THE PRESENT

After nearly a year of sending care packages and flowers (invariably returned to sender), calling, writing, engaging those close to her to speak on his behalf, and showing up every visiting day, Val had to face the reality that he'd been pursuing an illusory dream that would never be realized. He needed to shake off the tumbleweeds and get out of Dodge. He answered all necessary emails, returned phone calls, and temporarily placed *Parent Trace* in the capable hands of his new partner. He packed a bag and took the red-eye flight to Fiji.

Val returned a month later, tanned, refreshed, and ready to begin life anew, for the most part. Notwithstanding all the work he'd done on himself while in Fiji, his first thought when his feet touched US ground was to place a call to PJ. Maybe a month without hearing from him weakened her resolve. He gave himself a mental slap to the head and relinquished the thought. He knew her too well. She was lost to him, a reality he was hard-pressed to accept, but had little choice. He went straight to his brownstone and checked in with his business partner. He then made two phone calls. The first to his mother; the second, to Patricia Wellington.

***

A quiet tranche of concrete, hosting a small patch of shade along the western edge of the prison yard, would often find PJ savoring the restorative sights and sounds of nature—meager as they were—in birdsong, azure-blue skies, and a distant but clear view of the bursting colors of seasonal flowers that painted the hillside under the shifting shades of sunlight. Her mind vacant, as she leaned against the twelve-foot stone retaining wall, listening to and observing a world she was no longer part of.

Still taunted by as yet unanswerable questions, she wondered how she would survive the gloom, the bitterness, the thinly veiled rage that seeped from everyone around her? *Is this what the rest of her life held? Could she live with the thought that she'd never again breathe the air of freedom? Had the promise she'd made to herself to fight back completely evaporated? No!* She could not allow that to happen. She would not be swallowed up by the abased demon that ruled these parts. There were things she could do…things she knew she had to do.

The following day she requested to work in the library, where she would begin her crusade to bring down a venal justice system. She researched and kept a journal. She wrote every night, often until daybreak. She devised a communications code and used friends on the outside to assist in obtaining information she could not obtain through her library research. She got to know some of the more benign inmates and developed a following. On inspiration, she requested a meeting with the warden. Two weeks later, she was escorted to her office.

"Thank you for seeing me, Warden," PJ said politely, folding her hands in her lap.

"What can I do for you, Ms. Hollinger?"

She did not hesitate. "I would like your permission to teach a creative writing class," she said, observing the warden's reaction. The warden had no response. PJ cleared her throat and continued. "I believe that, as a creative outlet, it would benefit many of the women."

"How so?"

PJ took a breath. "The only freedom these women have are their thoughts. There is both an art and a science to relieving those thoughts on paper. It can be quite therapeutic. And self-affirming."

The warden thrummed her fingers on the desk. "Hmm. Interesting." She jotted something on her notepad. "Why don't you provide me with a plan, in writing, including what you will need, and I will think about it."

PJ took out several sheets of paper from her pocket. "I've already done that." She unfolded them, leaned forward, and placed the papers on the warden's desk. The guard standing at the door, took a step toward her, then stepped back when the warden's hand went up. "It's all right, Stevens." She picked up the sheets and scanned them briefly. "You've certainly prepared well." She nodded to the guard, her cue that the meeting was over. "I will give it some thought," she said as PJ was escorted back to her cell.

Depressed over the news that her appeal was denied, PJ did not leave her cell for two days, wallowing in wretchedness. Where was the proverbial light at the end of the tunnel? Was this some sort of karmic penalty for an egregious past life? It took her those two days and several hot showers to snap out of her doldrums and back to working on *the plan*. Her spirits rose when, some two weeks after their initial meeting, the Warden summoned PJ to her office, giving her the go-ahead to organize a creative writing class—on a trial basis. "Let's give it a month or so and see how it works out."

***

"I've got news, my sista."

"If it's not good news, I'm hanging up."

"It's great news, darling."

"Well, make it quick, I'm only allowed ten minutes."

"Okay. Be grumpy. You have every right."

"So, what's the news?"

"You know, of course, that Victoria Abbott has been in physical therapy for over a year now. Making wonderful progress."

"I am so pleased to hear that."

"Here's one better; she's agreed to review the transcripts and help Wally file a second appeal. She's already found several discrepancies in Weiner's handling of the case."

"Weiner. I knew it! He was paid off."

"There's more…One of the investigators Wally hired followed the money, as they say, and he thinks he found Weiner in the Cayman Islands along with his dirty payoff."

"That is good news. Great news! I wish we could talk longer, but I have to go. There's a line waiting for the phone. I love you."

"I love you more," Charlie said. "There's something else you should know…" but the line had already disconnected.

CHAPTER FORTY-TWO

Victoria Abbott

Victoria Abbott was born in Water Hill, New York, one of the wealthiest towns in Nassau County. Although she maintained an apartment in Manhattan, her Long Island home on Abbott Lane—so named in honor of her grandfather, a World War I hero—became her long-standing sanctuary. Remaining single after a bitter divorce, she shared the sprawling mansion, nuzzled among the splendor of red dogwoods and pine birch, with her mother and sister.

After graduating Harvard Law School in 1995, Abbott practiced family law for several years. In 1999, while following a trial in which a woman had been given a life sentence for murdering her cruelly abusive husband, Abbott left the firm and hung out her own shingle as a women's advocate defense attorney. She gained prominence over the years defending women in high-profile cases. Never having lost a case, she was asked to accept the office of District Attorney—twice—and twice refused. "I am accountable only to my clients," she remarked to reporters, "and to myself. The crucible that has been melting down the justice system is well outside my comfort zone." When Walden Thurgood asked her to take on PJ Hollinger's case, she eagerly accepted. Now, at fifty-six, she struggled to attain a relatively normal life, a life that had taken a cataclysmic turn. After nearly a year of virtual non-existence, followed by another of laborious and painful physical therapy, she wondered if she had lost her taste for the courtroom.

"I know it has been a horror for you, Victoria," Thurgood said when he'd asked her to review the case. "You are our last hope, but I will understand if you prefer to stay out of this arena."

Abbott reached for her glasses. You're looking well, Walden."

"As are you, despite everything."

"Ah. I wish I felt as good as I look," she smiled feebly. "I hear Henry Weiner has vaporized."

"Yes. About that. I have two of the best private investigators on it," Thurgood said. "I've been briefed, but would rather not say anything until verified."

"Trust, but verify." She removed her glasses and turned her head toward the opaque glass window. "I'm told I will be graduating to crutches soon," she said, resting her head back onto the pillow. "Do you have the court transcripts?"

"I have everything."

"How much time do we have?"

"We have twenty-six of a thirty-day window."

She closed her eyes and released a heavy sigh. "Leave me whatever you have."

***

Basil Romano had a long and esteemed reputation with the NYPD. He used every contact he knew, past and present, to dig up insider information pertaining to the Hollinger case, some of which shocked even him. He passed on to PJ whatever details she needed for her exposé: *The Forgotten Women in Block 24: A First-Hand Account of a Corrupt and Indifferent Justice System.*

"Your buddy, Murphy, came to see me yesterday."

"Huh. What did that old codger want? I thought he'd retired by now."

"Stop. I know he's been helping you."

"You're so cute when you're pissed."

"Listen, to me." She leaned forward and took his hand. "I don't want you doing this anymore. You need to enjoy your retirement."

"What's left of it."

"You have plenty of…"

"What did Murphy tell you?"

"You must stop worrying and slow down."

"Come on. What did he tell you?"

"He told me you must stop worrying and slow down. He also told me you're having a biopsy next week."

"That blabbermouth!"

"Why didn't you tell me? We promised not to keep secrets from each other." She squeezed his hand. "Please, granddad, stay away from here. Take care of yourself!"

"Don't try to sweet talk me, girl."

PJ stood. "We can talk over the phone. Now go home and rest."

"You know you're making me feel old and feeble."

"You are old and feeble." She pulled him up by his hands and put her arms around him. "I love you. Go home."

***

It took nineteen months—a gestation period that saw the hoped-for outcome of a successful appeal for *The People v. Penelope Jane Hollinger*. Charlie's tongue was burning to give PJ the news, but her husband convinced her that Victoria Abbott should have the pleasure.

It was about four p.m. when PJ began wrapping up her Wednesday writing class. The project was in its second year and had won the warden a commendation for reducing violent incidents by twenty per cent. She'd rolled the thought around her mind for days, and in a moment of conscience, credited PJ Hollinger with the idea…mostly.

PJ walked back to her cell pondering the last few chapters of her manuscript, which was already nearly four-hundred pages. When she got to her room, a woman on crutches, partially hidden by the long shadow of a late afternoon sun, stepped forward.

"Hello, Ms. Hollinger."

Stunned by the unexpected visitor, PJ tensed.

"I'm so sorry, I didn't mean to startle you." Victoria Abbott said. "Do you remember me?"

It took PJ a second or two to focus her eyes. "Of course I remember you. But I never thought I'd see you here, Ms. Abbott." Suddenly the years became a day. "It seems an eternity ago, yet only yesterday."

"Time is the moving image of eternity."

"Plato."

"Plato, indeed." Abbott hobbled across the room, attempting to sit on the bench opposite PJ's bunk.

"Here, let me take those for you," PJ offered, relieving Abbott of her crutches.

"I'm still getting used to them. "

"I can't tell you how relieved I was to hear of the strides you've made in your recovery," PJ said.

"I had much unfinished business to attend to, which is why I'm here."

"You've heard, I'm sure, that my appeal had been denied," PJ said.

"That is no longer an issue."

PJ's eyes widened. "What do you mean?"

"I mean, the shit has hit the fan, if you'll pardon my lively tongue." Abbott reached across and took PJ's hand. "We found the driver who took two years off my life. He was very talkative after I explained how prison life can be deadly. In addition, I had my junior partner fly to Frascati to reinterview the witness who saw you running, and lo and behold, only two sentences of her deposition were introduced at trial…with Weiner's full knowledge. "

"I hope he's been disbarred, at the very least."

"Oh, he will be more than disbarred if I have anything to do with it...which I do...He will be going to prison. It is incumbent upon the associate attorney to proceed with the intentions of the defense counsel should she be indisposed. Had he followed procedure, he would have filed a change of venue motion as well as advise you to choose a bench trial. I knew this would be the best approach given the rising tide against you in New York. He did none of that."

"He was paid off, wasn't he?"

"It certainly appears that way. His luck ran out in the Cayman Islands. He is being extradited from Israel as we speak. He thought he could find asylum in his country of birth, but they were having none of it."

"My God. This entire fiasco is like a Netflix series."

"And it's only the beginning. There's going to be a Congressional hearing. You will likely be asked to testify, given the subject of your electrifying book." PJ looked at Abbott in surprise.

"Walden gave me a copy of your manuscript. It's mind-bending."

PJ had to chuckle. "Mind-bending. Love it."

"Who is your publisher?"

"Happily, I am mulling over two offers from tier-one publishing houses. There are still some legal issues to iron out, given my current address."

Both remained quiet for a time, while Abbott considered what she was about to say. "You should also know that the section of the statement attested to by our witness in Frascati that had been redacted, made it clear that Candace Baker arrived at the Frascati house *after* you were seen running up the street."

PJ covered her mouth to muffle a scream. "Does that mean the verdict is negated?"

"Well…"

"Shouldn't it be declared a mistrial?"

"Let me explain, PJ."

"Please."

Abbott sat back and took a deep breath. "I hope you don't mind, but I made a decision before consulting with you. Based on my appeals brief of judicial misconduct and malfeasance, the judges panel offered two options: a mistrial, which would mean another trial and a continuance of your incarceration...or...a reduced sentence."

PJ paled, her face screaming disappointment. "And?"

"And in your best interest, I opted for a reduced sentence."

"What? Why?"

"I did not want to see you go through another series of anxiety-ridden interrogations, and opening wounds that hadn't even begun to heal. I felt strongly that the option I chose was the better one."

"But shouldn't that have been my decision?"

"PJ, I've been doing this for many a year." Abbott smiled so broadly, PJ thought her lips would crack.

"I don't understand. Why are you smiling?"

"The appeals court reduced your sentence to involuntary manslaughter...with time served. After the final paperwork, which should only take a few days—at my insistence—you will be released."

PJ was unaware of the tears streaming down her face.

"Here's the icing on the cake," Abbott said. "Walden Thurgood has convinced the Senator from New York to use his influence to defer probation."

Unbelieving, her heart propelling blood through her arteries faster than a pumpjack, PJ had to ask Abbott to repeat what she'd just said.

"You heard me correctly. Before the end of the week, you will walk out of here a free woman!"

CHAPTER FORTY-THREE

The Beginning

She needed to call Charlie. But there would not be sufficient phone time to say everything she wanted to. She opted to write her—a missive that took ten pages of lined, legal-size sheets of paper laden with every fear, every pain, every tear, and every small step forward that accounted for her nearly five years of prison life. She closed, reminding Charlie that she could never have come through it without her *sista-from-a-different-mista* holding her up each time she was about to fall. When she finished, she crossed her arms on the desk and buried her head in the well of their fold…and sobbed until she fell asleep.

He was there. She could see him in the distance. Her heart leapt. His arms reached for her. He was so far away. She ran to him. But didn't seem to get anywhere as though she were on a gerbil treadmill. The faster she ran, the farther away he would drift. "PJ." He called to her. Her heart pounded. "I'm coming, my darling!"

When she awoke, it was four a.m. The light bulb in the lamp on her desk had burned itself out. She felt disoriented, and vaguely sad. So sad her lips quivered as tears came to her eyes. She must have been dreaming. A profoundly sorrowful dream. But she could not remember it.

Five days after Abbott's incredible news, PJ stood outside the gates of the Women's Correctional complex, her face turned up to the heavens, drinking in its warmth, and appreciating its light after what had been the darkest days of her life. She gulped in gallons of free, fresh air, thankful beyond anything she could name for the taste, smell, and feel of freedom.

When the limo pulled up, the door flew open and Charlie burst out just as the driver braked to a stop. They ran into each other's arms, sobbing.

"Let's get the hell out of this bloody place," Charlie hooted.

ONE YEAR LATER

On a mild New York Sunday afternoon, PJ left the hotel. A walk along the familiar streets of the city she loved seemed fitting before returning to Los Angeles. The streets were uncrowded and the traffic moderate. After several blocks, she looked up, appreciating as she had never before the puffs of multi-formed clouds suspended like mobiles in an endless cerulean sky. She took a deep breath, forever thankful for being able to breathe the air of freedom…a luxury so cavalierly accepted until one is deprived of it.

She turned left toward Fifth Avenue, took another left up Fifth and stopped in front of St. Patrick's Cathedral, an iconic New York City landmark. Always awed by its magnificent white marble Gothic architecture, she thought about going inside, but instead continued her promenade, taking some time to window shop. She walked, one block after another, not allowing a single thought to spoil her stroll. Stopping at Starbucks for a latte, she continued across Fifth to Madison, then took a left on Park and 61st up to 86th Street. It was close to four when she headed back to the hotel. She waited for the light to change before crossing. She stepped off the curb, and stopped cold. *Oh, my God!* She backed onto the sidewalk and stood there, numb.

Their eyes met, as only eyes who have known every part of each other do. The man put down the child he was carrying and turned to say something to the woman beside him, then walked across the street in a dreamlike trance. "PJ," was all his quaking voice would allow. They stared at each other, unable to speak. Finally, he put his arms around her, his lips brushing her cheek. They remained so until she gently pushed away, leaving some space between them. "Force of habit," he said, his fingers tenderly coaxing away that undisciplined wave of hair that always seemed to dip over her left brow. His eyes could not pretend not to notice the one-inch scar at the hairline, just above her temple. "Jesus, PJ."

"A minor scuffle," she smiled.

He let his fingers gently trace the scar. "You still take my breath away." A passing cloud momentarily blocked the sun. "Ah," he sighed. "A Harbinger?"

"Just a cloud."

He took her hand. "How have you been? When did you…when were you released? What are you doing in New York? Where are you staying?"

With a soft chuckle she told him to slow down. "One question at a time."

"We have so much to catch up with," he said.

"I'm killing two birds," she said. "I was fortunate, with a little help from my friends, to land a job as editorial manager for NewsLine. I'm here attending their tenth annual conference—my first."

"That's great…isn't it?"

"It is. Affords me lots of breathing room."

"And the second dead bird?"

"Promoting my book."

"The one with the endless title."

"Yes," she laughed. "It's doing very well…ten weeks, so far, on the New York Times Best Seller list…after its second release."

"I know. I've read it. Twice. Went through two boxes of Kleenex.

"Sorry."

"I could not be happier for you…truly. I hope it leads to the changes you envision."

"Unfortunately," she sighed, "Reform is a blind snail making its way from one tree to another."

"That's not very optimistic."

"Realistic." She smiled warmly and squeezed his hand. "But behind all the rain there is still a sun. For better or for worse, things always manage to fall into place…that's just how the Universe works."

"You deserve every good and wonderful thing," he said, choking back tears. "I wanted to be the one to give them to you."

She looked away, giving herself a moment to hold up the floodgates that were threatening to rupture. "Someone once said, 'to love is to suffer.'"

"A gross understatement."

PJ glanced over his shoulder at the boy clinging to his mother, his tiny fingers reaching out for his dad.

"He looks just like you."

"He's the reason I get out of bed every morning."

"Your wife—I assume she's your wife—she's lovely." Her gaze remained a few seconds longer. "Isn't that…"

"Patti…Patricia Wellington."

She looked at him, her emerald eyes clouded with dew. "I'm so pleased that things have worked out for you, Val. All I've ever wanted was for you to have a wonderful life, to be happy."

"I know that. I do have pinches of happiness. But the dream-life I thought was mine has long passed me by." He hugged her again. She tried to pull away, but he held her close.

"Val."

He dropped his arms and stepped back. "How long are you in New York? Can I see you?"

Her frown answered before she said the words. "You know that would not be a good idea. Besides, I'm going back to LA tomorrow." She touched his face. "You have a family now. A beautiful child to raise. Let that be enough. We have lovely memories," she said. "But we can't rewrite the past. If we held onto the sorrow of what might have been, our lives would be unendurable."

They stood awhile, unwilling to let go of each other's hands. "What's your son's name?"

"Parker Jamison Wellington Kendall."

"That's quite a mouthful."

Val turned and gave a reassuring wave to his son. "He likes being called, PJ."

She closed her eyes, as if darkness would dissolve the stabbing pain in her heart.

He kissed her lightly on the lips. "I will never stop loving you, PJ Hollinger."

She met his gaze one last time, her eyes misty with unspoken sorrow. "Nor I, you," she whispered, her words smothered beneath the blast of a taxi horn.

R.S. Raniere was born and raised in Brooklyn, New York, moved to the suburbs of New Jersey in the mid-seventies, and eventually to Georgia where she used her master's degree in English to teach composition and literature. The author writes novels, short stories, poetry, and Christian non-fiction. A member of *Home Town Novel Writer's Association* and *Atlanta Writers Club*, her publishing credits include a short story in an anthology: *Diverse Voices,* published by The Heritage Writers' Group (2016); a poem in *Atlanta Review* (Spring/Summer 2015); faith-based articles in *Agape Review (2021),* and a short story in *Avalon Literary Review (*Summer 2022). Her novels include *Shades of Darkness,* and *Shades of Darkness Book Two: Trail of Lies.* E-mail: Talktome925@zohomail.com. Or Visit website: **RSRaniereLit.com.**